Roman's Return

Roman's Adventures, Book 3

By

Amber Anthony

Copyright © 2020 Amber Anthony

Paperback ISBN: 978-1-7343822-2-8
eBook ISBN: 978-1-3938325-2-2
Library of Congress Control Number: 2020912316
Published in the United States by Amber Anthony
WriteAmberAnthony@gmail.com

Cover Design
Kelly A. Martin, KAM.Design

Photo Credits
DepositPhotos: romancephotos, romancephotos, Obrik, crbellette
Shutterstock: allstars

Dedication

This book is dedicated to our Cover Design Artist, Kelly A. Martin of KAM.Design. Years ago, when we republished Blood Rising, our book was assigned to Kelly.

From the moment we completed the interest form until we saw our eBook for sale, we were unendingly grateful for her talent and vision.

When there was the opportunity to have a book video for Appetite for Blood, we thought of no other artist.

We celebrate our thirteenth collaboration with her by dedicating this book to her steadfast contributions to the beauty of our books.

Thank you, Kelly.

Forward

Here are some island terms used in this book with their meanings, so everyone is comfortable as they appear within the story.

Lavalava:

Today the fashion remains common in island and beach areas. The lavalava is fabric secured around the waist by overhand knotting of the upper corners of the cloth, men usually allow them to hang in front and often extend to the knee or mid-calf, depending on the activity or occasion.

Pāreu:

A pāreu/sarong is a piece of fabric usually between 4-5 feet in length that is worn as a loose-fitting skirt or dress. The Pāreu, on the other hand, was developed in Tahiti and adapted to Western fabric when European explorers introduced it in the 1700s. In Hawaii, the names are often interchangeable.

The Legend of Kauila at Punalu'u

Kauila, the Hawaiian Turtle Goddess, was born on the black sandy shores of Punalu'u. Several websites recount this legend.

Malama na Honu (Protect the Turtles) is a tax-exempt non-profit entity that was created in 2007. The organization is made up of over 95 dedicated and knowledgeable volunteer "Honu Guardians" who are on the beach every day of the year to prevent intentional and inadvertent harassment of the Hawaiian Green Sea Turtles as they bask peacefully on the beach. The volunteers provide educational outreach to the public by imparting facts about the turtles, explaining their behaviors, and creating an awareness of the ongoing need to protect this "threatened" species.

Manō

n. Shark (general name).

Prologue

Twenty Years Ago
Dolly, Texas

Amarillo was what everyone expected from Texas: hot, dry, dusty, and riddled with tumbleweeds. January had brought a snow-blinding blizzard mixed with ice, but of course, Kirk Roman had still been on the inside. The guards complained of the weather on the roads, and Kirk had shivered under the thin blanket and inadequate heat in his cell. At his release in mid-April, there was a reprieve from winter's ice and summer's swelter, and Kirk enjoyed Spring.

Now he spent his days in Dolly either on the back of a horse rounding up lost steers or doing one of the many chores ever-present on a ranch. He had no complaints. The back of a horse, even on the wettest spring day, was freedom. After being locked up for three years for a crime his wife committed, being told when to get up, when to go to sleep, when to eat, when to execute every bodily function, freedom was heady stuff.

Today was his first day off since he wandered into town a week ago. The two hundred and fifty dollars in his pocket was from the great State of Texas. Dolly was as far as the bus would take him on a prison release ticket. He had his heart set on a sturdy Deakin's Delight breakfast, which the billboard bragged had the best steak, eggs, pancakes, and coffee in town.

The breakfast lived up to its reputation, and the beauty and spunk of his server was a bonus. The young woman in the worn green gingham uniform with a faded kelly green apron was a welcome surprise. Tammy's sardonic sense of humor matched his own. Her brown doe-eyes carried her smile from her plump pink lips. She was as bright as the Texas sunshine, and she warmed up his day considerably.

She gave him a wink as she bent a little closer than necessary to pick up his well-cleaned plate. "That was an outstanding breakfast." He wiped his mouth with a coarse cloth napkin and laid it on the worn counter. "Your billboard is no exaggeration."

She nodded, eyes wide. "You're not from around these parts."

"Well, Dolly's my home for now at the Rocking Horse Ranch."

She rested his plate on her forearm and cocked a hip. "Are you Charlie's new Vet?"

With a tilt of his head and a raised brow, Kirk dismissed that idea. "I am a vet, but the Navy kind. Now I'm riding the fences. I'm waiting while an option is up in the air, if it bounces my way, I'm out of here."

"Well, you gotta eat dinner. It's chicken fried steak night at Teddy's Honky Tonk. Best in the county."

"Better than yours?" He gestured to the picture on the wall.

"It's better because I don't have to stand there cooking it. Plus, The Tornado Boys are back from Austin, and they really put on a show. Fifty cent longnecks all night."

"I don't drink."

"Good Christian boy, huh?"

"I don't know how good I am. But I don't drink. Does Teddy's serve anything else?"

"How about some Texas sweet tea?"

"That's nothing like Long Island Iced Tea, is it?"

"Come again?" The look she gave him was genuinely bewildered.

"I'd enjoy some chicken fried steak if you'd have some with me?"

****

The waking sun spit morning through the eyelet curtains over Tammy's double bed. Kirk lay on his belly with his arm across her. His hand cupped her breast, his breathing was deep and steady. *My God, that man is a love machine. No wonder he's sleeping so soundly.* Now in the light, she read part of his tattoo. 'The Only Easy Day was Yesterday' ran inside his right forearm. She remembered seeing the eagle, mounting an anchor crossed by a trident and pistol over his heart while he did such a grand job of mounting her.

She looked over to him. *Are his eyes really that blue?* Right now, his thick eyelashes fluttered in sleep, but his handsome face grinned broadly. *What a scamp.* "Having sweet dreams?"

His chest rumbled his chuckle. "In this bed? You bet."

The cellphone on the bedstand throbbed with "Anchors Away". Tammy jumped from him as his lightning response had him up and sitting with the phone to his ear.

"Roman."

Tammy rose and walked naked to the tiny half bath off her bedroom, eavesdropping on his conversation.

"What? When?" These words had Kirk pacing the room, picking up his clothes and dropping them on the bed. "I didn't need the money, I got a job. I'm a ranch hand." He sat on the side of the bed, scratching his morning scruff. "I figured that would be my rainy day fund." He stuck the phone between his shoulder and his ear as he unballed his socks and began dressing. "I didn't expect you to move this fast." Tammy figured this was the end of that magnificent body in her bed by the gist of the conversation. "Of course, I trusted you, I just thought it would be a few months."

Kirk shot a grin her way as he slid commando into his jeans. "So, you have the ticket reserved for me out of Amarillo to Vegas?" Tammy pouted, he wasn't only leaving, he was going to Vegas. "I travel light, just a duffle. Sure, I guess old Charlie won't get my forty-eight-hour notice, but then again, I'll probably not be back this way. Thanks, Evan. I'll see you in Vegas." He closed the call and slid on his western shirt. With each snap, her sadness echoed in the small bedroom.

"That was that option you were talking about?"

"To my great surprise, it's come about. I just thought the guy was being nice when he sent a cell phone and debit card to the prison for my release."

She tightened her robe and blanched at his words. "Prison?"

"Yeah, I was a guest of the state for a few years. Would it change your opinion of me if I said I didn't do it? That I got out early for saving people's lives?"

She nodded to his sneakers. "That's what you're doing working a ranch and wearing sneakers."

"Well, that and they were out of my size boots at Monroe's. I didn't feel like borrowing a truck to drive to Amarillo. Now I won't need them." He patted his wallet in his back pocket.

"I guess I should say it's been nice knowing you."

Kirk caught her up in a hearty embrace. "Oh, come on. It was better than that. We had a good time last night, didn't we? If I were staying here, I'd like to think we'd have had a lot more good times."

Tammy leaned back in his embrace. "I'm not sure my husband would like that."

Kirk's brows rose. "Husband?" He looked around the small bedroom and saw no evidence of a male occupant. "It seems I'm not the only one who neglected to mention crucial details of their life."

Tammy pouted again and wrapped her arms around his neck. "Two weeks ago, Shuggy took off for parts unknown. I don't look for him to come back anytime soon. Assuming he's still alive. He has some stupid friends."

"I hope your luck improves. What if you took some hospitality courses at the junior college and headed to Dallas?"

She dropped out of his arms and started stripping the bed. "I've got to hang around here to get my divorce started, plus, Daddy needs me at the diner." She watched Kirk, his dark head hung as his gaze followed her around the bed.

"Don't sell yourself short, Tammy. You're a hell of a woman, you deserve a good man." He sat down to tie his sneakers. "I'd give you a ride to the diner, but I can see we're right behind it. Is that your Dad's place next door?"

Tammy stood forlornly holding the bedsheets. "Don't worry about him, he can't see my back door from the kitchen."

Kirk nodded. "I'll see myself out."

"But Daddy probably saw your truck when he went to open."

Kirk's head dropped lower between his shoulders as he moved toward the borrowed truck.

Tammy listened to the old truck's engine turn over, stepping to 'his' side of the bed to strip the pillowcase. She noticed his Turk's Head rope bracelet on the nightstand. She shrugged. *There's no catching him now.* She dropped the fairly new band into her keepsake cigar box. *It will be waiting for him if he ever swings back this way.*

Chapter One

Skyler Kingston drove her Volkswagen Beetle convertible circa 1979 from her aunt's home in St Pete, across the Sunshine Skyway to Sarasota. It was her daddy's car, and she treated it like a Bentley.

Aunt Sherry trusted her to drive to the University of South Florida in Tampa for an admissions interview, Sky decided she'd take the long way to Tampa by way of The Central Coast Art Institute in Sarasota. That way, she'd knock out two interviews in one day.

Driving Daddy's bug is the best! Top-down, she knew the lemon yellow convertible garnered appreciative stares from the boys. She did not realize they were admiring her and not the car. Her long, crème soda blonde hair was a gorgeous hue blended of ash and golden shades. The Florida humidity triggered tempting tendrils at her high cheekbones, and with her humongous sunglasses, no one saw her brilliant zircon blue eyes.

Out of the car, boys often fastened their attention on her kissibly wide mouth with just the hint of a pout. The little dimple in her chin went with the twin dimples just above her buttocks. She never gave them much thought, but she lived in low-rider cutoffs, and guys seemed to notice them along with her limber and lissome legs.

Her family, meaning her father, Air Force General Henry (Hank) Kingston, was not in favor of the art institute. When she first mentioned it, his response was, "I'm not sending you to crayon college." When she explained their variety of art majors, his response was horribly similar.

He'd worked the last two years to get her an appointment to the Air Force Academy, but migraine headaches negated that option. Who knew the curse of migraines that began with her periods would save her from a military career she did not want. She couldn't think of anything she wanted to do less after a lifetime of being a military brat. She had dreams, and they were about creating art.

Sky walked on air back to her car. The tour of the Central Coast Art Institute campus was jaw-dropping if you were a true artist. Plus, the dorms were not barracks. The Dean of Admissions couldn't have been more helpful. Her mind made up. She wasn't looking at any other options. *Now, all I have to do is tell Dad.* She cringed.

****

Present Day

Dolly, Texas

After school was Tammy's favorite time of day. Her son, nineteen-year-old Conner, and his best friends Gif and Buddy ate off the same platter of dumpster fries and treated their sweethearts to root beer floats. They were made expressly with diet root beer as requested by Ginny, Gif's ever-dieting girlfriend.

Conner was by far the tallest and best developed of the trio. His coal dark hair was longer than she wanted, but Tessa, his girlfriend, liked it that way. He'd inherited Tammy's brown eyes, damn near black. She'd often wished that with his coloring, Conner would have his father's brilliant blue eyes. At least he had his dad's heavy fringe of lashes, and that was something. He also had his dad's perfect inverted triangle build, enhanced by growing up working on a ranch. But it was his face that stopped all female hearts from the time Conner could sit up. When he smiled, his entire face advertised his joy.

All in all, he was a perfect blend of Tammy and Kirk. He owned his version of his father's grace and physical ease. He never met a stranger.

It was hard to believe he would graduate from high school in a week. By that time, she'd have the ultimate graduation gift waiting for him, a move to the beaches of sunny Florida. Embry-Riddle Aeronautical University would be a few miles away. She could finance his dream of becoming a pilot. Enlisting in the Air Force wouldn't be necessary. She wanted to watch him grow in his college years, she wasn't ready to give him up. If he wanted to enter the Air Force as an officer and pilot, his university studies would support that. The hard part? Breaking the news to Conner.

The bell on the door announced the postman bearing a sizeable brown package. "Tammy, you been shopping online again?"

"No, Beau, I ordered new signs for the diner." The postman left with a tip of his cap, and her hands rested flat on the box, not wanting to open it until she signed the last of the papers. Tonight her lawyer would help her close the deal. Tomorrow, she would give Conner the news. She grinned. Female hearts would break all over the county at the word he was leaving town.

****

Sky took her place among the local vendors in St. Pete Pier Park. Her high school art teacher allowed her space in his stall on weekends and holidays. Sky sat under the booth's canopy and drew pastels from photos of clients. That way, they could enjoy downtown restaurants and come back later for the completed portrait. It was all cash, and she was sitting on a nice chunk of green paper.

An octogenarian with what looked like an equally aged poodle passed by her several times with a longing look. At last, she stopped and asked. "How much to have Penny's portrait done?" She nodded toward the dog.

Sky smiled. "Twenty-five dollars."

The white-haired woman's face fell. "Oh, dear." Sky noticed her frayed sneakers and faded clothing. "Your work is lovely, but that is out of my budget." The copper poodle rode in a wire utility cart. "I want a picture of Penny because I don't know how much longer she'll be with me." The dog panted heavily.

Sky's eyes filled with hot tears of sympathy. "You know what? I would be happy to do it for free if you let me take a picture of both of you with the portrait after it's done. I could display it for advertising."

The woman's face brightened as if she'd won the lottery. "Oh, would you? That would be such a wonderful gift."

Sky picked up her phone. "Let me get a few pictures of Penny. Do you have a treat that would make her put her ears up and look at you?"

"She's not supposed to have ham, but she loves it. I suppose a tiny piece of my sandwich won't hurt her." Pictures snapped, Sky went to work as her new friend sat beside her under the large awning and ate her lunch.

****

Conner dropped his backpack on the kitchen table and exploded. "You did what?" Tammy's smile evaporated, and she took a step back, clutching the paperwork to her heart. "You sold out our family legacy? The land, the diner, the houses?"

"Conner, you're headed into adulthood. What do you want with two acres of frontage in this town?"

"It's not the two acres along the state road. It's the forty acres back. It's Grandpa's diner. It's the house I grew up in."

Tammy smacked her hands on her hips and bent into the argument. "You've barely worked a day in that diner. I'd say I have seniority and sweat equity to sell out." She dropped the papers on the table. "I'm thirty-nine. I'll be damned if I'm a short-order cook for the rest of my life. Seven days a week, eighteen hours a day, no vacations since when?"

Conner paced the kitchen, running both hands through his hair. "But, Mom. We had vacations."

"Yeah, driving to Air Force bases for air shows. Glad you had a good time."

"It was more than a good time, look at the scout badges and rank I earned. Look what I learned. It's all going to count when I enlist."

"If I had known that's what I was feeding, I'd have taken you to Six Flags."

"Don't you get it? My whole focus since I was six years old, was becoming an Air Force Pilot. Grandpa understood."

"Your Grandpa served in a simpler time. Pilots fought each other. Now war is like a video game. In three years, there probably won't be pilots."

Conner shook his head and turned away to cut off his next words.

"You work six months like I have for the last twenty-five years and tell me what you think about selling out and moving to Florida." Tammy

8

mirrored his pacing and spoke under her breath. "You little ingrate, I did not expect this from you."

"Were you so wrapped in the diner that you weren't paying attention? Why do you think my Eagle Scout project was restoring the local park's remote control airplane field? Why do you think I enrolled in JROTC?"

"You were an only child, and you never sat still."

"Mom, Why do you think Aviation was my first Scout badge?"

"So, you could fly the hell out of here like I'm going to."

"Yeah, you think that's why I worked to get into honors classes? Paid for my own SAT prep? Instead of football games on Friday night, I spent time with Chip learning how to maintain his aircraft."

Tammy threw up her hands and turned away from him, shaking her head, mumbling. "Like I said, I thought you were bored."

"All I've ever dreamed about is earning that Air Force flight suit. I don't want you to pay for college. I'm enlisting."

Tammy fisted her hands at her side and groaned. "In Florida, our lives will be different. We can have fun. This is the first time I've had time and money to be with you."

"You raised an independent son. You have to face that." Conner shouldered his backpack. "If you're done with this town and the diner, I understand. You should go and do what you want to do."

Tammy's eyes burned. "Well, thank you, young man, for permission. What could be better than your blessing?"

Conner gave her a straight lipped expression. "Not arguing with my mother about what I want to do with my life?"

"You think you know so much? Live your life. See me in a year. Find me on the beach." Tammy shoved the paperwork into the envelope and stormed back into her bedroom.

****

Conner dropped into his desk in homeroom and buried his face in his backpack. Tessa ran her hand lightly down his back and bent over to whisper in his ear. "What's the matter, Con? Did you stay out last night after you dropped me home?"

He raised his head, and the sight of his girlfriend softened his anger toward his mother. "Mom's sold everything, and she's moving to Daytona Beach, Florida."

"I love the beach, I can see your mom rocking the beach life."

Conner narrowed his eyes at her. "Without even talking to me, she decided I was going to aeronautical school out there, and she was going to waste the money to send me."

Tessa slipped into the desk next to him and inclined her head sarcastically. "Poor baby, college in Florida. What a terrible mother to offer you that."

Conner shook his head. "What, do you women stick together?"

"My family has to scrimp to make up the difference between my grants and expenses at the community college. Plus, I have to live in Dolly and commute to Amarillo." Tessa shoved her books into the well below the desk seat and opened her textbook. Shaking her head, she refused to look at him as she chewed on her Bic pen.

"I'm sorry, sugar." Conner leaned across the aisle and brushed a hand down her arm affectionately. "I'm blown away, she kept all this a secret till this morning."

Tessa chewed on the pen until she spoke. "You want to join the Air Force. You can visit her from anywhere."

Conner slumped back, his long legs bracketing the desk in front of him as he folded his arms and sulked. "It pisses her off that I want to enlist. I swear I wish I had my dad to speak up for me."

****

Conner's motorcycle churned up the dust as he fishtailed to a stop in front of the diner. He'd never seen the parking lot empty. When he got to the door, he knew why. A red-lettered sign announced, "Closed! The Deakins family thanks you for fifty years of patronage." Another sign on a metal post beaten into the hard Texas dirt said, "Watch this space for the new home of Criterion Oil."

He put the bike back into gear and rode to the grey two-bedroom home behind the diner. The flat expanse of their brown land shimmered under the Texas heat. Home, the only home Conner knew, was a single story concrete rectangle. Tan brick ran halfway up the exterior to meet pale yellow paint in need of refreshment. The one car garage door was open, revealing the fruit of his mom's work.

Parking his bike, he sat for a moment examining the road dirt on his half-helmet. Restless sweat streamed down the center of Conner's back as he measured his words. He had thought all day about this morning's quarrel with his mom. Conner still had questions. How to approach his mom was the foremost.

The living room furniture stood on the driveway, and benches held plants, lamps, and stacks of books. The front door was open, and he heard his mom grunting as she stacked small moving boxes.

Conner hung up his helmet and jacket and put on a placid smile. "Let me help you with that, Mom. Is your truck going to make it to Daytona?" He counted the few boxes she was stacking.

Tammy dusted her hands on her rump and chuckled. "If you're not taking me up on my offer, I'll ship this stuff and fly there alone. I'm selling everything, including that dump of a truck."

"Before you have everything packed up, could I get my birth certificate? Where are we planning to stay until I graduate?"

Tammy never stopped moving. "Graduation is this Saturday. I'm out bright and early Sunday." She went to a banker's box of papers and retrieved a cigar box, handing it to him mutely.

Conner had never seen this. He lifted the brass clasp, and there was Cleopatra extending a hand to Marc Antony. This had been his mom's secret box, kept in a nightstand drawer. Now there were only two things inside. The tobacco aroma, still strong, was imbued into the folded birth certificate. He lifted the paper, and a dingy white rope bracelet fell from its folds. Conner disregarded it and read the birth certificate. "Mom, why did you name me Conner Roman Jameson? Are we Italian?"

Tammy groaned. She carried a camp chair and trod into the near empty living room. Popping open the folding chair she took in a deep breath and wiped hair away from her face. "Get me an iced tea. It's a long story."

As Conner prowled into the kitchen of the small house, he kept up his interrogation. "I don't even remember why my name is Jameson, and your name is Deakins." Conner tucked the box under his arm, carrying the tea in one hand and the bracelet in the other. "And what's this?" Conner shook the bracelet at her.

Tammy rubbed her eyes with the heels of her hands and drew in a deep breath. When he handed her the iced tea and sat cross-legged on the floor, she began. "Let me tell you about life, son." She took a long swallow. "I had a husband by the last name of Jameson. He left before you were born, never to be heard from again." She looked up at him from under her bangs. "But he was not your daddy." Conner's shoulders wilted. "Your daddy worked at the ranch. He treated me good, but I knew while I was with him, he wasn't going to be here forever. I couldn't leave your grandpa, and by the time I found out I was pregnant, I figured it would be better to stay home. Shuggy Jameson, my runaround husband, took off, and I couldn't find him to file for divorce. I figured if they ever caught him, they could hold him responsible for child support."

"Is that why you dragged me from town to town, and I missed so much school I had to repeat the first grade?"

"Yes, I got word he moved to Tulsa. That was bunk. Still, I drove through all the small towns between here and Tulsa. We slept many a night in the truck."

Conner's wry smile emerged. "I thought we were camping..."

Tammy shook her head. "Yeah, right."

Conner stared between the bracelet and the birth certificate. "Was this my dad's?" Tammy nodded. "So, Roman was my father's first name?"

A dreamy look overtook her eyes as she sat back in the folding chair. "Kirk was his first name. Kirk Roman."

Chapter Two

Present Day
Honolulu, Hawaii

Kirk Roman and his wife, Jordan, waited behind the temporary stage at Queen's Surf Beach in Waikiki. Their exercise and health show celebrated three months of week over week high ratings on the local PBS station. There was network talk of taking the show nationwide.

On an exercise mat under a palm tree, Jax, his son, did pushups to emphasize his special forces physique. The director pointed out Kirk's taped marks on the stage floor while the hair and makeup artist fussed over Jordan. Kirk turned to the director. "Can you move those women at the foot of the stage? They squeal every time Jax comes on."

The director gave him an incredulous look. "Move them? I wish we had twenty more. They're ratings gold. We want them to squeal."

Kirk's face was a thundercloud. "It's damn distracting."

"Don't be jealous." Jordan patted his back, reassuringly. "Some of those little white-haired women over there are from Silver SEAL. They'd squeal for you if you took off your shirt."

Kirk looked at his muscle shirt emblazoned with his gym logo. "You don't think I'm showing enough?" He stepped within a breath of his wife and raised a brow. "I'm married now."

The director harrumphed. "I don't care what color hair they have, are they squealing yet? What we will do is rotate the audience for each episode, so it doesn't look like we did three shows in one day."

Jordan tittered. "Oh, the magic of television."

Kirk looked back at Jax's pre-show routine and stepped away to drop and perform a few pushups. He looked up at Jordan. "Happy now?"

She smirked. "Take off your shirt."

Conner rode in Buddy's truck to the Amarillo airport, duffle in the truck bed. "I appreciate you letting me use your computer to look up my dad. What a kick, my dad was a SEAL. He ought to know something about the service."

Buddy nodded along with the radio and broke out in a grin. "Yeah, and when your daddy lets you move in, remember who to invite to Hawaii. Don't worry about your motorcycle, you know I'll take good care of it while you're there."

Conner pointed an accusing finger. "Don't take her off-road."

"Yeah, yeah, yeah. So you have to fly Amarillo to Dallas to Honolulu, right? When do you sleep?"

Conner pulled his straw cowboy hat down and folded his arms over his chest. "When I'm dead."

Buddy chuckled. "You may be dead when he opens his front door and sees you standing there. That takes stones to show up unannounced. He don't even know you exist. Hope he don't have a bad ticker."

Conner chuffed out a deep breath. "We're all going to find out about his ticker."

****

Skyler was not a bad girl. She wasn't a flirt. Through high school, she would pair up for formal dances but generally hung out with five other artists. It was never serious. The thought of going all the way with one of them was like kissing your brother. *Ewwe.*

But there was one guy she reconnected with the weekend their art club visited the University of South Florida Art Department. The life model was one of her high school's alumni, and she'd crushed on him for two years before he graduated and slipped from her grasp. *Why did he wait until he was a college freshman to ask me out?*

She felt like she was ditching her friends when she drove over to USF's campus to spend the night in his dorm room. The allure of sleeping with an art class life model ran dry by Easter. When she drove off the campus for the last time, why did the song, "I Like 'em Big and Stupid', come to mind?

On the other hand, wasn't she the recipient of the Visual Arts Academy Award two years in a row? She volunteered in the middle school art program. When it came time to cross the stage, she squeaked in as the tenth student of the Decem Decori. She laughed to herself, what a fancy name for the top ten students. *Talk about ostentatious.* She loved her art teachers, and that's how she stayed out of trouble. So why did she switch out her Honolulu ticket for an earlier date without her father knowing?

She fibbed to her Aunt Sherry, who was like a mother to her, that she was meeting her father there. And she would... eventually. She had to build up the courage first.

On the flight into Dallas, Sky felt privileged to get the last window seat available. She chuckled to herself, daddy would have said she had ants in her pants. It would be a long travel day if she didn't quell that lump of guilt in the pit of her stomach.

The woman who sat next to her conversed above the cabin noise nonstop across the aisle with her friend. *If she thinks I'm givin up my window seat for them to sit together, she has another think coming. I have headphones, and I'm not afraid to use them, at least until Dallas.*

****

After boarding the plane in Dallas, Conner Roman Jameson settled back in his 'extra comfort' window seat on the Hawaiian Air flight. He appreciated the extra five inches. He swore he would not recline his seat, no matter how long this flight was. He plugged in his phone, stuffed his headphones in his ears, and waited to see who would sit next to him.

Conner shifted in his leather seat and watched pre-flight entertainment. An excited young beauty approached, gazing up at the seat numbers as her backpack bumped along the seats. *If her smile wasn't so contagious, she wouldn't get away with that nonsense.*

She halted at his row and bit her bottom lip. "I believe I have the window seat." She held up the people behind her while he grimaced, unbuckled, and ducked to move out of her way. She climbed into her seat, arms wrapped around the backpack. *I wonder if she realizes she has to stow that above us?* Conner stood out of the aisle, in front of his seat, giving her a chance to realize her mistake.

15

"Are you in the right row?" Her blonde head tilted quizzically. Huge upturned and brilliantly blue eyes blinked at him.

Conner pulled the boarding pass out of his back pocket and studied it. "You know what? I am the aisle seat. I'm sorry."

She flashed a smile. "No worries."

"Can I help you with that backpack? It has to go above."

In a daze, she shivered and oh'd back to him. "Let me grab my stuff." She dug for a blowup pillow, a Kindle, and headphones. "Thank you." She passed the bright teal bag to him.

"Are you a blacksmith?" He hefted the heavy bag jokingly. "I didn't know they made travel anvils."

"I've carried it through two airports so far. My daddy says, don't bring what you can't carry."

Conner carefully moved his perfectly shaped straw cowboy hat to the side and pushed her bag securely in the bin. While he stood over her, he enjoyed the high definition fit of her cropped leggings. Her filmy gauze top danced with her movement as she buckled into her seat.

He took his seat and turned to her. "If you tighten up those straps, that backpack won't fight you."

She lowered her Kindle and hesitated. "Yeah…" When she twisted up her long hair, the movement generated a sexy aura of fresh and vibrant orange. When her hands settled to her lap, the sensual jasmine and rose tickled his senses. The longer he sat next to her, the more he fell under her sensual cachet. *She smells great.* "Is this your first visit to Hawaii?" She fairly bubbled over with cheerfulness.

"Yeah. Going to visit a dad I've never met."

****

"Wow." She glanced up at the flight attendant and smiled and then looked back at Conner. "I'll trade you the one you don't know for the one I already have."

"Ouch. Is he in Hawaii?"

Sky accepted the cola in the flimsy plastic cup. "I have a week on my own, then we collide."

Conner tore into his snack mix. "At least you know what the reception will be. I keep trying to plan for every contingency. Where I

16

come from, he could meet me at the door with a rifle calling me a bastard and ordering me off his land."

Her pink lips pursed around her straw as her brows rose in the center. She spoke cautiously. "Where's home?"

He gestured with his thumb and forefinger. "Little town outside Amarillo."

"Thank goodness. I thought you'd tell me Tombstone."

Conner eased back in his seat. His hand washed over his top lip. "Nobody back home has mustaches like that."

She smiled. "See there, it's not as bad as you were imagining. What if he welcomes you with open arms?"

****

When the cabin lights dimmed, the low LEDs glistened off her blonde hair. Conner sat captivated by the spun gold effect. Her blonde was natural, he could see by her groomed brows and her thick golden eyelashes. It was a natural slide down her straight and pert nose to her plump lips puckered in slumber. Why did he wonder how kissable those lips were? The faint pattern of freckles that saddled her nose splayed across her collarbones and disappeared into a silky crevice of cleavage.

He had the most irresistible desire to raise the seat arm between them and draw her into his side while she slept. *I'd never be able to explain that.* Whenever the attendants came by, he requested her favorite soda and snacks. If this was all they were getting, they would land hungry.

When the inflight screen showed they were still a couple of hours away from landing, Conner sunk back in his seat. He adjusted the wings of his headrest to keep an eye on her. The gauzy top rose and fell with the rhythm of her relaxed sleep, and he was toast.

****

When Sky moved in her slumber, her earring caught on her hair, and she woke. The airplane angel had visited. On her tray was a can of soda, nut bars, and three bags of Hawaiian snack mix. She looked to her right, and the guy next to her had the same setup. She flagged the attendant for a cup of ice and gestured to the items on the tray. "Thanks for thinking of us while we slept."

17

The flamboyantly handsome attendant winked at her seatmate. "All that is from your cowboy. He thought you'd need some grub on the trail."

Sky gazed adoringly at Conner. "Awe." The attendant raised a brow and moseyed off.

Didn't he have dark eyes? The kind of deep brown eyes that pulled you into an eddy and held you there. The lashes fanned on his cheek were impossibly long and thick. Yes, his dark eyes sparkled when he talked about flying. *How much would I love to see that same sparkle if he talked about me?*

The larger than life young man next to her slept folded up like origami. His long booted legs stretched into every available inch of the bulkhead. Those blue jeans should be illegal. The white wear marks hinted where he stowed his valuables. She saw the outline of a phone, a wallet, keys. The frayed fly flap rippled over well-used brass fly buttons.

Why am I looking at his fly? Can he see me? Sky slid toward the window but watching him from that distance only made her appreciation of him more obvious.

The flight attendant cruised by, they exchanged glances, he dipped his chin. "Emm humm." And then he was gone.

The guy's plaid shirt fit snugly over well-muscled arms resting folded across his chest. The colorful plaid caressed his torso the way she would like to caress him. She'd seen handsome guys before. Dated a couple, but this cowboy was a mystery wafting away from her like campfire smoke. Hickory dark brown hair fell over his forehead, and wanton curls rested on his shirt collar. No earring, no ink showing. Thick sideburns cut straight and a little longish. With his chin tucked to his chest, his lips had a particularly alluring pout. His profile was classic. Hundreds of years of sculpture glorified men like him. *God, he's perfect. I wish he was available.*

****

By the time the young couple strolled to baggage claim, they knew each other's names. He had a girlfriend, she had nobody serious. She drove a classic Beetle, and he rode a Harley Softail. More than anything, he wanted to fly, and she wanted to paint. Every dime in his bank account was earned summers and weekends at the airfield and saddling up horses for trail rides and mock roundups. He could spot a dude from Ohio faster than a Texas two-step. Her money came from sitting at the St. Pete Pier doing portraits. She could identify the perfect angle to draw the best features out of any subject. Both were nervous about being with their family.

****

Conner fiddled with his phone. "Ain't that a kicker?" His hand dropped to his side as he shook his head.

"What is?"

"I almost ordered a Lyft in Amarillo." He turned off his phone and restarted it. "This should fix it."

The belt began chugging past them bearing bags tossed haphazardly. Sky's gaze darted from Conner to the sluggish beltway. "Didn't you say you're going to my youth hostel in Manoa?"

His phone lit up and recognized its location. "Yes, I am. If I can get a Lyft."

Her teal bag rumbled up to her, and before she could lunge for it, he picked it up with one hand. "Is there another one like this?"

Sky winced, squeaked, and pointed. "Yes. It's the bigger one coming up."

Conner laughed at the shapely girl with the butterfly colored luggage. "Watch this." He picked up the small black hard-side suitcase and put it beside her two stout suitcases, backpack, and shoulder bag. "Are we both here for the same amount of time? I guess I'm asking for a car with a large trunk."

****

Sky watched her new friend order their ride. *Am I nuts? Well, it is a ride-share.* They exited the sweeping doors of Daniel K. Inouye International Airport. In a sea of lei-wearing Aloha shirts, he stood a head above the rest in his cowboy hat. Its square set flattered his sculpted features. Shadowy stubble accented where a full beard could be in a week. With his military surplus duffle over his shoulder, he shifted from foot to foot in his faded 501 jeans and well-worn boots. He rolled up the sleeves of his plaid western shirt to compensate for the heat. The

19

Amber Anthony

working cowboy tan ended at his wrists, and his forearms were muscled under a dusting of dark hair. Conner's look was not tourist cowboy. It was authentic.

****

Sky and Conner parted as they unlocked their doors across the hall from each other at the hostel. He held up a bottle of water and an orange from the lobby counter. "This isn't going to cut it for more than a couple of hours. How about we reconnect at one?"

Sky leaned against her open door. "Have you ever seen the ocean?" He shook his head. "You paid for the Lyft, let me get lunch, okay? We'll eat on the beach."

Conner dropped his bag inside his door and tipped his hat to her. "It's been a real pleasure, Miss Kingston."

Sky curtsied. "Why, thank you, Mr. Jameson."

She blushed the second she closed the door to her tiny room. Within ten minutes, her toiletries were on the desk, and her clothing suitcase sat open on the luggage stand in what they called a closet. Throwing herself on the creaky double bed, she breathed in the soft island air.

Freedom! I can come and go as I please. No one to tell me what to do and when to do it. She looked at her watch. *Plenty of time for a shower and a nap. Before I shower, let me find some ice for this soda. Ice for the soda? More like ice to cool down what he heated up.*

She donned her terry cloth robe, grabbed her toiletry bucket, picked up the wafer of a towel the hostel provided, and with her key, headed toward the shower.

Chapter Three

Hot sand, cool saltwater, bright sun, and bikinis no bigger than a bandanna. The midday sun bore down on him as he lay on his belly on the beach towel. Girls walked past him, dibbling water on him, and vanished, their laughter lingering behind.

As the water ran down the crease of his buttocks, he realized he was nekkid. *Is that why they were laughing? My white ass? Hell, my whole body is glow-in-the-dark white.*

Sky emerged from the turquoise ocean in a minuscule white bikini, her tanned flesh glowed. *Is she gliding my way?* The sky and ocean shimmered as one behind her. She illuminated the beach as if she were the sun.

She dropped on her knees before him. "I'm so glad you're here. I've missed you, Conner." She leaned back on her heels and extended her hand. "Come swim with me, as dolphins do."

The primal ache of his bedbound erection sprung him off his belly and onto his back. The hostel bedroom's air was stale, and the sheets felt coarse. His cock throbbed hard as a railroad spike as he thanked God that the beach scene was a dream. *Jesus Christ, that girl.* He checked his phone for a noon alarm and willed away his woodie.

****

Sky dropped her robe and got the warm water running. She stepped under the spray, working on disciplining her thoughts to painting on the beach versus painting her new friend in the nude. No matter how diligently she tried to keep her thoughts on landscapes and boats at sea, Conner Jameson's handsome face and strong body distracted her. *I could watch him lift luggage all day if he'd take off that shirt. I'll bet his back is cut and I'm curious, with his height, does he have a six-pack or an eight pack?*

She turned away from the showerhead to rinse out the shampoo, and her hand instinctively found its way where the silky soapy foam collected from her body. *Is it true what they say about the size of a man's hands and feet? I sure would like to find out. Those hands of his swept up my luggage like it was a sack lunch.* She shook her head. *But, no, Skyer, that would be wrong. He has a girlfriend.*

****

Sky sat in the hostel's patio area and slipped on her sunglasses as she fished through her fringed Anushka hobo bag. Once she found cologne she spritzed once and stowed it in the matching makeup bag. *Aunt Sherry couldn't have thought of a more beautiful graduation gift. She knows I love peacocks.* The palm trees swayed overhead as she heard a shuffling sound. She was still processing being halfway around the world. Although Florida and Hawaii were considered wonderland by the other forty-eight states, this was a different flavor of paradise. *How do you strategize against a General?* She shook her head to dispel that thought. *First thing, relax and get to know this cowboy.*

Conner grinned as he approached. "How do you walk in these things?"

"You've never worn slippers?" Sky leaned over, concealing her laughter.

"Bedroom slippers, I've worn bedroom slippers. In Texas, these are called thongs, and you only wear them in the shower or the pool."

Sky stood up and shouldered her bag. "In a hot minute you're going to find out in Hawaii you're never far from water. C'mon, let's have an adventure. I've signed out two bikes for the day because the horses are on the north side of the island."

Conner approached the bike next to hers and shot a finger at her. "You're funny. I like you."

When they stopped at a traffic light, Sky asked, "Do you eat sushi?"

His dark eyes narrowed. "Do I look like a catfish?" His full lips curled into a smirk. "I don't eat bait." He chuckled at her wilting offer. "Awe, Sky, I do like to try new things, just not tiny pieces of raw fish." He hitched the waist of his jeans, and Sky's attention returned to his penetrating dark eyes.

"I know right where to take you. Let's pedal over to Sea and Sky Tacos, you can build your own plate."

They rode up to the sidewalk tables with the bright red umbrellas. They parked, locked the bikes, and walked to the counter. Sky loved watching him discover the island take on Mexican food. She buried a grin as he rubbed his belly. "Hungry much?"

There he stood, a guy out of his usual element. His hands splayed on his hips, one knee bent as the other foot tapped some secret tune. Hickory colored hair moved in the restaurant air conditioning and he combed it back from his forehead like a well-practiced routine. His pink beast of a tongue wiped his bottom lip. "I'm so glad I didn't have to leave tacos at home." He gave a mischievous grin. "They call this Mexican fusion, huh? Not Tex-Mex?"

He stood back and watched her place her order. When it was his turn, he gestured to the server. "Taco plate, one corn, one flour. Brown rice, pinto beans." He turned to Sky and shook his head. "Garlic shrimp or steak? I'm going with what I know." He turned back to the server. "Steak, please. Jalapenos, guacamole, tomatillo salsa, and make it a combo." When he stepped away with his tray, it groaned under the weight of his special requests.

In the midst of the busy sidewalk eatery Sky spread her paper napkin over her lap. "I'm going to give you a taste of my garlic shrimp taco, and you're going to regret that you didn't order it."

"I can always go back for dessert, but I have a feeling, your company is sweet enough for me." As he prepared to eat, his brows danced with good humor. His grin was effortless and went all the way to the creases of his eyes.

Sky blushed into her plate of food as she watched him wrap as much as he could into each shell and demolish the serving in voracious bites. She shook her head. He had the longest, thickest eyelashes she'd ever seen.

Holding two hands full of food Conner looked up and caught her. "What?"

"Just enjoying your healthy appetite." She sipped on her drink.

Conner wiped his hands and raised a brow. He pointed for emphasis. "I'm going to ask you a question. I want you to think about it before you answer."

Sky looked away to the street and back to him curiously. *What is he going to ask me? Oh, here it comes.* She spoke cautiously. "Okay…"

Conner nodded as he took a long draw on his soda. His lips on that straw… She squirmed on the bench. "If you had to choose between eating tacos every day or being on a health kick for the rest of your life…" She kept nodding along with him. "Would you choose hard or soft tacos?"

She snorted out a laugh. *If I say hard, he's going to take it one way, if I say soft, how is he going to take it?* "Well, some days are hard, some days are soft." She closed her eyes and winced. *I cannot believe I said that.*

Conner took a big bite of his second taco and nodded actively. "We have a lot in common. I do like you."

Sky grinned. "Well, I like you, too." She nodded at his quickly disappearing food. "You were hungry."

"Well, all we got was crackers and the front desk offered me that orange, I'm really hungry."

She reached across the table and ruffled the black lock of hair that always flopped onto his forehead. "Your hair and eyes are so dark, do you have Polynesian heritage?"

"Nope. My mother says I'm dark Irish, and my dad's a mainland transplant."

They ate in silence as conversation lagged. She looked to his empty plate. "Do you paint?"

He put down his drink and nodded. "Yeah, barns, fences, bathrooms, bunkhouses."

"For a second, I thought you meant you painted barn art. That's a dying skill."

"Barn art? No time to sit and look at art on a barn, there's work to do." He chuckled. "I get it, you mean art painting. I was so bad at it, they made me the art class model. They wrapped me in a sheet and had me pose."

I bet they did. She controlled her swoon and backed away to view him as a subject. "Well, I'm fresh out of sheets, but if you take your shirt off, I'd love to paint you."

Conner surveyed the tan bodies all around him. "You don't have enough white paint. Maybe in a week or so..." He held out his forearms, and she bit her lip at the stark reality of his pale arms.

"You do have some catching up to do. Are you wearing sunscreen now?"

He nodded as he dug for the can in his backpack. "I have my orders from the guy at the front desk."

"The best way to do it is a little time in, a little time out of the sun. When they cleared their trays, Sky noticed Conner reading the dessert menu. "Still hungry?"

He nodded, watching people walk with bowls across the street. "Is that ice cream?"

She caught his hand and dragged him to the crosswalk. "Better than ice cream, shave ice."

The influx of tourists built around them. For Sky, everything was here for the two of them. After demolishing large towers of fruity colored ice, they ambled toward their bikes. Standing at the end of the block, watching the clouds dancing over the beach, Sky giggled. "How's your day going? Mine is pretty fantastic."

Conner stood, arms across his broad chest. He shifted back on one foot, looking down at her as they stood waiting for the signal. "Yeah, why is that?"

"I don't know. I'm here in paradise. I'm doing what I want to do. I get to be seen on these gorgeous streets with a great looking guy."

Conner scoped out the young, vibrantly dressed tourists. "Yeah, together, we do fit on a postcard, don't we?" He checked his watch.

"Do we need to leave?" Sky's joy flagged.

Conner shifted his footing and frowned at his thongs. "I've got to pick up a couple of things, get a haircut, and some sneakers. I'm pedaling back to the hostel and grabbing a ride to a couple of places."

Sky nodded, walking beside him. "Sneakers are a good idea, those slippers look like an accident waiting to happen."

"I know, right? What are you gonna to do?"

"Probably sort my supplies, organize them in the backpack and find out where's the best place to paint on the beach."

They got on the bikes and made good time moving against traffic. After they returned the bikes, Sky followed him into the lobby, where he consulted the bulletin board for local services. When Sky approached the reception desk about painting, a tanned gal in barely anything sidled up to Conner and tapped a finger on his shoulder. She was buff, probably a surfer judging from her physique. "I know a great shopping center, not too far. I can give you a ride."

Conner's gaze swept the bronze girl from her bare feet to the sun-streaks in her spiky hair. "Awe, that's nice of you, but I gotta do a lotta things that take time. I don't want to hold you up. That's nice of yah."

Sky silently pumped her fist in her head. *Thank-you.*

****

Back in her room, all Sky wanted to do was open her Kindle and cry. The bad news courtesy of the front desk was sales were not permitted on the beach. She sighed. *I can do portraits for my portfolio. I'll figure something out. Maybe Conner will pose for me?*

Chapter Four

The following morning Conner examined himself in the hostel dormitory mirror. Yesterday he found a cheap but sharp haircut. When he couldn't raise Tessa on the phone, he ironed his white western shirt, polished his boots, and his silver belt buckle. The only flash he wore was the ostrich basketweave belt with his granddad's engraved buckle. An extra close shave accentuated his square jaw. His gut churned like the ice cream machine at the diner. Surprised to see his hands shake slightly, Conner drew in a deep breath and clenched both hands to steady them. He hadn't expected to be so nervous. How could this invisible father mean this much? What if he had a bunch of kids? What if Conner wasn't welcome?

He eschewed breakfast, didn't even want coffee. He'd eat after his gut settled down, which probably wouldn't be until his big reveal. The rideshare driver let him off in the circular drive, and Conner closed the car door feeling he was closing the door on his past. That hit and run jackass he thought was his father was nobody. Now he was about to meet a living, breathing man. How would they get along?

Conner took the concrete steps slowly, moving out of the way of two gabbing women who paid him no mind as they flew past him to the sidewalk. He caught the door before it closed and stood for a second. The place known as Silver SEAL Fitness Center was unlike any gym in Texas. High tech machines lined the walls, clanking with the rhythm of sweating athletes. High-velocity music drove folks on treadmills. A freshly scented gust of cool air hit him. Televisions played news, sports, and an exercise class. *Is that my Dad leading the class?* He ran his damp palms down the thighs of his new 501s right before he went tharn.

"May I help you?" He thought he heard a woman's voice. "If you were looking for the gym, you've found it." Now, if he could only find his tongue, he walked toward the pretty lady with a warm voice. He wondered if his eyes looked as round as they felt.

"Yes, ma'am. I was looking to speak to Kirk... ahh... Mr. Roman." Time flowed like molasses.

The woman studied his face as she bit her bottom lip. "Is he expecting you?" She looked away at the monitor and flashed back to scrutinizing him.

"No, ma'am. I don't think he's expecting me." He held his cowboy hat in his hand. A lock of black hair fell over his forehead.

The pretty lady cocked her head and leaned toward him confidentially. "May I tell him your name and the reason for your visit?"

Conner's dark brows knitted. "My name is Conner Jameson. The subject of my visit is kinda personal if you don't mind me saying."

"Okay... Excuse me." She turned to her assistant. "Bonnie, I'll be right back." Bonnie moved to the counter mesmerized by the cowboy.

****

Jordan took the stairs like a gazelle. *When I get a hold of Des, I am asking for lottery numbers.* She slid into Kirk's office doorway. "Turn on the lobby cameras from my angle."

Kirk looked up. "We got trouble?"

"Depends on what you mean..." Jordan smirked, her arms crossed over her logo shirt, and the smirk turned into a laugh. "Who's visiting us today?"

"This kid?" Kirk leaned closer to the monitor. "Is he one of those film stars?" Kirk put on his eyeglasses and enlarged the image. "What boneheaded thing did Jax do eighteen years ago? What is that kid eighteen, nineteen? Is this a long lost grandson?"

"Oh, dear..." Jordan's chuckle slowed. "He didn't ask for Jax. He asked for Mr. Kirk Roman." Kirk pushed back from the desk and reared in the chair, his eyes scanning the ceiling while his fingers did the math. "Remember Des's prediction? By this time next year, you'll be settled with all your children around you?"

Kirk stood abruptly. "You don't believe that poppycock."

"Maybe not, but I believe my eyes. Do you want me to bring the young man down, or do you want to come upstairs so I can watch?"

Kirk paled. "Why don't we go up together?"

****

To settle his nerves, Conner picked up the gym brochure and scanned it, absorbing no information, but it gave him something to do with his hands. From the corner of his eye, he saw the woman returning, and beside her was a tall man with greyer features than his photos. Features that were eerily familiar. Would he look like this in a few decades? He dropped the brochure and found himself standing almost at attention. *What the hell am I gonna say?*

His father stopped in front of him and put out his hand. "I'm Kirk Roman, you're Mr. Jameson?"

Conner swallowed roughly. "Yes, sir. I'm... I'm Tammy's son. I'm... your son." Conner thought he actually might pass out. He pulled what he had learned was a Turk's Head bracelet from his pocket. "Mom said you left this... on... with her..."

It was his father's turn to swallow convulsively. He accepted the bracelet from his son. "Ah, yeah, my bracelet." He gestured to the woman beside him. "This is my wife, Jordan." He paused as if wondering what to say next.

His wife spoke up. "Welcome, Conner, why don't we all go down to Kirk's office? I'll bring some refreshments, and you two can talk." The two men stood floundering as she pressed a gentle hand to their shoulders and steered them downstairs. "Bonnie, keep an eye on the front desk and..." She pantomimed zipping her lip at the girl who shrugged silently.

She led the way to the office and motioned to the pair of chairs in front of the desk. "You two sit here and get to know each other. I'll be right back."

****

Conner's mind was at once jumbled and completely blank. *Is this how shock feels?*

Kirk's words took a moment. "It's been some time since I've seen your mother. How is she?"

Conner, relieved to talk about anything other than himself, perked up. "She hit the mother lode. An oil company bought all forty acres and paid her a hefty sum. She's already in Daytona Beach, Florida. She wants one of those duplexes so she can live on one side and rent out the other."

Kirk worked the cords of the bracelet in his two hands, his finger tracing the in and out pattern of the white rope. "Well, that sounds like a great plan. What are you doing here? Thinking of moving to Hawaii?"

Conner sat military straight. "No, sir. One day I'm going to be an Air Force Pilot. I heard you were in the service." He tucked his chin for a second. "I... Mom... she's not keen on the idea of me enlisting..." He swallowed hard. "I wanted to talk to a man I trusted about it. Grandpa died a year ago..."

There was a heavy silence for a beat.

"You just met me, and you trust me? Well, that's quite an honor, son. I'm glad you came to me."

Conner's words spilled out. "So, you believe me?"

Kirk leaned across the divide and put his hand over Conner's. "I do look in the mirror every day, and I remember being... young and full of spit. Yes, son, I believe you. I'm sorry I didn't know about you."

"Until a few days ago, I didn't know about you. Mom gave me my birth certificate and that bracelet. I wondered who Roman was. Then she told me the story of my middle name." Conner balled his fists on his knees. "Who keeps stuff like that from a kid?"

Kirk's held breath escaped with a gust, his brow rose, and he shook his head. "Back then, we still used phone books to find people. She knew no way to contact me. Maybe she hoped her husband would come back if he knew there was a child."

"If she was married, why did you sleep with her?" His dark brown eyes expressed his ache. Kirk returned the pained look. "You didn't know, did you?"

"It was my first day off. I went in to buy boots and stopped for breakfast. Tammy was the kindest, most genuine person I'd met in years. We hit it off. She invited me to meet her for chicken fried steak. We danced into a whirlwind." Conner's jaw dropped silently. "I got the call to come out here as we were waking up. I was on a plane that night."

Conner stuttered out. "You never looked for a wedding ring?"

Kirk shrugged. "She didn't wear one. As I was getting dressed, I told her I thought we'd have had a lot more good times. And she told me she wasn't sure her husband would like that. I think that was kind of her defense against me sliding out of bed and out of town. She did say he'd just taken off on her, and she was waiting to file for a divorce."

Conner shook his head. "She never even dated after I was born. We were close, but not close enough for the truth." He stood and turned from Kirk, seeking the wall of blinds facing the exercise room. His head dropped as he wiped his eyes.

Kirk took in a deep breath, moved to Conner's side, and cupped his son's shoulders. "She was probably trying to protect you." They stood in pensive silence, the base thumped above them, throbbing like an anxious heartbeat. "It takes a lot to tear up your old dad, but I think this is one for the books." His chuckle grew more emotional as they stood in the sounds of their sniffling. "If I had known, you and I would have been in each other's lives from the start."

Conner turned to his father and let the older man embrace him in a bear hug. They compressed nineteen years of emotion into a few seconds. Kirk cleared his throat as he put on the bracelet. "This will remind me that things lost can be found."

There was a quick knock, and the door opened, Jordan backed in with a tray of fruit and bottles of sparkling water. "This was all I had on short notice…" She put down the tray and scurried out, closing the door behind her.

Kirk led his son to sit down as he poured glasses of water for both of them. "I can see you're a cowboy, did you ever work on The Rocking Horse?"

Conner's familiar smile spread. "Oh, heck, they stopped punching cows when I was a kid. They've gone Hollywood. It's a full out dude ranch now. All those bankers from New York are flying in on private planes, bringing their families to play cowboy. I gassed their private jets and saddled their horses."

Kirk laughed. "And I'll bet you've broken a few hearts."

Conner ducked his head. "I try not to, but sometimes I still get text messages."

31

Jordan returned, sticking her head around the door. Kirk turned and waved her in, and she leaned against the edge of the desk. "Where are you staying, Conner? We're so delighted you're here. We'd love for you to stay with us."

"Well, thank you, ma'am, but..."

"Jordan."

"Yes, m'am..., Jordan. I'm at the hostel in Manoa. I'm not here to impose."

Jordan gave Kirk a nod. Kirk tapped the boy's knee. "Family isn't an imposition. How did you get here?"

"Lyft."

Kirk stood immediately. "You can at least join us for lunch. My schedule is clear, I want you to meet your brother."

"My brother?"

Kirk's arm encircled Conner's shoulder. "Don't get any ideas from him. He thinks he's a superhero."

Conner paused, scrutinizing Kirk and Jordan as he followed them up the stairs.

Chapter Five

Sky turned on the shower full force. Would it wash away all the emotion she saw last evening at the beach? She was alone, and Conner was off doing things to prepare to meet his father. She watched families playing everywhere. Scenes of daddies and their little girls assaulted her heart.

Growing up with him in the military meant time with her father was heightened by visiting resorts together and staying in strange cities twice a year. Paris Disney was no replacement for Christmas morning under a homestyle tree. As she grew older, she realized her father did the best he could. On the other hand, as she got older, she found herself warier and warier of their interactions. He wanted to be a dad, but he was a stranger. She wanted to please him, but his goals for her were different from her own.

She'd ducked two of his calls since she arrived, and now she felt guilty. He was in the military after all, what if something happened to him and she hadn't answered his last call? Last night she watched a father give his daughter away in a beautiful beach wedding. What if she never got to do that with her father? She would gather her wits and make that call after she got out of the shower.

Toweling off, Sky picked up her phone and hit return call. He answered on the second ring as if the phone was at arm's length. "Kingston."

"Daddy? Hi, Daddy. Sorry I missed your calls yesterday. I was out."

"Out where? Your aunt tells me you are in Hawaii. Are you?"

She had never heard this tone from him before. On the other hand, she'd never traveled halfway around the world on a whim. "Yes, as a matter of fact, I am in Hawaii. I decided I needed time to think before we got together out here."

Her father's tone gentled somewhat. "I'm looking forward to Hawaii, too. I got a nice two-bedroom suite. We'll make some great memories."

"Don't we always?"

"Where are you now?"

"The hostel in Manoa."

He laughed. "Roughing it? Is it safe? I can get you checked into a single at the resort with a phone call."

Sky returned his laughter. "Oh, Daddy, I'm safe. It's secure, and although it's a shade shabby, it's clean."

"Pick out your favorite restaurant and make our reservations. We can invite Aunt Jordan and her new husband."

Sky pouted. "Aunt Jordan got married to someone other than you?"

Hank chuckled. "He asked first. I shoulda never told him to make a move."

"Well, why did you give her up? I love Aunt Jordan…" Sky huffed out in disappointment. "I thought during this trip, you would have popped the question."

Hank sighed. "Oh, peanut. I guess I was away from her too much."

This trip is a bust. I can't charge for my art. The boy I met has a girlfriend. And now Aunt Jordan is married. Crap.

Hank waded into the long silence. "Now, don't fret. I've got some great news to talk about when I get there.

Sky shut down. "I'm looking forward to meeting you at the Coconut Palms in six days. Love you, Daddy." Sky looked heavenward.

Judge, I'm amending my complaint. This trip is a bust. Aunt Jordan is married. I can't charge for my art. The boy I met has a girlfriend, and my father probably has a new plan for my life. Double Crap. Time to eat my feelings at the Rainbow Drive-In.

****

As Jordan's convertible cut through the tourist congestion, the hotel traffic gave way to Kapi'olani Regional Park's greenery. The scent of the pervasive plumeria trees rode on the soft breezes coming off the surf to their right.

Conner couldn't contain himself. "Look how blue that ocean is, the ground is incredibly green, the flowers are like colorful birds. I've never seen anything like it." His head swiveled to see a flock of white birds fly and dive in formation. "I've never seen birds fly like a school of fish, what are they?"

Kirk turned in his seat. "Those? They're the bird of Ku. He's one of the four great Hawaiian gods. But you can call them White Fairy Terns."

"They're cool!" Conner's attention followed the flock as it rose and dove from tree to fragrant tree. "Those flowers, the bright colored ones – they were made into leis, some of the people on my flight got them." Conner settled back in his seat. "I thought there was nothing finer than flying an airplane at sunrise, but this is paradise."

Jordan exchanged a glance with Kirk and nodded. "We think so."

Conner dug for his phone. "Kirk, will we be close to a beach? I want to swim at Waikiki, and I think we passed it." Conner looked back from where they came.

"We've got you covered. The beaches are free for everyone. Even in neighborhoods there are easements to get to the water." Kirk gestured to the left. "On the other side of the island is the Banzai Pipeline, we'll go up there and watch the preschoolers put me to shame on their surfboards."

Conner's jaw dropped. "You don't surf?"

Kirk shook his head. "Not like those little kids."

Conner marveled. "The water is unbelievable, so many colors of blue. The air is so clean."

Within a few blocks, the foot of Diamondhead abutted Diamondhead Road. Conner gawked at being this close to the gently sloping mountain. "It looked big from downtown, but man, that is huge."

Jordan smiled back at him in the rearview mirror. "And I thought things were just big in Texas."

They got caught behind tourists in a rented Polaris Slingshot automobile. The open-air, 3-wheeled roadster convertible moved at a glacial rate as the woman knelt in the passenger seat, snapping photographs.

Conner leaned over the side of Jordan's convertible. "That thing looks like the Batmobile, and it should be going a hundred miles an hour..."

Kirk hunkered in the front seat. "Looks are deceiving." He checked his watch. "At this rate, you could have let me off at Lē'ahi Park, and I could have swum home."

"But then you wouldn't have had our delightful company. Besides, Jax and Kameo are probably behind us, I doubt they're ahead of us."

The Slingshot's driver goosed the accelerator, and the woman nearly toppled out of the car. With a scream, the tourists disappeared ahead.

Jordan pulled her car through gates ornately decorated with dolphins into the porte-cochre, and Conner sat spellbound. Kirk exited the car and watched his son's reaction to the estate.

Focusing on the massive etched glass double doors and wide steps, Conner stood in place and did a 360-degree turn. "Is this a condo complex? Where do you park?" Kirk dug for his key fob and phone. He opened the double garage doors to reveal his motorcycle and Jordan's parking space. "Is that your bike?"

"Yep. I don't ride much since I got hitched, but it's mine." Kirk hit the security app on his phone, and the etched doors made an audible click. "Come on in, let's go out to the pool."

Kirk and Jordan entered the foyer and slid out of their shoes. Conner noticed the collection of footwear parked at the door. Kirk turned back to his son. "Those boots are going to get cumbersome. You need to get yourself a pair of slippers."

Conner's brows joined in dismay. "Those things? I've got some. I wear 'em in the shower. They aren't fit for the street."

Jordan smiled. "We have an extra pair somewhere you can wear by the pool. Meanwhile, park those beauties right here." She watched him sit on the bench in his stocking feet. "Socks, too." His feet were as white as his ankles. He rolled up the cuffs of his jeans. "Do you have a swimsuit? Want to borrow one?" She gestured to the view through the living area. The white walls gave way to massive sliding doors that opened the home to nature and the ocean view.

Conner stood, eyes wide at the elegance of the low slung furniture and exotic electronics, but his jaw dropped at the ocean's never-ending surf pounding within feet of the back property line. "Hot damn." He followed them, taking in every detail. "Where is your apartment?"

Kirk came back from the patio. "Son, I'm the caretaker of this spread. It's the home of a friend of mine. He used to be my business partner. You've heard of Evan Silver?"

"Him, *the* Evan Silver? The computer guy?"

"Yeah…Anyway, I used to live in the pool house, but that's a long story. We're in the main house now until our condo is rehabbed. If you wanted to bunk with us, you could stay in the pool house for privacy, come and go as you please…" Kirk walked him through the kitchen out to the garden with the water feature and the quaint cottage.

Conner blinked. "I thought I was bringing all the surprises, but you got me."

Jordan entered from the hallway carrying a few pairs of board shorts and slippers. "Jax is on his way now. Why don't you use the powder room and get comfortable?" She showed Connor the way and left to join Kirk.

****

Powder room? This bathroom is larger than my bedroom at home. The window looked out into a walled Zen garden. Conner backed to the glass, his broad shoulders framed by the exotic plants, and it looked like he was sitting next to Buddha. He snapped a selfie and texted it over to Sky.

'I've met the most interesting people in Honolulu, how about you?'

The floor to ceiling mirror magnified his cowboy tan. Before he could get into his swimsuit, his phone pinged. Sky sent a selfie shooting a peace sign standing on a beach.

'I did meet this handsome cowboy, wish he was at the beach with me. Can you get over here later? I'm on Waikiki on the beach behind the statue of Duke. It's a

*landmark. I'll be here till 8 pm but come earlier for the
sunset of your life'.*

He stared at the cleavage in her bikini and shifted from foot to foot.
That bikini makes her a landmark herself.

'I'll find some way. See you there."

Standing in the loose board shorts, he was pasty white from his
chest to his size thirteen feet. *Oh, jeez.* He scratched at the patch of black
hair in the center of his chest and realized how much whiter it made his
skin. Thankfully, the board shorts ran to above his knees. He tied the
knot and prayed they stayed up. *But my ass is just as white as my thighs, how
would they know the difference?*

Before he left the powder room, he rolled his underwear into his
jeans pocket and folded them up to fit under the counter. The shirt? He
was wearing it.

"There he is," Kirk called cheerfully to Jordan. "We thought you
got lost. Take a look at the juice selection out here, we have soda and
water, too."

Conner stared at the commercial beverage cooler. *Mango, papaya,
pineapple, orange, grapefruit... Coke, Pepsi, Sprite, Root Beer, how many different
sparkling waters?* "Ice water?"

Jordan met him with a tall tumbler of ice water garnished with a
slice of lime. "I'll bet you're thirsty after that flight yesterday."

Kirk stretched out on a teak lounger, his hands behind his head.
"You need to do some private pool time before you hit the beach. You
are prime sunburn material."

Jordan brought a can of sunscreen and offered it to him. "Get rid
of that shirt, and let's get you protected." Suddenly, Conner felt like he
was a ten year old on vacation with his parents. He slid out of his shirt
as Kirk stood up and began spraying his back and legs. "Rub that in so
it doesn't streak."

Chapter Six

Conner rubbed in the white spray, which was just about the color of his skin and he lamented that fact. He was distracted by musical laughter and lusty snickers. The most stunningly beautiful woman in the world ran in with a man chuckling behind her. The dark-haired man caught the woman in a playful embrace, and they froze, looking at Kirk, Jordan, and Conner.

"Kameo, this must be my new little brother." He dropped the woman to her feet and faced his dad. "But I wanted a pony." And then he took strides to catch Conner in a two-handed shake. "Kid, I'm your brother. Jax, short for Jaxson, and this is my wife, Kameo. That's Dr. Kameo Roman." He gestured his thumbs back to himself. "Yes, I'm Mr. Dr. Roman. Are you ready for this crazy family?"

Conner stood gobsmacked until Kameo stepped up to shake his hand, and then she hugged him. "Welcome to your Ohana, little bro."

At that point, Conner was spellbound by her tropical scent and the weighty shoulder length of silky black hair that had a life of its own. One of those plumerias was pinned behind her left ear.

She is heaven. What is she wearing? The bikini top defied gravity. The flowing skirt that wrapped her round hips wasn't actually a skirt, it was clothe tied at her hip, and the split went all the way up to show the tie of her bikini bottoms. *Her legs go on for days. My brother is the luckiest son of a bitch on earth.*

Jax walked up to Conner, put an arm around Kameo, and patted his cheek. "Yeah, I'm the luckiest bastard on this island." He exchanged a smirk with his father, who shook his head at Jax.

Conner nodded numbly. "Uh-huh."

Kameo slipped out of Jax's embrace and waved him off. "Stop that. You're embarrassing me." She raised her brow at Jax. "We're here to welcome your brother."

****

After a long lunch, with many revelations, Kirk and Jax walked Conner out to the garage. Kirk gestured at his Harley. "You said you ride, why don't you use my bike while you're here?" He took a full-face helmet off the wall. "This has Bluetooth. You can pair your phone for navigation and hands-free calls." Kirk pulled a riding jacket off a hanger. "I left the body armor in this. Might be a little large, but people will see you."

Conner slid into the jacket and shifted his shoulders. He leaned into Kirk for a hug and a handshake. "I don't know how to thank you. Man, this is fancy gear."

"I'm glad to do it. Isn't that what dads are for?"

Conner and Kirk exchanged silent smiles. Conner cleared his throat." At home, I wear a jeans jacket and Mom makes me wear a half helmet. Nothing like this."

Kirk handed over the keys and slapped his son on the back. "Only thanks I need is your promise always to wear your gear." Conner nodded. "Are you coming to the gym tomorrow?"

"If I'm going to stay awhile, I'm job hunting tomorrow." He held the helmet, ready to ride. Jax and Kirk exchanged a look. "But I gotta eat, can we get together for lunch?"

Jax pulled out his wallet and passed cash into his brother's hand. "Bring lunch with you unless you want a granola bar and a smoothie. Bring some for me, too."

Kirk gave both sons an exasperated look and stammered. "There is a café across the street. It's not granola bars all the time." Conner donned the helmet and slid up the face mask. "Around one?"

Kirk nodded. "I'm really glad you're here. I know you want your privacy, but don't be a stranger." They hugged briefly, and Conner turned back to Jax as Kirk left.

Jax stood, a knowing expression on his face, his arms folded over his tank top after he slid his sunnies on top of his head. He finished with a smirking nod. "You might have hidden your phone from dad, but you've already got a date..." Jax playfully punched his brother's shoulder.

Conner nodded. "There is this girl... just a friend. Besides, I've got a girlfriend back home."

"You work fast, been here twenty-four hours, and you're heading off to meet a beautiful *friend*. But seriously, kid, I know you need to pick up a few things. Living in a hostel, you need some snacks and stuff."

Conner looked around and considered. "Stuff, huh?"

"Let me lead you back to the hostel, and we'll stop at the store and pick up a few things. I'll let Kameo know." Jax texted Kameo, and Conner mounted the bike. "Do you know where the statue of Duke is?"

Jax laughed. "I'll hook you up." The brothers roared out of the driveway in the pickup truck and motorcycle.

****

Conner entered his hostel's private room. Stark as it was, it looked about the size of his bedroom at home, and it was clean. Jax carried the cooler, ice, and snacks in and set them next to the one plastic chair with the tennis balls on the feet. Conner dumped the shopping bag on the bed. He held up the red board shorts, the beach blanket, and a towel. "Thanks for the shopping trip."

Jax picked up the thirty-six count box of Trojans. "I want you to be the only surprise child on this island. Promise me, you'll carry a couple at all times. But not in your wallet." Jax opened one of the tins of Altoids and dumped them on the bedspread. "Carry them here. The heat won't degrade them."

"But I've got Tessa back home."

Jax smirked and nodded. "The TSA allows people to pack condoms. Meanwhile, be prepared."

Conner watched in mute amazement as he accepted the filled tin from his brother. "Did your doctor wife teach you that?"

Jax stared at him for a moment, laughed, and shook his head. "Kid, if you join the service, your drill sergeant will be amazed at your readiness." Conner slipped the tin into his back pocket and nodded. When he looked at his phone, Jax chuckled. "I'll head back and let

41

everyone know you're settled in." Jax stopped at the door and turned. "Have a good night."

****

Conner sat in the silence of the stark hostel bedroom, still tingling from the way the Romans accepted him. Sorting through the snacks and sodas, he dutifully stowed the remaining Trojans in the bottom of his duffle bag. He answered his phone on the second ring. "Hey, baby. I wish you could be out here with me. My dad is so cool. You'd…"

"I'm going to Vanderbilt." Tessa screeched into the phone.

Conner jerked the phone from his ear. "Vanderbilt? I didn't know that was a possibility."

"It was a long shot, I got in as an alternate. My cousin lives in Nashville with her husband, and I'll be summering with them so I can find a job and get my housing situated." She took a breath. "I leave the day after tomorrow!" *Again with the screech.*

His heart sobered. "How are we going to say good-bye, baby?"

Tessa's voice lost all her triumphant glee. "Con, it's been great, you've been the best boyfriend a girl could have. But we're adults now, and we need to…"

"You're breaking up with me?"

"You left me."

Conner tapped his foot and ground his jaw. "I came out here to meet my dad." Dead silence. Not even static. "I guess since you're wiping your feet on my heart, I might as well stay."

"I'm so glad you understand, Con." Garbled voices came through the phone speaker. Her hand muffled more sounds. "Hold, on Decker, let me get off this call."

"Decker? Is he going to Vanderbilt, too?"

"One thing doesn't have anything to do with the other."

"Right." He made a fist and then let it go. "Don't let me keep you. Have a good life, Tessa."

"Well, you too. Send me a postcard, okay? Mom will forward it." Tessa hung up.

Sonnofabitch. Decker Cargill. Hadn't he seen the Cargill label on all the meat delivered to the diner? Decker's family lived on a ranch that spanned the land between Amarillo and Canyon, Texas.

He went to a boarding school in Austin. How fuckin' fast did he move on Tessa? Has she been seeing him all along? What a stretch for a billionaire's son to be involved with the daughter of a hick town general store owner.

Conner shook his head to clear his thoughts. Realization dawned like a gong. *I'm in paradise, and I'm single.*

Getting used to tourist drivers on the Waikiki streets, Conner followed his navigation system's directions to the bronze statue of Duke on Kalakaua Avenue. Sundays, parking meters weren't enforced, so he parked, locked the helmet to the engine guard, and took off on foot with his backpack to find Sky.

It was a little after six, and the sun looked like it had awhile before it set. The caressing warmth of that sun couldn't be the same orange orb that flashed harsh in Texas. The sand glistened before him, shadowed by tall palms dancing in the beach breeze. The music of people's conversations, children playing, and the heartbeat of the waves invigorated him. *Oh, Lord, look at me now.*

He rolled his shoulders and stood tall. Everything about this place was surreal after nineteen years of school, scout projects, and two part time jobs. Conner silently scanned the beach for Sky. He wanted to see her first so that he could savor the sight of her pale blonde hair and tan shoulders. Was she wearing cutoffs or a bikini bottom? *Her selfie didn't show that.* Did she have a tattoo? He didn't... yet. *Man, I love Hawaii.*

She sat, facing east, sketching Diamondhead. Her serious expression at her task impressed him. He'd never seen anyone so young be so serious about a craft. Did he look like this when he co-piloted with Chip? He knew he was serious when he rode with Chip, the topdressing pilot. Chip let him do everything except land and take off. Man, he loved it. *Flying is life.*

He straightened his tank top, let his board shorts ride low on his hips the way Jax did and slid his sunnies onto his face. With a deep breath, he headed across the sand to his beach bunny.

Evidently, every man on the beach headed for his beach bunny. *I have to rethink that my brother is the luckiest son of a bitch on this island.* What a stroke of luck that his steady girl cut him loose. *I was shocked, but that door closed, and what a window I'm looking through.* When he saw two surfers with boards hanging over Sky's easel, Conner's first inclination was to shoo them off. He hung back and watched her style.

Head down over her palette, she mixed colors and half-listened to their come-ons. With a tilt of her blonde curls, she lowered her sunglasses, and after an extended silence, she waved her brush between them. "Does this usually work for you?" The two college-aged guys exchanged looks, the alpha male bent closer and said something indecipherable. Sky brandished the long paintbrush like an epee, and he backed off.

The wingman caught his buddy by the shoulder and turned him away. Leaning back to Sky, he shook his head. "This season is just beginning, with an attitude like that, you're going to be alone… a lot."

Sky smiled, sipped from her smoothie, and declared. "I won't be alone, I just won't be you either of you."

Damn, girl. That's a smackdown. It made Conner wonder what the alpha guy had said. She didn't strike him as a mean girl. The surfers bumped boards leaving for the shoreline. Conner took his time approaching her from the front. "I got here as soon as I could. How's your painting going?" He walked behind her to see the horizontal canvas full of bright azure sky, a multicolored mountain, and an abandoned red beach bucket with a yellow shovel. "What are you calling this?"

Sky looked over her sunglasses and giggled. "Mountain and bucket?"

He nodded appreciatively as he stuck his thumb out to check the perspective between the bucket and Diamondhead. "At least they're both sitting still for you."

Chapter Seven

Sky bit the end of her paintbrush and grinned. "I can't sell anything on the beach, but here's my plan: I take their photo, and we meet over at the shave ice stand, they pay me, and I ship the piece. Clever, huh?" Her brow rose with her satisfied smirk.

"You work fast. Speaking of work, tomorrow, I have to look for a job. Even temporary work."

"How long are you staying?"

He winced. "I haven't bought my return ticket yet..."

"Oh, you do need a job. There are horse ranches all over this island."

He stretched out his blanket, laid on his side and propped his head on his hand, in rapt attention to her pose on the small folding stool. "You're a piece of art just sitting there, I wish I could draw." She blushed. "Do I make you nervous watching you?"

She began cleaning her brush. "I was only killing time until you got here. Let me pack this stuff on my bike, and we can go for a walk. How about some of those garlic shrimp?" Sky shook out a gauzy dress and slipped it over her bathing suit. Conner watched the fringe dance over her knees as she walked.

****

Sky hefted her art supplies over one shoulder. "You like rice?"

Conner stopped abruptly. "Is that a loaded question. Why?"

Sky waved him to join her. "Everything at the Moose Pub is served with rice, but you'll like it. Especially since..." She leaned close to his ear and whispered... "there's no sushi." She laughed at his response when they bumped hips.

He caught her with both hands. "Steady as she goes, lead on." When he let go, her electricity surged through him.

Sky jabbered about the restaurant, and as he followed, all he could think was how soft her skin felt.

"… they rock happy hour with the music and videos, but we can play darts or pool…"

If she bends over a pool table, I am officially done.

Sky's voice captivated him. "You know you're in Hawaii when you see this on the menu." She pointed. "Kalua pig quesadilla." She turned to him and slowly licked her lips. He shuddered. "All that steak in Texas, have you ever had teriyaki sirloin steak?"

I feel like I've been staked. Sweet mother.

Conner approached the host station, and they were seated near the pool tables. He felt her gaze through the menu.

Her big blue eyes searched his face with concern. "You haven't said a word about your dad. Did it not go well?"

Without glancing up from the menu, he nodded. "It went great. You're gonna love my family. I've got an older brother. He was a SEAL, and his wife is a doctor."

Sky put down her menu. "I always wanted a brother. But what about your dad?"

Conner put down his menu and shook his head. "It was so funny. I go into his gym, and this really nice lady stares real hard at me. I told her I'm here to see Kirk Roman, and they come back, and it was like a dream. We sat in dad's office, and his wife brought some drinks and stuff. He's so cool. He said he was honored I came to him for advice and that if he had known about me, we would have been close. Then his wife asks me to move into this mansion on the water…"

Sky's chin rested in her hands, her eyes wide at his tale. "Are you going to leave the hostel?" Her tone sagged.

Conner shook his head. "They offered me a pool house, you ought to see it, it's bigger than the house I grew up in."

She tucked her chin, and her hands fell into her lap. "So, when are you moving?"

Conner waved the thought away. "I can't impose like that, besides, you're showing me the ropes around here. If I left, I'd have to take you."

Sky blushed at his comment and bit at her bottom lip. The server came by with their drinks and hovered, waiting for their order. Once they ordered, they each relaxed back into the booth, gazing across the table at each other.

Conner stuck out a leg. "How do you like my jams? Jordan loaned them to me and said they were mine if I liked them. Do you like them?"

"Is Jordan your brother?"

Conner grinned. "Naw, my dad got married last Christmas to this woman he knew for eighteen years. Man, I am not waiting for eighteen years to stake a claim." He watched her complexion pale. "Did I say something wrong?"

Sky's index finger flew up. "Your dad took eighteen years to," she used air quotes, 'Stake a claim'?" Her jaw hung open.

"I guess he moves kinda slow? Yeah, she worked for him, and it was something a friend said that got him to ask her out."

Sky leaned across the table, stony-faced. "Her name is Jordan, a unisex name?"

Conner chuckled. "The men in my family have gorgeous wives. Jordan has beautiful silver hair. She's so athletic..."

Sky threw both hands up and groaned. "Your daddy married my Aunt Jordan. She was my dad's girlfriend." Sky buried her face in her arms, and her words were muffled. "I cannot frigging believe this. You and I are almost kin."

Conner's brows gathered. "Is that a bad thing?"

"No, that's a great thing, but she was supposed to be my mom!"

Conner got up from his side of the booth and slid next to Sky. "Well, angel, you can join my family at any time."

Sky leaned away from him. "Shouldn't you ask your girlfriend, first?"

Conner slid away from her. "Funny thing about that..."

****

After three games of pool and five games of darts, Sky made it clear she was not into letting men win. They drained their ice teas, and Conner picked up the check. Hand in hand, they strolled toward the beach. The breezes blew tendrils of soft blonde hair back from her happy face. She hadn't stopped grinning since he told her he was done with the girl in Texas. *Will I ever admit she was done with me first? It doesn't matter, I am trading up.*

Each time they got to a stoplight and waited to walk, he thought about crushing her into his arms and telling her what a revelation she was in the few hours he knew her. *She is gutsy, hell, she got on an airplane all by herself and flew off to be alone in Hawaii. She picked the hostel when she could have made a beeline for Aunt Jordan.* She wasn't like the girls he knew in Texas, and he was gladder for it.

When they hit the beach post-sunset, the surf was darker. The waves made their insistent advances and further retreats as high tide moved to low tide. They found few people as he slipped his hand out of hers and gently placed it at the small of her back. They wandered along the shore, stepping out of the seafoam. "You need to get out of those sneakers."

"I thought of that." He stood back on the packed wet sand and traded his Chucks for the slippers in his backpack.

She opened up her beach towel a few feet back on the dry sand and dropped her pack on it. "Join me, wading?"

Conner dropped his pack to join hers. He would have followed her anywhere. Once they were a few feet into the caressing water, Conner caught her by the hips. "These days, I know I need permission. I hope you won't deny me a kiss."

Sky's expression was radiant. She poked him in the chest. "You broke up with your girlfriend. I can't get over that." She hugged herself with a shiver.

"Get over it, please, I know I did." He wrapped both arms around her. "You're shivering. Are you cold?"

She wrapped her arms around his waist and pressed her cheek to his heart. "You tell me. Do I feel cold to you?"

Conner's hand smoothed the curls buffeted by the beach breeze. "You feel like heaven, angel. Pure heaven."

"Since your momma raised such a gentleman, why not let me kiss you back?"

He caught her around the shoulders, and when he expected it would be just another kiss, it became wonderful. Her lips were stained with the shave ice blue raspberry color, and the flavor enticed him. When Sky Kingston kissed him, he knew he'd been kissed. In the calf-deep water, they ended their reverie only when a huge wave swept them to their knees. When it was necessary to come up for air, she blinked at him. He blinked at her.

"That was one big kiss. Is that a Texas kiss?"

His cheeks flushed with optimism. "Did I lasso your heart?"

"With just one kiss?" They struggled to their feet. "You'll have to try it again tonight after you follow me home to make sure I'm safe."

"But I have a motorcycle, and you have a bicycle..."

Sky tapped her finger on his bottom lip. "Come with me. I have a plan." They made their way to the bike rack. "Drive your bike over here. I've got to make a phone call."

****

Sky dialed Aunt Jordan's cell. "Aunt Jordan, it's Sky. I was wondering if you could do me a favor?" Sky heard muffled words and grinned at her plan.

"Sky, oh, where are you? Your dad is coming out soon, will you be with him?"

"Actually, I'm in town right now. I hate to impose at this hour, but I'm down at Waikiki near Duke's statue."

"Well, what are you doing there?"

Sky buried her chuckle. "I'm staying in Manoa until Daddy gets here. I'm on a bicycle, and the guy I met at the beach wants to give me a ride on his motorcycle. Can you come and get my bike?"

Sky heard she was on speaker by the noise Jordan's husband made.

"Sky, you stay right there. Do not go with a boy on a motorcycle. Give me fifteen minutes, stay under a street light."

Sky heard the throaty sound of the Harley, and Conner kept it in neutral, the steel horse throbbing with power between his legs. *He broke up with his girlfriend.* The words spun in her head until she blinked back to reality.

"Okay, I'll wait right here." Sky ended the call and turned to Conner. "Aunt Jordan is coming to pick up my bicycle. But I've played a mean trick on her. I thought I had to. She didn't marry daddy."

Conner looked askance. "Okay." He turned off the bike. "It's going to take a while for her to get here."

Sky's expression brightened. *Good, more than good. Aloha, cowboy!* She shook her head and grinned. "May I sit with you on the bike? It's getting a little chilly."

Conner got off the bike and stalked to her, his eyes dark and hungry. "It would be a pleasure to keep you warm, angel." He slipped out of his jacket and wrapped it lovingly around her shoulders. When she felt cocooned in the scent of leather and his cologne, she lifted her face for a kiss. His hands framed her cheeks and drew her to him. His moan filled her with a primal hunger she'd never felt in a public place.

She was in imminent danger of having sinful fantasies. So much happened in the last three hours. Her head spun at the feeling of him being this close, their lips within breathing space. His arms cuddled her close to his chest, and their lips danced in breathless joy. He pressed his forehead against hers. She felt his hands reach and grab the sides of her arms as if to steady them. Nose to nose, eyes closed, they took a deep breath at the same time, sharing the moment and inhaling the shared oxygen. Their spirits soared.

Cars zipped past them. Bicycles blew by them, barely missing them. It was not until headlights swept over them, and a car door opened that they heard Jordan's squeal.

Chapter Eight

"Skyler Kingston, is that you? What are you doing?"

Conner raised his dark head, still gazing in Sky's eyes. "I'm just keeping her warm, Jordan."

Kirk flew to his side. "She looks warm to me. I think you can back off." He turned to Sky. "Honey, I haven't seen you in how long?"

Sky dreamily looked up at Kirk Roman. "Hi, Mr. Roman. I haven't been here in two years." She huddled by herself within his jacket. Conner separated and shuffled from foot to foot.

"Hey, Dad. Thanks for coming to get Sky's bike."

Jordan hovered maternally. "Sky, this is not a surprise. You knew."

Sky shrugged. "Not until dinner tonight when Conner told me about his dad and his new wife." Sky threw up her hands. "I gave him hell because you were supposed to marry Daddy."

Kirk paced around the group, scratching at his neck. "What?"

Sky turned on him. Her hands on her hips. "Don't pretend. Daddy has been courting Jordan as long as I can remember. I wanted her for a mom."

Kirk bent over her, mirroring her posture. "Well, missy, in all those years, he wasn't froggy enough to jump. So last August, he dared me to stake my claim."

Sky held her ground and gave Jordan an exasperated look. "Men."

Jordan engulfed her in a hug. "Oh, honey. They'll always be a mystery. Your daddy is a good man, and I love him, but I was never in love with him. I'll always be your Aunt Jordan."

Kirk turned to Conner. "This is my best friend's little peanut. His only daughter. His only child."

Conner mouthed to Sky. "Peanut?"

Kirk was in his face. "Look at me, mister. If something's starting here, you better be a gentleman. Because the hurtin' that I'd put on you is nothing like the swoop down General Kingston will inflict."

Sky mouthed back to him. "Sorry."

Jordan cooled off. "Where did you think you were riding on the back of the Harley tonight?"

Conner stepped up. "Sky came out earlier on the bicycle to paint, and when I showed up, we had dinner and walked on the beach, I couldn't get the bike back to the hostel, that's why she called you."

Jordan was appalled. "The hostel? The same hostel where you're staying?"

Conner nodded. "We met on the plane from Dallas. We both had reservations at the hostel."

Sky looked dreamily at Jordan. "It was fate. You know how you bare your soul to people on a plane, thinking you'll never see them again? It was kismet."

Kirk put his head in his hand and then abruptly snapped it up. With a shaking finger, he warned Conner. "Souls better be the only thing you've bared."

"Kirk!" Jordan caught him and pressed him behind her. "Let's get this bike back to the hostel. Go ahead, Skyler, get in the car."

Sky and Conner brushed fingertips before he reclaimed the jacket and mounted the Harley.

****

Sky pouted in the back seat. "I could have ridden with Con on the Harley."

Jordan swiveled in the front seat. "Honey, summer romances are fun and exciting, but they're also heartbreaking…"

Kirk lifted his gaze to the rearview mirror. "You are not dressed to be on the back of a motorcycle."

Sky slid down in the back seat, arms crossed over her chest. Jordan waved him off. "In a minute. Honey, is this what your Aunt Sherry would want for you? Fly into town, and within twenty-four hours, you're in a liplock with a boy you barely know?"

Sky shook with controlled outrage. The longer she sat mute, the worse Jordan's words felt. They rode in stony silence all the way to the hostel.

Kirk pulled up to the parking lot and lifted the bike from the trunk. He stood, staring into the night, listening for the sound of his Harley.

Sky exited the car with as much dignity as she could salvage. She thanked them for coming to pick her up in a barely audible voice, walked the bike back to the hostel's rack, and returned to her room without a backward glance.

****

Kirk and Jordan sat in the car, waiting for Conner. Jordan smoothed back her ponytail. "How was that for a rude awakening?"

Kirk winced. "I guess I didn't dodge this part of childrearing. Do we step back or step in?"

Jordan leaned against her window, her hand over her face. "I think we've already stepped in it."

Kirk nodded. "These technically aren't our kids, they're eighteen and nineteen, and we've warned them. Now they're going to do what kids do. All we can do is be there for them."

The bike's headlight bounced as Conner entered the parking lot. Conner parked the bike, and helmet in hand turned to his dad. "Do you want the bike back?" He stood, poised for the worst.

Kirk looked away and then back at Conner. "No, son, I don't want the bike back. How would you do everything you want to do this summer without wheels?" They stood like awkward mirror images. "Son, we flew off the handle. I apologize."

Conner bounced the helmet on his hip. Grasping for reason, He chuffed out. "We weren't doing anything wrong."

Kirk moved closer and dropped his hand on Conner's shoulder. "You were on the most romantic beach in the world, of course, you didn't. Don't let her break your heart."

Conner's jaw was set as he nodded at his dad. "Okay."

He walked down the hallway, digesting the swift sword of parental judgment. Hesitating, Conner stood in the hallway between their two doors, mind racing. He stopped in front of Sky's door, feeling terrible for the way his family treated them and knocked softly. "Sky? You in there?" He looked at the light coming from under the door and heard the bed squeak. Her silent shadow stood for a beat before she answered.

"Yes."

He shifted, leaning closer to the doorjamb. "Are you okay?"

"No."

Conner pressed his hand flat against the door. It moved slightly. He watched the door press back to him, believing she pressed her hand to his. "Angel, is there anything I can do about that?" *Was that a sniffle? Did they make her cry?*

"No. Not tonight."

Conner's head rose to the heavens for inspiration. His lips were drawn tight, and he shook his head. "How about a nice breakfast tomorrow before I job hunt? I can drop you at the beach afterward, and you can relax or paint or do whatever you want." Silence. He watched the door move back. *She dropped her hand?* Her shadow still darkened the light under the door. "Sky?" He heard another sob.

"Okay. What time?"

"Seven. You pick the place."

"Thank you, Conner." He stepped back from the door and heard it center in the jamb. "That will be a nice way to start my day."

"Seven it is."

Chapter Nine

The sun warmed up the early morning air as Sky attached the umbrella to her folding chair to shield her as she sketched Conner's fabulous profile from memory. *He might be my most beautiful subject yet.* She paused a moment in bright reflection on their kisses. Steamy kisses to begin her dreams. Something fluttered in the pit of her stomach. *That boy could really kiss.*

A few tourists stopped by to check out her work, but no one took up her offer to meet across the street to purchase their portrait. Everyone hurried in vacation mode, not thinking a portrait would be their best souvenir.

"What are you sketching there, Sky?" A familiar voice asked from behind. Sky's back tightened, recalling last night's high emotions.

Sky turned slowly. "Aunt Jordan." Sky's grip on the paintbrush and palette never loosened. *Jordan Perry was one of my favorite adults.* She grew up watching her dad tippy-toe around this woman, while she longed for a normal life with a mom at home and a dad in the military. Without enthusiasm she offered, "Congratulations on your marriage. I wish you'd married dad…"

Jordan's expression went from joyful to neutral immediately. "You think he could handle you and me together?"

Sky kept her hands occupied to avoid a hug. "Nope, but I wish you were my mom. And I would have grown up normal, like the other military brats."

Jordan sat down on the beach blanket. "Thank you, sweetheart, for your faith in me. I didn't do a very good job of mothering last night." Sky sat silent, her gaze sweeping all around the blanket, but not at Jordan. "I didn't recognize Conner. I imagined the worst."

"Then that's what you expected from me? I'm sorry I didn't tell you I was with Conner. When he told me you'd married his dad, I was devastated. I don't know what I was thinking to prank you like that. We didn't set up the kiss."

Jordan lowered her sunglasses and smiled softly. "It just happened."

Sky nodded. "I really like him, Aunt Jordan. On the plane, he was kind and interesting and worried about whether his dad would accept him."

Jordan's nod was understanding. "He seems to be all those things."

Sky put down her palette and brush. "While we were on the plane, he said nice things about his girlfriend." Sky hugged herself and leaned toward Jordan. "But you know what? I think she broke up with him, I don't get that they decided to separate."

Jordan's head bobbed from side to side, and she bit her sunglass earpiece. "If that's true, be aware that people on the rebound often mistake infatuation for something more." She shook her head. "Don't get your heart broken."

Sky grinned. "Have you looked at him? What a way to go."

Jordan laughed. "He does have the family good looks."

Sky pointed to the beach. "How did you know I'd be here?"

"Conner called after he dropped you off. He wanted to tell us he was job hunting, and you were painting. He confirmed his lunch date with his dad." Jordan pulled an insulated tumbler out of her bag. "I brought you my specialty orange-fig smoothie. People say it's delicious."

Sky sipped and smiled. "Thanks, Aunt Jordan."

Jordan regarded the easel. "Last week, when I talked to your dad, he said you've really blossomed as an artist." She gestured toward Sky in her pāreu. "And I can see you've blossomed as a young woman as well. Did Conner tell you, we own a fitness center, do you want to continue working out?"

Sky held up the tumbler. "This is yummy. Did daddy ask you to spy on me?"

Jordan laughed. "No, I decided to spy on you all by myself. I wanted to talk." She pointed to the canvas. "In reality, I want to see your art."

Sky nodded to the canvas. "This is my preliminary blocking. You can't see how handsome he is yet."

Jordan bent closer to see the geometric colors blocking the profile and shoulders. "Looks promising. Handsome? Is it Conner?"

"Usually, I'd have a photo to show you, but this is from memory. He's hard to forget."

Jordan's brow rose. "They all are."

Sky giggled. She pulled out her phone. "Anyway, these are pictures from my portfolio."

Jordan's face lit up. "Sky, are these the before photos? Or are these the portraits?"

"No, no, these are my portraits."

Jordan shook her head. "They're magnificent. I would think they were pictures."

Sky made a dissatisfied face. "Well, not every art teacher would agree with you. I've been told more than once I need to employ more expressionism."

Jordan elbowed her playfully. "That's why you want to go to art school. To learn about everything and develop your own style."

Sky hugged her. "I love you, Aunt Jordan. I want to paint your portrait."

Jordan hugged her back. "I'd be grateful if you'd do my portrait. But today I'm here because I want you to consider a mural of our men for our gym. Have you ever done anything that big?"

Sky frowned in reflection. "Well, I did theater sets. It's just blocking on a larger scale."

Jordan winked at her. "I promise you, the subjects will be engaging. Each of them is easy on the eyes." She pulled out her phone. "Of course, Kirk is better looking when he's not breathing fire." Jordan showed her their wedding photo. Sky oh'd silently. "This is his other son, Jax."

Sky's brows rose. "Wow."

"He's married." Jordan giggled girlishly.

Sky giggled. "My only condition is… they have to pose for me, I'll photograph them."

Jordan welcomed her positive response. "You'll do it?"

Sky nodded. "It's rough work, but some artist has to do it. Another condition is, if you hate it, you have to say so."

Jordan gave a solemn nod. "Can you come with me now?"

Sky nodded. "If you want me to do some sketches, can we swing by the hostel and drop off my painting stuff and pick up my other gear?"

Chapter Ten

Conner followed the navigation system's directions down South King Street. Sushi restaurants sat, one after the other. *Dear Lord, please, not sushi.* When the pleasant voice said, "Your destination is on your left," he felt his empty stomach flop to his ankles. He parked the bike as a Jeep whipped into the parking lot like a street racer's drift. About to raise hell at the guy, he recognized Jax drop to the pavement with a natural smirk. "Kid, have we got some fish bait for you!" Jax pointed military style to the small brown wood building barely a foot off the busy road.

Conner turned from the blue and white storefront behind the parking lot. "I thought you were going to drag me in there." The oversized banners artistically displayed tiny pieces of fish and rice.

Kirk appeared from the other side of the Jeep, adjusting his cargo shorts. "Jax, stop it. This kid is a carnivore. Conner, this looks like a hole in the wall, but this is some of the best chicken skin in Honolulu."

Conner winced. "Chicken skin?"

****

Conner sat upright on the basic wooden stool at the small square table. "That was different. I've never eaten anything that good from a little pewter pot."

Kirk raised a brow. "You must have one hollow leg." He pointed his chopsticks to the stack of empty dishes next to his younger son. "Hopefully, you'll find a job that pays your grocery bills."

Conner's expression flagged. "I think I'll be wearing my belt tighter. I went to three ranches and two airports today. Even with my experience and training, nobody even wanted my number."

Jax shrugged with a frown. "The job market is kind of closed here. If you don't have Ohana in the business, you bus tables."

"I can't support myself bussing tables."

Kirk started to speak, hesitated, but forged ahead. "You do have Ohana in business here, you know. Why don't you come work for us?"

Conner shook his head, wringing his cloth napkin in his lap. "I can't ask for a handout, you're already loaning me your bike."

"Handout, hell…" Kirk proclaimed.

Jax cut in. "He'll work you like a coalmine mule." Jax distanced himself from his dad and mugged a comical face. "I bought into the business so he couldn't order me around."

Kirk accepted the check and pulled out his wallet. "Nope, that Kameo's job. I only keep you for your network ratings." He plopped the credit card down and passed it to the server. "If your torso doesn't hold the interest of women, 18 to 39, I'll have to recruit your not so little brother."

Conner went wide-eyed. "You're on TV?"

Jax gave his dad a look of mock disdain. "He calls it TV, it's the local public broadcasting channel."

"But, we may have a network offer to go nationwide." He winked at Conner. "Seriously, we could use a guy your age to attract a younger audience." The men stood up to leave. "But, you'd have to cut out the fried chicken skin…"

They exited into the bright Honolulu sun. Kirk tapped Conner's midsection. "Think about it, you could work on your physical training for boot camp on the job."

Conner slid his sunnies out of his cargo shorts and inclined his head. "If you think I could pull my weight…"

"Follow us to the gym, son. We'll get you set up."

****

Jax dragged Conner down to the basement storeroom. "You have to play the role of a fitness guru from the skin out." Jax stopped on the stair landing and poked into Conner's chest. "You, my boy, look like Casper the friendly ghost goes to college. I've gotta fix this." Conner followed his brother into a room of shelves and plastic totes marked with sizes. Jax opened a tote marked 'M' and drew out an ultra-tight, second-skin sleeveless compression shirt.

Conner spoke up. "I wear a large." He caught the plastic bag, preparing to throw it back.

Jax winked. "Not anymore. What's your waist size? Twenty eight-thirty?" Conner opened his mouth, and Jax tossed a pair of two-toned shorts at him. "These are next to skin fit without the squeeze, but don't put them on yet, I have to get you the right briefs."

Conner's complexion bloomed bright red. "Briefs, like tighty whities?"

Jax waved him off. "No, the sweat-wicking, keeps-you-cool technology, and your package stays put briefs."

"What package am I delivering, here, Jax? Is this a secret Magic Mike location?"

Jax shoved the tote back in the rack. "Man, you can be distracting by hitching your gear every ten minutes. You want a video to catch you with a hitch in your giddy-up?" Jax moved conspiratorially close. "Fact is that the women get off on that. So, make it count when you do."

Conner silently repeated his brother's advice, standing there holding three pieces of clothing that looked like they were junior high sized. "These shorts are mighty short."

Jax led him through the hall to Kirk's office and his private bathroom. "Look, the briefs have a three-inch leg, the shorts have a seven-inch leg. If you've got a leg longer than that, God bless you. Now get in there, towels are on the shelf. Shave again, get cleaned up, and dressed for your orientation and publicity shots."

Conner flinched. "But, I'm as pale as Casper."

Jax fist-bumped him. "That's what Photoshop is for."

Conner stared at the private bathroom. *This is an executive washroom.* He stripped down, still conscious of his pale complexion, showered, lathered up and shaved in the shower stall mirror.

He got out to wrap up in the most luxurious bath sheet ever. *Life is good.* His face was riddled with tiny bloody slices from the new razor. He stuck toilet paper to each spot and averted the white fabric from his jaw as he carefully pulled the skin tight compression shirt over his torso. He gasped at the look. *Jeez, I feel like I'm in a porno.* The grey briefs had to be the tightest underwear he'd ever shimmied into. *Yeah, I'm locked in.* He caught his sack, adjusted everything into the gusset, and let out a breath. *Ooh, it's like my nuts are being cuddled.*

He chuckled out loud and willed away his stiffy. He looked down. *Stop that.* The two-toned blue shorts were cut high on the side with a shaped hem. When he turned around, it looked like the light fabric followed the shape of his ass. *I might as well be nekkid.*

As he tossed the towels in the hamper and wiped the counter clean, he got used to moving with the insanely soft fabrics. Before he turned off the bathroom light, he posed in the mirror, a la Schwarzenegger, winked at himself and shut off the light announcing. "I'll be back."

He found a pair of trainers and low cut socks on the bench in his dad's office. Jax's note said. "These are the largest we have, 13s, hope they fit." Was he supposed to wait for Jax or just head upstairs?

Chapter Eleven

Skyler, being nobody's fool, had taken her time at the hostel to freshen up. She lightly smoked her zircon blue eyes with brown eyeliner and finished with mascara and brow gel. Being a natural blonde, sometimes her lashes needed a boost. With a swipe of blusher and touch of gloss, she twisted up her long blonde hair, so the tendrils curled around her face demurely. With a spritz of light cologne, she joined Jordan in the lobby.

"Well, aren't you one smart cookie?" Jordan stood, gathering her purse. "May I help you carry any of your supplies?" They each shouldered a tote bag and left to assess the task of glorifying three bodies in a mural.

****

Skyler studied the expanse of white drywall. "I'll have to prime it."

Jordan nodded. "Make us a list."

"You want the wall divided into three parts? Why not four, why aren't you up here?"

"Let me explain our demographic. You've seen Kirk and Conner, but you haven't met our ratings king."

Sky nodded, glanced around the room of exercise machines and free weights, and noted only one man on the rowing machine and another hitting the heavy bag. The majority of the machines were occupied by women of various ages and fitness levels.

She bit the end of her pencil and calculated the size of the figures from the examples of the poses Jordan suggested with their brochure. Her job would be on par with the artists of the first Olympics. *Thank God they aren't going to be nude. But with their audience, that might be a plus. The flip side? Do I want to see Aunt Jordan's husband naked? New thought, new thought.* She blinked hard and expelled a breath.

****

Conner felt more than conspicuous in his duds. With each step, he wondered if he'd ever feel fully clothed. He stopped at the top of the stairs, still not familiar with the large gym. Scanning the room for Kirk or Jax, he didn't see them. Jordan was giving instructions to a girl on the free weight bench.

As he walked toward Jordan, machines on his right and left stopped their rhythmic clanking. Women turned to smile and stare at him. He nodded, smiling sheepishly. Halting behind the girl on the bench, he said. "Sorry to interrupt, Ma'am, I'm lookin' for my dad or Jax?"

The girl on the bench spun around, her sundress foaming over her knees as she dropped a pad into her lap. "Conner?"

"Sky!" He jerked both arms into every position he could figure that would cover the brevity of his clothing. He finished, his hands clasped in front of his crotch, wearing a stupid-ass grin.

Jordan's head swiveled between the two of them. "I believe you two know each other."

Sky turned to her, her eyes enormous, and her voice low. "Remember the sketch from this morning? I am redoing it in this outfit."

Jordon mouthed an 'Oh' and tried to rescue the awkwardness. "Conner, I see Jax dressed you."

Conner cleared his throat. "Yeah. But not with much."

Jordan hesitated. "Oh, look, there are Jax and Kirk." She pointed to the closed cable monitor above them. "They're in the sparing room. Come on, Sky, let me introduce you to Jax."

Jordan led the way, and Conner dropped back to speak with his sweetheart. "I can't believe you're the first girl to see me in these ridiculous clothes."

Sky's attention was focused totally on his poor face with the dots of bloody toilet paper. "What clothes? All I see is bloody tissues." She dropped her gaze appreciatively and shook her head. "These are not ridiculous. Oh, Conner…"

His hands flew to the dots of dried paper. "Is it bad? Do I look bad?"

"No, they'll come right off." She gave a quick, friendly kiss to his jaw at the bottom of the staircase. Then he heard his dad clearing his throat.

"That's some fancy medical attention you're getting there, son. Jordan, watch, and learn." Kirk caught his wife to his side and pecked her on the cheek. "So, this is our new artist?"

Jordan jumped in. "Kirk, she's agreed. And wait till you see her work."

Kirk moved forward, both hands straight ahead to separate the two kids. He looked into Conner's dark eyes. "We need you to center yourself and get ready for your headshots." Kirk stepped back, wiped at his mouth, and shook his head. "I still can't believe these two kids met on the airplane."

Sky smiled and hugged her drawing tablet. "Kismet."

Jax ambled up, stuck out his hand to Skyler. "Hi, Skyler. I'm Jax, the brother." He turned to Conner and spoke low. "There's a pocket in the back of those shorts for your... Altoids tin." Conner's hand flew back to feel the horizontal zipper in the waistband of the shorts.

****

By the end of business that day, Jordan returned to the gym with a pair of jeans and her helmet for Sky. Sky understood Kirk's rules about motorcycle gear. She couldn't help but wish Conner was in that skin-tight athletic wear, but he wore his usual shirt, cargo shorts, and sneakers by the time they climbed onto the bike for the ride to the hostel.

As they stood in the parking garage, Kirk asked. "You coming to work tomorrow? We open at seven, but employees report at six forty-five."

Conner's eyes flashed, and he looked at Sky. "Six forty-five? Am I wearing that get up again?"

Kirk held a Silver SEAL gym bag. "Employee gear is in here, it will be in your locker when you arrive." Conner nodded, they lowered their face shields and drove off.

Conner and Sky wore helmets with communication systems that allowed them to talk while riding safely. Sky held on to his torso. At the light, he put down one foot, and the engine purred between their legs. "Maybe you could model some athletic wear for me."

Conner shook his head. "You might as well draw me nekkid."

Sky giggled. "Is that a possibility?"

Conner put the bike in gear and goosed it. "Whoa."

When they parked the bike at the hostel and removed their helmets, they both wore unmistakable grins. Sky did a little dance. "We both have jobs in the same gym. Can you believe it?

Conner laughed. "We need to celebrate. Do they deliver pizza in Honolulu?"

Chapter Twelve

Sky giggled as she set up her phone and Bluetooth speakers on Conner's desk. "I've never had a room party before. Good practice for college."

Conner offered her a soda from his cooler. "You know your smile is contagious." She blushed as she twisted off the soda's cap. "It looks like you and Jordan got things ironed out."

Sky bobbed her head and thought. "Yeah. We both had apologies to make. Everything is cool now!"

There was a knock at the door. "Island Pizza."

Conner held open the door, paid the guy and returned to the double bed covered with the beach blanket "You asked for a pizza with extra cheese, no pineapple. I added an order of wings and garlic knots. You have to help, cause tomorrow I start Kirk's diet."

He sat at the opposite corner of the beach blanket and savored the sight of her on his bed. She bit the pizza and then drew the stringy cheese back from her lips. *Was it a sin to watch a girl eat?* Apparently so, judging by the feelings he developed as she went about enjoying a meal. Everything about her was vibrant.

Conner dove for the opportunity to grab a garlic knot, and their fingers tangled on the same buttery bread. Sky slid it his way. "Tonight you eat whatever you want, the diet starts tomorrow. Aunt Jordan gave me a list of their favorite natural food restaurants. Like that's something I'm supposed to do. Once Daddy gets here, it's steak three times a day."

Conner nodded as he chewed. He swallowed. "I think I'm going to like your Daddy."

"You might have a lot in common. He's from Oklahoma." She jumped off the bed and bent over the cooler. "Need another tea or soda?"

Conner thought he needed a bucket of ice. *Don't bend over like that.* "I think I'll need some of that, what was it? Shave ice?" *Anything to get me out of the privacy of this room. She's killing me.* "Have you noticed the island breezes?"

Sky took a double-take. "They're kind of famous."

Conner held up a halting hand as he moved off the bed and began a slow pace in the small room. "You see, the heat isn't like Texas..."

"Thank God!"

"No, it's what the island heat does to me... to you..."

"Huh?"

"I wake up in paradise, and everything smells like heaven. And then at the end of the day all of that heaven..." He stammered for the words. He felt Sky's scrutiny as his nostrils flared. He turned away from her and scratched at his neck as he shook out his waistband.

"Conner, are you alright? Is riding the motorcycle in the sun affecting you?"

He turned on his heel. "Sky, damn it, woman, you're driving me nuts with your scent when you come too close. I'm losing a battle with my body." He stood as far away from her as the cubicle of a room allowed. "I'm an animal."

Sky took in a deep breath as she held her sundress bodice to her nose. "I'm sweaty, and my perfume is too heavy now."

"It's you, it's your musk, and it is driving me..."

"Conner, I just hide it better than you. Do you know how I want to melt into you every time I get on that motorcycle?" He nodded mutely. "That bike throbbing between my legs, my nose at your neck, and my arms around your waist."

Conner briskly moved to the door. "Sky, you need to leave, please."

Sky rose glacially and swept up her phone and speaker. She avoided his personal space and backed to the door jamb. "You know, it wouldn't be horrible if you did make love to me."

"It wouldn't be? Wouldn't it be too soon? Wouldn't you think I was rushing you?"

Sky's chin dropped as he spoke, and she answered from under her golden eyelashes. "Would you think I was easy?"

Conner retreated away from the door and stood, hands splayed on his hips, his heel bobbing up and down. "Nothing about meeting the right woman is easy. I could mess this up in a heartbeat. And that's the last thing I want to do."

Sky dropped her phone and speaker on the chair and slowly approached him. He stood statue-straight. She held out her hand. "Let's get some shave ice and cool down."

****

The 'wind therapy' on their ride to the gym perked up their early morning lethargy. They bounced up the stairs on the dot of 6:45. Kirk, standing in the lobby, checked his watch. "I'm impressed. Both of you here, bright and shiny."

Conner wilted from the sarcasm. "You told us what time to be here."

Jax approached with a stack of clean towels for the front desk. "New rules, no sarcasm on the first day." Jax turned to Conner. "I told you he'd work you like a coal mine mule."

Conner watched the other gym employees straggle in, glancing at the wall clock. "I thought you said six forty-five. What are they doing coming at 6:50?"

Kirk threw an arm around his son's neck to lead him to the exercise studio. "Let me tell you what happens when you own the place..."

"My folks owned the diner. I know what happens."

Jordan greeted both the young people with an orange and fig smoothie. "Good morning, this is for energy, as if you two kids need more energy."

Conner admired his stepmom's vibrant personality as he followed Kirk down the stairs, and Sky followed Jordan.

****

Jordan's eyes twinkled as she led Sky back to the front desk. "You can only imagine your father's surprise when we chatted online last night."

Sky's complexion blanched. "You told Daddy?"

"Was it supposed to be a secret?"

"You told him about Conner?" Sky whispered. "Does he realize how good looking he is?"

69

Jordan shook her head. "Your daddy knows that the two of you are extremely healthy and attractive."

"Is that supposed to be some kind of code?" Sky pulled out her telephone and checked for messages. "At least he's not blowing up my phone with texts." She glanced at her reflection in the mirror. "Wow, my face is red."

Jordon nodded, looking through drawers under the counter. "Honey, your face *is* a little red. You might have a smidgen of beard burn. This might help." Jordan handed her a tube of cortisone crème and then snatched it back. "Of course, the only thing that really helps is repeated exposure."

Sky grabbed the cream. "I won't get the chance for any exposure if Daddy sees me like this." She leaned close and examined every angle of her complexion. "It's like the whole world knows. We didn't neck all night."

Jordan gave her a knowing look. "It only takes him with a heavy beard and you with a tea rose complexion." She chuckled. "I'm guessing your daddy has given a few cases of beard burn himself."

Sky stuffed her fingers in her ears. "I don't even want to think of that." With dawning realization, she dropped her hands to her side. "By the way, did he give you beard burn?"

"I'll never tell."

Sky brought her smoothie to her lips. "Conner's a dead man."

"Give your dad some credit, he spent his life working with young people."

"I can't think about this anymore. I have to get to work." She readied her sketchpad and headed to the fitness machine area. Sky blocked three areas of the wall and checked them against the landscape of machinery to make sure the athletic figures would stand as compelling physical examples of sports fitness. She reached into her case and came up with her supplies. It was nine forty-five, and she was well on her start for blocking the mural. She moved around the painter applying the primer to the previously painted wall.

A man half-interested in rowing came to a stop when Sky sat down and began blocking on her sketchpad. After a few moments, she felt his gaze. "Are you looking for your trainer, sir?"

The man released the bar and dropped his feet to the floor. "No, I'm sorry, I was watching you work."

Sky turned pink. "Well, not much to watch."

He was bearded, his hair a little wild. His middle-aged fit body was more developed in his arms and shoulders. "I paint a little myself."

"Oh, you do? What's your medium?"

"Oils mostly. I wield a mean palette knife." He gestured his strokes. "Heavy on the impasto."

Sky stopped sketching. "Oh, I am so photorealist. Hopefully, one day I can loosen up."

"Do you live on the island?"

"No, I'm just visiting my Aunt Jordan. She lives here, and in the fall, I'm going to Central Coast Art Institute in Sarasota."

The stranger nodded. "Ahuh."

"I'm so excited to be able to learn in such a diverse place. I'll be able to concentrate on my art."

He smiled broadly. "You're going to love it. Art school was the best. So many ideas. That's a good school. You have to be accomplished to get in. Congratulations."

Sky hugged herself. "I still can't believe they like my work." She gestured to the wall. "Isn't it fantastic the Romans trust me to paint an athletic mural here? I mean, I've done theatre sets, it's the same principle."

The stranger's smile grew as Sky talked. "With that attitude, you'll be back here next summer doing street art for the festival."

"Oh, I don't know about that. What I want to do is portraits. I didn't know you can't sell them on the beach. I got here earning money on the St. Pete Pier!"

He wiped his neck with a towel. "Is your art online somewhere?"

She snorted. "On my phone, my tablet." She reached for her tablet and opened her gallery. "Here they are." He accepted it, swiped through, and returned to several of the pieces for longer looks." He hummed like her art teacher when he saw something he liked, or at least that's what she hoped.

He held out the tablet with a photo of an aged woman. "The woman and the dog are sweet, but the woman alone says so much more."

"She doesn't know I painted her. She didn't have the cash for a picture of her and her dog but look at her." Sky gestured to the aura of knowledge in the woman's expression. "Poor lady didn't have the twenty-five dollars for the dog's portrait, so I gave it to her."

Handing back the tablet, the man expressed surprise. "You got to Hawaii on twenty-five dollar portraits?"

Sky shrugged. "Partly."

He stood and smiled. "Keep up the good work. Don't let anyone kill your muse."

****

Jordan approached her after the man on the rowing machine left. "I see you met Rando."

Sky smiled. "Is that his name? We didn't exchange names."

Jordan laughed. "So, you don't know who that was?"

Sky shook her head. "He was nice, is he famous?"

Jordan's expression glowed. "He looked at your portfolio. He owns major galleries in Oahu and San Francisco. Look him up, he's Randolph Kane, K-a-n-e."

Sky swiped through images on Google for him, his art, and the audience his work attracted.

Jordan continued. "His portrait of Lunalilo hangs in the National Portrait Gallery in Washington."

Sky gushed. "His work is in museums all over the world, and he works out here? That is so cool."

Jordan grinned. "He is a real person, and he is a very nice man. How wonderful that he took an interest in the mural you're doing."

Sky looked from her pad to the wall. "Yeah, no pressure there..." She was silently thrilled.

Chapter Thirteen

Friday morning, Conner lay in bed, swiping through his phone's browser. The words 'open cockpits, hands-on aviation, and hangar tours' caught his eye. He missed flying, and the thought of taking an 'aviator's tour', with a behind-the-scenes look at Ford Island's Hangar 79, got his fly-boy heart beating fast.

If he jumped on the bike and left with rush hour traffic, he might get one of the hundred and fifty tickets for the Fighter Ace 360 Flight Simulator. It would be hard to choose between the sci-fi starfighter and the World War II experience. He thought he'd feel closer to his grandpa if he flew a P-38 in a heart-thumping dogfight over the tropical waters of the Pacific.

He hadn't even gotten out of bed when Sky knocked. "Hey, sleepyhead. It's our day off."

Conner's hand smacked at his face. *Our day off. Oh, Jeeze, is she going to want to do this or what?* "Give me fifteen minutes, I'll meet you in the lobby." He heard her flip-flops move along as he jumped into jeans and a tee-shirt. He jockeyed for space in front of the mirror in the shared bathrooms and was in the lobby with three minutes to spare.

Sky turned toward him, and her sundress rippled at her knees. She held a pair of blue jeans over her arm, and when she saw him, she broke away from two guys bending her ear on comparing surf excursions. "Sorry, guys, my pilot's here." The two tourists stood gape-mouthed as she glided to him. Her hand caressed his freshly shaven face. "Did we make specific plans for today?"

Conner grinned. "Not exactly, but…" He held out his phone. "Don't you want to fly beside me in a P-38?"

Sky removed her sunglasses. "Huh? I can't fly."

"No, this is a simulator, and if we leave now, we might get one of today's limited tickets."

"Where?" *Did she sound interested?*

Conner caught her daypack, and they stowed their gear in the bike's saddlebags. "Near Pearl. It could be a great day if you want to come. If not, I can drop you somewhere." *No pressure.*

"Why wouldn't I?" Sky pulled on her jeans under her dress and waited to get on the bike.

Conner adjusted his helmet with a nod and smiled. "You've never expressed any interest in flying, but it's my passion and not having flown for the past two weeks I'm itchin' to get airborne."

Sky climbed on the bike and held on. "Then fly us there." She held out a hand. "By local speed limits."

Conner nodded and replied via the helmet to helmet communication system. "Hold on, then."

****

This is his ultimate desire? Flying? The entire road trip, Sky couldn't inject a word into Conner's tales of sitting in a top dresser's cockpit. When they arrived, his feet barely touched the ground. Eight-year-old boys on the shuttle to the aviation museum were more contained.

It was only a simulator, but Conner played it to the limit. His ducking and weaving evasions rolled her stomach as much as the P-38. He, on the other hand, was ecstatic. She knew that because of his totally intent body language throughout their 'flight'. Conner exited first, turned, and held out his hand to steady Sky. Gripping the railing to exit the simulator, Sky swallowed hard to settle her queasy tummy. *If he could climb right back in, he would.*

"Are you okay, angel?"

"Yeah, what a rush."

Conner's excitement didn't end with the experience. His ebony eyes were dilated, his face flushed, and a light dew of perspiration glowed on his forehead. "That was so cool. Oh, man, now that I've tried this, the old topdresser won't be as exciting." Sky watched an elderly volunteer's ear prick up at Conner's comment. He moved toward Conner with a handout.

"Topdresser?" The man grinned, and his wrinkled face brightened.

Conner extended a hand. "Yes, sir, back in Texas."

"Kid," the man pointed to the simulator, "keep flying like that, and they'll put you in a flight suit."

Conner's eyes lit up as he rolled his shoulders to work off the excess adrenaline. "I sure hope so."

"Then it's a good thing you're on our side." The volunteer handed Conner a printout of his flight.

Conner stared at the score. "Pretty good."

****

Sky's blue eyes shimmered with empathy as Conner made thoughtful trips up and down each aisle of the gift shop. He held up the kid's sized flight suit. "Man, I never had anything like this when I was a kid."

Sky laughed along with him. "It's a shame they don't make that thing in your size."

He returned it to the rack and arched a brow. "Oh, but they do. Of course, I have to earn mine."

Her smile held bravely. "I remember Daddy's, sort of… I have a photo of him in his flight suit in my bedroom back home."

Conner beamed from within. "I can't wait to meet your dad. He didn't happen to go to the Air Force Academy, did he?"

Her smile snapped off. "No." She felt his scrutiny at her emotional shutdown.

Conner slowed and turned to her. "As much as I'd like to talk to your dad, I don't want to take up all his time. You probably don't see him much."

Sky nodded. "I don't. It's like he has a whole other family, and that's the Air Force."

"Yeah, I can see how a General would feel that way."

Sky turned to a row of commemorative pins, magnets, and mugs. She laughed ironically and held up a cup. "This is perfect for you."

He read it. "I love the smell of jet fuel in the morning." He shook his head. "As true as that is, I'd probably break it before I got it home. But it's perfect."

If he could leave only footprints and take only memories of his time in the P-38, he'd stuff as many tangibles from the gift shop as he could into his saddlebags. "If you were a mom, would this mean something?" He held up the gold plated Pacific Aviation Museum Christmas ornament.

"If you picked it out for me, it would." Sky hugged herself, awash in his unbridled enthusiasm for all things aviation.

Conner dug into his pocket. "Angel, why don't you grab us some bottled water at the café?" He held out cash.

"Oh, I've got it, Con. It looks like you have some shopping to do. I'll have a seat in the café and check-in with Aunt Jordan." She'd watched him debate the brightly colored Aloha shirt with bomber planes versus the night flight Aloha shirt. He bit at his bottom lip as he picked up the one that was twenty dollars less. She wanted to go back and buy him the one he kept returning to.

She watched him from a distance, working out her feelings for his dream. It was love at first sight, at least for her. Then it was two steps back with a girlfriend, one step forward with her calling from Texas to break up, and now this major drawback, Con was enlisting in the Air Force this fall.

No matter who Con spoke with, his admiration for the history and respect for the volunteers bubbled up like a Cub Scout. To him, the retired military volunteers were rock stars. *Then why do I feel times with my Air Force General Dad are just rocky?*

Before they climbed back on the bike they had done everything available at the Pearl Harbor historic sites. Sky was weary and had just enough energy to hold on for the ride back to Waikiki. She had to admit her emotions sapped her vigor for the day. This whole day was an eye-opener. *That's what you get when you fall in love at first sight.*

Before they put on their helmets, Sky's hand rested on his shoulder. "Conner, do you ever think about the women these pilots leave behind?"

He looked over his shoulder. "What do you mean?"

Sky's gaze swept the Pearl Harbor area. "I can't be here in all this history and not feel the sacrifices. For every man who died here, there was a sweetheart, a wife, a wife with little children, families who would never have these men at their dinner table again."

Conner bit his bottom lip for a beat "These men were doing what they were called to do."

****

Conner couldn't help but notice Sky's flagging gusto by her lack of conversation. Playing it by ear, he steered toward a quiet restaurant a few blocks off the beach. "How about a quiet dinner before we head back to the hostel? Yah gotta eat." He waited for a beat for her reply. "You okay, angel?"

"I'm good." She sighed. "Sure, a quiet place will be nice."

They took the back corner booth in a café with a menu heavy on comfort food. When she excused herself to use the lady's room, Conner pulled the tag off the stuffed plush pilot bear and sat it in front of her iced tea. When she returned to the table, he felt her unending gaze. He pointed to the bear. "Someone was looking for you."

Sky sat, and her face flushed. Her brilliant blue eyes shimmered for a split second, and she recovered to hold the bear to her heart. "You are the sweetest, absolutely."

"I didn't mean to make you cry. What's wrong, angel?"

Still holding the bear, Sky began. "I need to tell you how I feel about something…"

Conner cocked his head. "Okay." His word drew out. *Is she breaking up with me after six days? My new record.*

"My dad worked on me for two years to go to Colorado Springs."

Conner shook his head. "Shouldn't you be there right now?"

Sky dropped her chin. "Two things kept me out of the Academy, migraines, and the fact I didn't want to be there."

"Oh, man, you were that close to my dream."

Sky sat the bear on the table and wrung her hands in her lap. "But it's not my dream. I wish I could give it to you, but then I'd lose you, too."

"Lose me, angel? What are you talking about?"

"I feel like the military has eaten up my life. When one family member serves, everyone serves. That life is not for everyone, it's not for me."

Conner sat gobsmacked. "I had no idea you had such negative feelings about the military."

"I don't have negative feelings about the military, it's just not for me. My dad has an incredible career, where else could he achieve what he's done? But it's not for me."

Conner shook his head. "What is for you? What do you want to do?"

"I'm going to tell Dad I'm studying art. You have your passion, I have mine."

"I'm sorry you feel jammed up with your dad. I know how that feels because of my mom. Ever get the feeling they're trying to live their lives through us?"

The tension seemed to float off her shoulders as she sat back in the padded booth. "I'm glad we've had this talk." She picked up the bear and planted a kiss on his nose."

Conner pointed at the stuffed bear. "It was his idea."

Chapter Fourteen

Sky stood at hostel check-in. "Good morning, I'm checking out!" She called to a clerk behind a half-open door.

"How was your stay? Everything cool?" The hippy kind of guy smiled as he accepted her key card.

"Oh, yeah, so much so that I want to reserve a place for a couple of weeks at the end of the month."

The guy in the tie-dyed shirt shrugged. "Oh, man, bummer. I can't do a couple of weeks, you get one more week because it's a two week limit per year. Otherwise, everyone would crash here indefinitely."

Sky's heart sank. "Yeah, I'll call you about that week. I don't want to sleep on the beach."

"Yeah, you could do that, but not with all that luggage." He gestured to the stack standing behind her.

Sky accepted her receipt and turned away, her hopes dashed. She pulled out her phone and texted Conner.

Did U know there's a 2 wk a yr limit at the hostel?

Sky pushed her wheeled luggage to the sidewalk and waited for her Lyft to her dad's resort. No answer yet from Conner, he was at work.

Bell services led her to the suite she would share with her father. An island-themed living room separated the two bedrooms. Sky indicated she was taking the bedroom with the simple ensuite bath and tipped the porter.

She peeked her head into the master bath with its bubble tub and steam shower, plotting a time she could send dad off with Kirk and Jordan. The robes were fluffy and white, the rooms smelled like plumeria, and all she had to do was prepare for the battle of her life, against a General.

Sky took extra care with her appearance. After styling her hair and applying makeup, she slipped into her freshly ironed sundress and strove to look like an adult. She had all the brochures for Central Coast Art Institute in her purse and made sure she uploaded her portfolio on her phone.

When her father's text arrived, Sky headed toward the hotel's portico. A white Mustang convertible pulled into the arrival drive and her eyes widened.

Wow, Dad, he's looking fresh and ready for the next new thing. When did he ever wear an Aloha shirt? He's lost weight, and his arms look like he's working out. Holy crap.

She bounded down the walk before he could turn off the car or get out. "Wow, Daddy, you look like you could have fun."

His smile grew wide, and he nodded actively. "I've been known to have fun."

The trunk popped, and General Hank Kingston got out of the car and waved hello to the bell captain. The taller than average General commanded attention with his grey brush cut. His Mount Rushmore type of face was clean-shaven and tanned by years in the desert. As long as Sky remembered, his broad shoulders and chest were exactly where every one of their reunions began and ended. *There is nothing like Daddy's hugs.*

"General Kingston checking in."

The team rolled to the car and began loading luggage on the trolly.

Sky ran to his side, and they hugged hello. The bell captain checked her tablet and handed Hank a small card. "Download our app, use this code, and your phone will unlock your room."

He nodded a thank you and pocketed the card. "If you'll have the bags taken to my suite, I'm taking my little girl out to lunch."

"Of course, sir."

As Sky watched the staff trundle off, she turned back to her dad. "Well, how about we go to Duke's? If you drive fast, we can get a parking space."

Hank dropped behind the wheel and waited for her to get comfortable. They buckled in, and he pulled back into traffic. "How do you feel now that you're a high school graduate?" He dipped his sunnies and looked at her for a split second.

"I feel ready."

He nodded, both hands on the steering wheel. "To get started on your engineering degree? If you do well in your first two years, you could go to MIT."

Sky sat sideways and sighed. "Dad, can we not talk about this in the car?" They rode in uncomfortable silence all the way to the valet stand.

Hank handed the key to the car park as the valet opened Sky's door. Her father scooped her into a bear hug, which she returned. "It's good to see you, peanut. You look beautiful."

"Awe, Daddy. It's good to see you, too." She melted beside him as he hooked an arm around her shoulders and led her to the restaurant. "While we're eating, let's just catch up. No college talk."

Hank stepped back from her and set his jaw. "Truce for now?"

She nodded, her blonde ponytail bobbing over her shoulder.

****

As the server took away the empty dishes, Hank sat back and adjusted his dinner napkin. "Now that we've eaten, I have a little announcement."

Sky's brow arched. "Well, I know you're not proposing to Aunt Jordan, so..."

"The Air Force offered me a generous bonus to re-up for four more years, and there's a real possibility I would retire as a Major General."

Sky put her elbows on the table and rested her chin in her hands. "Oooh, two stars." Her brows waggled. "How dangerous is your post?"

Hank held out his hands as if weighing two sides. "Their generosity was based on the fact no one else wants the job, and I am familiar with the players. So in answer to your question, not as dangerous as the Pentagon. Those land sharks are too much for me. But more dangerous than Andrews."

Sky tsked. "What I'm asking is, how likely are you to get shot?"

Hank laughed. "Versus walking in D.C.?"

Sky shrugged and shook her head. "Daddy, I'm serious."

"Okay, peanut. I'm as safe there as you are here."

"Well, then if it's something you really want to do, if it's your life's calling, I say go for it."

"My life's calling?" Hank sent her an assessing look. "Okay."

The piece of Hula Pie sat between them with two forks. As Hank stirred cream into his coffee Jordan's voice reverberated in his brain. The words burned his conscience. 'Just listen to the girl, don't start in with your agenda'. He hadn't done a very good job of that. Promising himself to be more open, he prompted her with a wave of his fork over the pie's whipped cream. "Ladies first, dig in."

Sky slid her fork to the chocolate cookie crust and slid out a bite, smiling around her fork. The macadamia nut ice cream and hot fudge slid to his side of the plate. "I know you don't get much hot fudge on post."

"Tell me what you came to Hawaii to think about before college?" He scooped the toasted macadamia nuts into the hot fudge and let it sit in his mouth. *The better to keep my mouth shut.*

"Daddy, I don't want to study engineering."

"Then, English?"

"Neither of those are what I want to do with my life."

Hank swallowed hard, and his pause lingered. "What are you saying?"

Sky tucked her chin and tried again. "I don't want a career in those fields."

"Peanut, you have the aptitude to become a talented engineer. It's a lucrative profession."

"Dad, I don't want to spend my days looking at a computer and figures. I can't see myself succeeding in that structure."

Hank put down his fork. "Succeeding in that structure? Cut the crap."

"Dad, I never envisioned loving numbers."

Hank slid the pie to the side and raised his hand for the check. "We'll finish this at the hotel."

Sky winced. "So you can yell at me?"

Hank didn't answer. He didn't speak to her as they left the restaurant, on the drive to the hotel, or as they walked the extremely long hallway to their room.

****

When the door closed, her father began. "No more crap. If you don't want to study something you can use in the real world, you tell me what you want to do."

Sky drew a deep breath. "I don't want to learn to be a drone." His bushy brows furrowed, and his jaw tightened. "I don't want that kind of regimentation. I want expressive freedom. My love is art, not math." She raised her brows. "Honest enough?"

Hank sat, one hand fisted resting on his thigh, his fingers clenching and unclenching. He gave out a gust of a deep breath and stewed in silence. When Hank opened his mouth, he closed it again, shook his head, and smacked the table next to him. "After losing an appointment to Colorado Springs, you still have the opportunity to excel in the civilian world. You settle for what, art?"

"My love is art."

Hank's lips straightened and went white. "They call them starving artists for a reason. I push you because I know what's best for you."

Sky paced the room. "What's next? An arranged marriage?"

Hank went florid. "Point heard. Not taken."

Sky shook her head. "The more you force this, the bigger the embarrassment I will be. I would struggle, and I would fail miserably in engineering. If you have a shred of respect for us as father and daughter, you're going to let me decline the scholarships and pursue a degree at Central Coast Art Institute."

Hank snorted. "And work as what?"

Sky braced herself. "Art restorer, art educator, portrait artist."

"Right." Hank folded his arms over his chest. "I'll bet those jobs are plentiful."

"Right now, I'm painting a mural for Silver SEAL."

Hank shook his head. "It's family. Who else hires a kid with no experience?"

Sky's chin dropped, and her gaze rose from under her lashes. "I've already made contacts with a gallery owner who wants to follow my work. All I can promise is that I'll find my way." She softened. "Daddy, it's not that I don't appreciate your advice. Thank you for believing I can do great things."

Hank stood with enthusiasm. "You have the brains, a strong body…"

Sky sat. "I don't have the will or desire, and you know more than most, that is essential." Hank deflated and sat back down. Sky closed the space between them to lay a gentle hand on his shoulder. "Thank you, Daddy."

He didn't look at her. "You must be busy with that mural. They probably need you at the gym right now." He handed his phone to her. "Order a ride and get over there." She accepted the phone and worked silently to order a ride.

Chapter Fifteen

Head up, chin out, red-eyed, Sky marched up the fitness center's steps, art supplies in hand. She yanked open the door and welcomed the cool, fragrant air that greeted her. Bonnie, at the check-in desk, raised a hand in greeting. "All your folks are in a meeting in Kirk's office."

Sky forced a smile. "That's okay, I'll just get to work." She unpacked the projector and put on the oversized white dress shirt she picked up at the charity shop as a smock. Within minutes she stroked paint on the walls with great emotion. As she worked the brush strokes into different widths and lengths, she stopped and stepped back regarding the energy of the figure. She placed Kirk in the center. Fists poised to strike, sporting a sheen of sweat over his bare chest. His cobalt blue eyes blazed fiercely as his artful lips curled in a come-on smile.

There was a catharsis to painting a life-size image like this. This 'Kirk' was larger than life. It was the way she felt about him and the way he welcomed her into his business. Sky emphasized his shoulder's musculature that packed the power into his fisted hands. A few times, she stopped to consult the closeups of his tattoos. *This has to be perfect.* In this pose, it was going to show. Inside his right forearm was 'The Only Easy Day Was Yesterday'. *Damn straight about that.* Would her relationship with her father ever be right? *I am such an embarrassment to him right now.*

Kirk's image painted itself as she fashioned the strokes. She stood back and took in a deep breath. Hearing a voice, she jumped.

Rando stood nodding approvingly. "Didn't you tell me you were a photorealist? I see a lot of release in this figure. Good effort."

Sky's eyes stung at his compliments. Tears erupted. "Really?"

"You caught Kirk's energy, you can't bottle that. Is this your first mural?"

Shy wiped at her eyes. "Well, I sort of cheated, I used a projector."

Rando smirked. "Michelangelo sketched his images on framed cloth, pierced the cloth with dots around the figures, sprinkled them with charcoal dust, and placed the cloth on the wet plaster of the Sistine Chapel's ceiling."

Sky giggled at that fact. "He basically painted by number?"

"Yup. Very sophisticated paint by number." Rando walked a semicircle to view the image's impact. "He's following me around the room. Great job, Sky. I'm going to let you work, don't want to hover." She shrugged, and the tears kept flowing. "What is this? I'm complimenting you."

She waved at him. "Don't go. Do you have a minute?" They sat down on opposite weight benches. "I had a huge fight with my father at lunch. He had me all set up for an engineering degree. I finally got the guts to say no. I told him I want to be an artist." She hiccupped. "He brutally said I'd starve."

He leaned forward. "Sky, ask anyone, I don't give undeserved praise. I've been in the art business for twenty years. I know when I see an artist who will sell. Your work will sell."

"You think I can support myself with painting?" Her eyes began to clear.

Rando put his hands on his knees and drew in a breath. "Any good art, be it books, music, or visual, will sell with the right exposure. The work is finding your market and positioning yourself there."

"That's the catch."

"That's right. That's why you must go to school. Study business, marketing, get a teaching certificate. Colleges foster art."

Sky felt an enormous weight lift. "I'm so glad you were here today. I needed to hear a professional opinion." She stood up with a little shiver. "I'm suddenly incredibly inspired, Mr. Kane. Thank you."

Rando gave her a nod and a smile, he gestured toward Jordan, who was giving them space but eyeing the discussion curiously. "I see one of your fans approaching." With a broad grin, he left.

****

Jordan smiled at Rando as they passed each other, and she approached Sky. "Oh, honey. This is wonderful. I can't wait for Hank to see your work."

Fat tears erupted again, followed by a muffled sob, and Sky fled to the ladies' locker room. Jordan counted to ten and then strolled down the steps. She smiled at two women holding the door open for her. They looked over their shoulders at the young girl in tears. "Is she okay?"

Jordan nodded. "Young emotions, all will be well." She checked it was only the two of them and then sat beside Sky. "Is this anything you can talk about?"

****

Jordan shot toward the office's open door. Kirk lounged behind his desk, bobbing in his chair, shooting the shit with Jax and Conner. "…and then I told her…"

Jax leaned back in the chair, long legs stretched in front of him with an accomplished grin. Conner watched the conversation wide-eyed as he leaned on the end of Kirk's desk.

The men watched Jordan's aggravated movement as she dug in a cabinet for a Bota Box of Nighthawk Black. She set the wine box on the edge of the counter and filled the shatterproof wine glass. She guzzled half the glass, refilled it, and turned to the men. One hand on her hip, the glass to her lips she growled. "I hate men."

Kirk looked at his sons. He waved a finger. "Either of you responsible for this?" He gestured at Jordan. They both shrank into their chairs. "Ah, Jordi, what did I do?" His sons skulked out of the office.

Jordan shook her glass at them. "Run, go ahead…"

"Honey." Kirk soothed in his most reasonable voice. "What can I do to make this better?"

"I want you to go over and kill Hank."

Kirk leaned an elbow on his desk and rested his chin, watching her drain the wine glass. "Hank just arrived today. He works fast. You're not upset about him not proposing, are you?" Kirk winced at his humor.

"If I had married him, I'd be responsible for his death. They always look at the spouse first."

Kirk nodded. "Good to know. So what did Kingy do?"

"He is tormenting his daughter."

"Aha. And as a man with no daughters, you want me to straighten him out."

"You're my husband, it's your job." Jordan glared.

****

Kirk knocked on the door of Hank's hotel suite. Hank yanked open the door. "Oh, it's you." He waved Kirk in holding a large bottled water. Hank's eyes and face were puffy. Kirk assumed it was from the long flight and overhydration. Every flat surface in the living room held empty water bottles.

Kirk picked one up and sniffed. "Yeah, good to see you, too, Teflon. So, ahh..."

"Whattaya want, Romeo?"

Kirk rubbed the back of his neck and walked to the glass door, looked at the beachfront view, shrugged, and turned back to Hank. "I heard there was an explosion in the room earlier. I thought I'd come by to check the wounded."

Hank fell into the sofa. "She wants to go to crayon college."

"Aha." Kirk turned on his heel. "She wants to be an artist."

Hank gestured with an open water bottle, splashing with each exclamation. "No, damn it. She wants to be a portrait artist and study art restoration at some fancy art institute." Hank drank a few gulps and then sat down the bottle. "All I see is an appliance box under the freeway where I can visit..."

Kirk tried to keep his smile neutral. "I can only imagine how disappointed you were about the Academy."

Hank's head dropped to the back of the sofa. "Oh, hell, candidates wash out all the time, they get better offers..." He waved that idea off. "The kicker today was that we've never even had a heated discussion about anything. We've never had a cross word... and it all came to this. I work with kids her age. Why did I not see this?"

Kirk sat on the coffee table across from Hank. "You can view them with objectivity. This is your little peanut. You want what's best whether she wants it or not."

Hank put up a foot over his knee and shook his head. "How did you get so damn smart?"

"Not my kid. I can see her objectively. You know last year you set me straight about Jax and Jordan. I'm just returning the favor. But I've got to tell you, Teflon, I've gotten to know your daughter in the last week, and no one is less likely to spend her days with a slide rule and pocket protector. Was she even active in the science fair?"

Hank shook his head. "Nope." Kirk began a grin that escalated to belly laughter. "What the fuck are you laughing about?"

"Her not pursuing your dreams is small potatoes compared to the fact that she's dating my son."

Hank leaned forward. "Dammit, I forgot about that."

Kirk waved his hand. "Problem solved. Why don't you get a nap, get cleaned up, and come by Evan's house for dinner? The family will be there, and you and Sky can walk on the beach if you need to."

****

Conner was in the mat room with Jax when Sky found him. The two men were wrapped around each other like pretzels shaken too long in shipping. It looked painful. Conner played the good sport as his purple belt brother swept the mat with him. "That's the best you've got? I was at bonfire once, and a guy disrespected his girl and I…"

Jax put him in a straight ankle lock before he could finish his words. "In five seconds, I've disabled you." He tightened the pressure a minuscule amount. "Do you doubt me?"

Conner's gaze met his. "No," he gasped.

Jax continued in an instructive tone. "Don't lose focus." He looked up to see Sky standing at the door. He released Conner immediately. "Okay." He slapped his brother's back. "Good lesson."

Conner rolled to his knees, one hand massaging his ankle, gasping as he rose. Jax left the room, winked at Sky as he passed. "Hi, Sky."

She made to approach Conner, but he held up a hand. "I deserved that, and I'm okay. Give me a minute."

Sky covered her mouth with one hand and waited. Conner smiled as he shook it off and walked to her. "You okay, angel? I said I was okay."

"I need… to sketch you." Her voice was intense.

You need me how? Like a hug? Like a kiss? Like full out skin to skin? "Right now?" Conner pulled his sweaty shirt away from his chest and back.

"Yes, it's an art emergency."

He shook his head. *Art emergency?* "Okay." Conner blinked. "Jordan says we're having a family dinner and you guys are coming…Why don't I shower and change, we can go to their house early. I'll ah… pose by the pool?"

Chapter Sixteen

Sky posed Conner in his board shorts sitting on the stone wall, the anxious ocean behind him. The fresh breeze that moved the restless waves stirred the atmosphere. Emotions felt sharp, on high alert. Conner studied her as she studied him. She was wound as tight as a violin string.

She hadn't said it, but he was guessing her time with her dad hadn't been pleasant. Under her tan, she seemed pale. More than once, he'd seen tears spring to her eyes over nothing. *What do I do for her? Listen? Answer the rhetorical questions? Pray the answers are right?*

Conner stretched out on his belly on the wide stone wall, his chin resting on his folded arms before him.

"Can you come up on your elbows a bit more? I want to see your chest." She walked, so her view was straight on. She put down the drawing pad and approached him, smoothing his jams' fabric over the back of his thigh. Her hand rested there on the flesh behind his knee. *She's not sketching.*

Conner rolled off the wall onto his feet on the beach. He held out both hands. "Walk with me, Sky."

With a perplexed expression on her face, Sky kicked off her slippers and came down the wall with measured fascination. Once her feet hit the sand, she barreled into his arms, pressing her cheek against his chest. "Oh, angel." He whispered into her ear, his inhalation giving her a shiver. He turned and leaned against the wall, spreading his legs for her to stand between. She wrapped her arms around his torso and stood laminated to him. He felt every emotional response churning inside.

"Kiss me, Conner." Her voice was so soft it evaporated on a vapor.

He squelched any internal confusion once his lips locked to hers. These were not the cute and tidy kisses they played with on the beach.

Nor were they the almost to the limit kisses in his room when they tossed the pizza box off the bed and rolled in each other's arms. These kisses expressed new demands. They told him her limits were gone. Her clothed body melted into his, and their hearts raced in tandem. Within his embrace, Sky wrestled her full sundress up far enough that they were belly to belly. "Sky, do you know what you're doing to me?"

Her hand ran down the front of his trunks and caught his reaction. "I do." Without seeking his gaze, she pressed tighter. "I don't think it was an art emergency as much as it was a hug emergency."

"Yeah, but you're hugging a certain part of me and…"

"And we're on the beach in front of your father's house." She raised her head as a light went on inside the house. "And I think the security lights just told me they are home."

Conner groaned. "Oh, angel." He lifted her chin and saw the haze of happiness that replaced her earlier sadness. "Yeah, they're home, and we've got to stop this. Bad timing." He pushed her away, and her dress fell back to her knees. His hands capped her shoulders. "I don't want a hay roll. I want you." His words made her glow, and his heart thumped in time with his sex. He pressed his length down his leg. "I've got to walk this off. Let's make a plan."

Sky giggled as she danced on the sand away from him.

He winced. "You see what you do to me?"

Sky hugged herself and twirled, her hair wild in the late afternoon sun. "See what you do to me?" She followed a few feet behind as Conner kicked at the cool water in the shin-deep surf. "So, Con, what's the plan?"

His hands planted on his hips, and he stared away his stiffy. Conner shook his head, smirking at her. "It doesn't help that you look so cute. Go away, put up your art stuff. Gimme a minute. Then we can synchronize our watches."

Sky bounded up the wall, looking back over her shoulder. "You're the best…"

*****

Sky brushed away the ocean breeze tangles in her hair and splashed cool water on her face while Conner went down the hall to change into his street clothes. She met Jordan in the kitchen and hugged her. "Is there anything I can help you with?"

Jordan looked around the refrigerator door. "Set the table? Dishes are over there." She pointed to the tall cabinets. "This will be casual, I'm cutting up grilled chicken for Caesar salads. I hope Hank still likes coconut crème pie. I found a mile high pie at the bakery." She held the pie on her fingertips. "What a diet buster."

Sky's brows arched. "I wish we could hide that from the guys." She accepted the pie and set it in the center of the huge kitchen island. Sherlock Holmes's voice announced. "You have a text. A text has come in."

Jordan's gaze narrowed. "That quite an assistant you have there."

Sky held the phone to her heart. "That's when Daddy's texts arrive." She ducked away from the kitchen to read.

Almost there, see you in ten.

The front door opened, and Kirk announced a la Ward Cleaver. "Honey, I'm home."

"We're in the kitchen, you got here before Sky and I ate the dessert."

Conner entered the kitchen. "Dessert? After I get my ass handed to me, I like to eat."

Kirk moved around the kitchen to hug Jordan. "If you're breathing, you like to eat. Your mother needed a diner to keep sufficient food on hand."

Still in Kirk's arms, Jordan winked at him. "You're a growing boy."

Conner pulled open the pita chips and removed the top from the hummus. "You meant for me to pull this out, right?"

Kirk nabbed a pita chip and a scoop of hummus before his son could inhale it. "So, I heard you tried force on Jax today. How'd that work out for you?"

Jordan watched intently. Sky winced at the memory of the interaction. Conner swallowed and lowered his head. "Not very well."

"And why is that, son?" Kirk asked.

"Because Jiu Jitsu is about technique and not brute force."

Kirk clapped Conner on the shoulder. "Lesson learned. Good."

The doorbell rang, and everyone looked at Sky. She nodded, and opening the front door, found her dad with his arms full. He had a floral arrangement in driftwood and a market sack. "This is for Jordan and Kirk." He placed them on the table in the foyer and extended his arms to Sky. "Get in here for a hug, peanut."

"I love you, Daddy."

"I love you, too, peanut." When they released their hug, they carried his items into the kitchen.

Hank placed the market sack on the island and removed a bottle of wine and a large loaf of cheesy garlic bread. "Man does not live by tofu alone. Here's your months' worth of carbs." Sky slid the floral arrangement to Kirk and Jordan. Hank pointed his beefy finger at it. "This is a decoration, not dinner."

Jordan admired the orchids in the driftwood. "But you know many orchids are edible."

Hank smacked his broad chest. "I'm a carnivore and a carbovore."

Kirk narrowed his gaze. "Hank, you know there's no such thing as a carbovore."

Hank shook his head. "Like you're the expert."

Kirk stared him down and clapped his hands once. "I want you to meet somebody special. He's been asking about you for days." Kirk pulled Conner forward. "Son, this is Brigadier General Kingston, also known as Teflon. Around here he's Hank. Hank, this is my youngest son, Conner Jameson."

Conner stood very straight, not exactly at attention, but close. He extended his hand. "It's a real honor to meet you, sir."

Hank shook hands with a twinkle in his eye. "I am Hank around here, Conner. It's a real pleasure to meet you. Whereabouts in Texas are you from?"

Conner nodded. "A little town outside Amarillo."

Hank strolled over to peck a kiss on Jordan's cheek. "Oh, the panhandle. I did basic at Lackland, down near San Antonio."

Conner nodded. "When I bugged my mom bad enough, we took a vacation to see the air show at Lackland. That's where I'll train in the fall."

Sky's heart warmed at the immediate connection between her father and Conner. She caught her dad's eye and winked at him. Sliding a tray of cut veggies near the hummus, she asked, "Who wants what to drink?"

Jordan placed a frosty pitcher on a trivet. "Fresh pineapple iced tea, beer, or wine." She nodded at Sky's phone. "Hank, do you know Sky's portfolio is on her phone?"

Conner gestured to the television in the next room. "Give me a few minutes, and I can get it in high def on the wall."

Sky relinquished her phone, and Conner went to work. The families stood next to each other at the long kitchen island and snacked as images appeared on the nine-foot screen. Hank stared transfixed. "Peanut, these are astounding. You are leagues ahead of where you were last year." The collection slowly scrolled, and he had comments on many. He laughed, "I love the expression on the dog's face." The profile she'd just completed on Conner scrolled on, and Hank held up a hand. "Hold it there, can you hold it?" Conner froze the frame. Hank marched up to the screen, then back to Conner. His head swiveled back and forth. "Wow. This is perfect. I'd think this was a photo of you." Hank turned to Kirk. "Poor kid looks just like you did when I met you."

Sky spoke shyly. "So, you like my work?"

He kissed her cheek. "It's beautiful, peanut. Which one do I get?"

"I'll tell you what. You pick out a subject, and I'll paint your very own." As she spoke, the last painting in the group scrolled past and on the wall was their recent excursion to Ford Island and Pearl Harbor.

Jordan smiled and pointed. "Oh, you visited the aviation museum?" The room laughed at the image of Conner holding the kid's flight suit in front of himself, his expression was positively childlike. Without Conner knowing, Sky caught photos of him talking with the aged volunteers. His animation was evident in still photos. Last, was a closeup of his flight simulator record in the cockpit.

Hank clapped him on the shoulder. "Well, look at you, ace. Of course, nobody's really firing back, but you cleared the sky."

Conner's energy from that day returned. He grinned wildly and wrung his hands. "You think so? It was just a game."

Kirk rocked a fist into Conner's shoulder. "That's my boy." He held out a plate to Hank. "Now, Conner, let us old farts fill our plates before you, the human locust, gets dinner."

****

Kirk and Jordan took a few moments after dinner to show Hank some World War II military maps they'd had framed for their new condo. Conner carried a pitcher of iced tea followed by Sky with the glasses and ice. They thought it would be a pleasant end to the evening if the family watched the Honolulu sunset together.

Conner whispered behind her. "How do you think they'd take if I said we want to sleep on the beach tonight?"

Sky's head whirled toward him. She almost unsettled the glasses. "Not well. Don't let his good ol' boy party demeanor fool you."

Conner moved close behind her, and as they both watched the adults in the pool house, Conner pressed his hips into her backside. "If you think any of this has dialed back, you're wrong. Seeing you as beautiful as you are makes me want you ten times worse."

Sky fell back on him and caught his hand to hold over her clothed nipple. "I'm feeling the agony, too, Conner. What are we going to do?"

"How hard does he sleep? You said it's a two-bedroom suite."

She looked over her shoulder. "Not that well, but we are on the first floor."

Conner stepped away from her and did a desperate dance. "He's a light sleeper, but you're on the first floor. Can you get away?"

Sky leaned on the table and gave him a frown. "I don't want it to be like that. I want to take our time. I want it to be romantic."

"You're killing me… What are we going to do?"

Chapter Seventeen

Jordan flipped off the overhead kitchen lights as Sky leaned on her elbows on the counter, watching the men involved in military talk. "You know how I know they're talking about military stuff?"

Jordan stood beside her and shrugged. "Tell me."

Sky sighed and pantomimed their movements. "Daddy is wowing Conner with his flying tales, and Kirk is doing sound effects. Are they twelve?"

Jordan put her arm around Sky's shoulders, and their heads touched. "In so many ways, they are."

In the kitchen's semi-darkness, the women stood unseen and watched the male bonding between Kirk and Conner complements of Hank's war tales. Jordan tipped her head toward them. "I saw some romantic sparks flying between you and Conner. It looks to me like you two are getting close."

Sky pushed away from the counter at the window and leaned back on the island, her arms crossed over her chest. She sighed, and her voice was thick with emotion. "We clicked on the airplane so well. Everything we do together we enjoy. It's just wrong that he's dead set on joining the Air Force."

Jordan leaned on the counter and turned to face Sky. "I don't know what you mean?"

"I mean, I won't live in military housing two years at a time. What's even worse is waving goodbye when they go somewhere the family can't follow. I can't sell artwork out of a closet on some remote base. We want different things."

"You've only known him for seven days. Is it that serious already?"

Sky twisted the end of her long ponytail. "It could be, I mean, look at him. He's smart and funny and built, and there is not a lazy bone in his body. I can't believe the military didn't tie him up in a bow with delayed enlistment when he was a senior."

"Conner and I had a long talk about mothering styles. She put her foot down. He'll do fine if the military is what he wants."

Sky nodded toward Conner's rapt attention to Hank. "Can you doubt that's what he wants?"

Jordan put a tea kettle on and pulled out two mugs and her collection of loose tea. "You have your work cut out for you at the gym, if you need to finish the mural more quickly, you could work at night. I'll understand if you leave when your Dad does."

Sky caught the counter with both hands and gawked at Jordan. "What?"

Jordan shook her head. "If you two hit your flash point, all reason will go out the window. Lord knows where you'll both end up."

Is this mothering code for 'you kids will screw and end up running away with the circus'? Sky's lips straightened. "When is Conner leaving?"

Jordan opened a drawer and pulled out a calendar. "I believe the date the recruiter gave him was the Wednesday after Labor Day."

Sky's shoulders sagged. "Well, I'm here with daddy for two weeks, then the hostel will only put me up for a week after that. At most, I have three weeks. Aunt Jordan, I'd be lying if I told you I don't want to sleep with him. Maybe that's what hurts the most. It could go two ways, we could find out we hate each other's guts, and fall goes on as planned…"

Jordan interjected. "Or you could be real adults about it and keep in touch. The years do fly by."

Sky chuckled. "I see how you injected his enlistment in there. Right, what is eight years anyway?"

Jordan poured the tea. "Whatever you do, I believe in you. I always have, and I believe in Conner."

****

Angel-

K, J & H leave 4 Kauai @ 0400 Thurs. Due back Sat. 1100.

Sky read the text shortly after she turned in around 1 AM. When she and her dad left dinner at the Roman's around 11 PM, they dropped the top on the Mustang and did a drive up to the North Shore and back. It was peaceful, just the wind and the brilliant indigo background for the millions of stars in the moonless sky.

She stared at the message and felt heat flush into parts she didn't know could flush. *Oh, my God. How can I live between now and Thursday?* She fought with herself over what to reply. *You Made My Day.*

YMMD! RU kidding me?

Conner replied pronto.

Nope.

Sky flipped over in the bed, muffling her laughter into her pillow. She was curious. *What are his plans?* She typed.

? r ur plans?

There was a delay, and Sky's heart quivered. The phone beeped, and his reply throbbed on the screen.

It's our 2 days off. Let me bring you breakfast. Stay in bed, Okay?

The island shook momentarily as she read and reread his text. *Stay in bed? Works for me.* She grinned as she replied.

WFM and a kiss emoji

Conner shot back the exact reply, and she could only imagine his spirits were riding as high as hers when she closed her eyes.

****

Hank and Conner sat on the sidelines while Jax and Kirk took turns beating each other up. Hank handed Conner a water bottle, gestured toward Kirk and Jax, and joked. "They think this is fun. In fact, your dad, he laughs that I call this place a sweat factory."

Conner nodded, rolled his shoulders, and rotated his neck. "I know I'm going to have some bruises. So, what do you like to do when you're in town, sir?"

Hank pointed to Kirk. "Before that son of a bitch married Jordan, I'd blow into town, eat out every night, go dancing and fly back to my command. She and I had a handshake agreement."

Conner narrowed his eyes. "Handshake agreement?"

Hank scoffed. "I like being with a pretty woman. My gal died seventeen years ago. In my career, it's not fair for a girlfriend to sit and wait for me to come back from some godforsaken hell hole."

Conner nodded mutely.

"I couldn't replace Sky's mom, but Jordan, she's a peach. She's good people. Tell me why *you* want to enlist?"

Conner's eyes lit up. "Yes, sir. I came out here to get some moral support and advice. I've always wanted to be a fighter pilot."

Hank's smile was kind. "That's a noble ambition. If you're smart enough, strong enough, and have good enough vision, then you just might be selected to begin the training to become a fighter pilot. I can see you're strong. How are your grades?"

Conner thought for a moment. "My SATs, my math, and reading scores were ninety-sixth percentile. I'm an Eagle Scout. I took JROTC in high school, and our local topdressing pilot used to take me up with him. He'd give me the instruments sometimes while we flew."

Hank looked impressed, which pleased Conner. "Tell you what, I'd be happy to put in a good word with the commandant of the Air Force Academy. We were in the same Master's program for Strategic Studies…. Once you're in, they can take a look at you."

"That would be aces, sir. I mean, I'll take college classes as soon as I can, wherever they send me…"

Hank interrupted. "Conner, I know you're eager to get started, but I think someone has shined you on."

Conner frowned. "Pardon me?"

Hank looked away for a minute and inclined his head back to Conner. "You go in now as an airman, you'll never be a pilot." Conner sagged back against the wall and shook his head. "Look, son, in every other branch, you can go into elite service without a college degree. Not in the Air Force. Our elite are our pilots, and if you want a shot at being a pilot, you go in with a degree."

Conner's eyes widened, and he sat up straight, shaking his head. "A college degree still doesn't mean I'll be a pilot?"

Hank nodded. "They're the best of the best, but you will be an officer if the Air Force is what you want. Now, from what you said last night, you have a mother who's intent on seeing you at the aeronautical university. If you want to be a pilot, you couldn't have a better start."

Conner's gaze searched the ceiling. "And then I'd have to go back and admit she was right."

Hank smacked his thigh. "In the buffet of life, sometimes you got to eat crow." Conner narrowed his eyes and winced. "You did tell her you were coming here to get advice."

Conner nodded peacefully. "I got to meet my dad and my family. I met you and Sky. I enjoyed beautiful Hawaii. Coming here was a good decision."

Hank held up a fist to bump. "There you go. And the fact that it confirms your mother's offer is just gravy. I'm expecting big things from you, young man."

"Thank you, sir."

****

Conner sat on the exam table, the paper stuck to the backs of his thighs. His foot swung from nervous energy. *I fly how many thousand miles to paradise and have to get cleared after my ex thinly admits to screwing around on me.* There was a knock on the door, and he answered. "Yeah."

The PA came in with an energetic air. Something told Conner this guy was ex-military. He consulted the tablet. "Mr. Jameson. How can we help you today?"

It took a second for Conner to speak. He raised his head and set his jaw, and then words tumbled out. "About a week ago, my girl called me long distance to tell me we were done." The PA nodded. "All the time on the phone she's cutting me loose, this guy is in the background telling her to hurry up. Like he has ants in his pants." The PA nodded. "So, I'm here to find out if I have something worse than ants."

The PA peered at him over his half-glasses. "Have you had any symptoms? Pain on urination, rash? Anything?"

"Nope, thank God."

The PA laughed. "Well, it was a good decision to come in. Let's do a couple of tests."

Conner walked out of the clinic, relieved, and peeled the Band-Aid off the recent blood draw site. *They said it would be a week before he'd have the results. Damn. A week is a lifetime.*

****

Hank and Sky stood on their suite's lanai, eating off the room service cart. Sky bit a piece of crisp bacon and shook her head. "Daddy, there is something criminal about you waking up at 0500 on your vacation. I have to get in and paint, but don't you ever sleep in?"

Hank poured more black coffee and chuckled. "I don't get enough time with you. Before you know it, you'll be finished with school, married, and spending your time adoring your husband with no time for me."

Sky nodded. "That's the way the songs make it sound. I'm glad you're enjoying the Romans."

Hank swatted a bear-sized hand at her. "Awe, peanut, I like to pull Kirk's chain. But I came here for us to have a good time. How much more work is there on that mural?"

Sky demolished the bacon on her plate and swallowed some juice. "I just blocked Jax's pose, and I'm laying in the background today. I've got a bit of work to do yet."

"You think you'll be finished by the time I leave?"

"Probably not, but I can get another week at the hostel."

Hank shivered and made a face. "Ah. I ran Conner by there yesterday… I'd rather get you a single here. You'd have the pool, safety, room service, security, clean linens…"

"Yeah, yeah. I get it, Daddy. Sure, I won't have to padlock my art supplies." *Privacy, clean linens, a king-size bed… sure.*

Hank looked at the time. "I've got to get you over to sweat heaven, or you'll be AWOL. Plus, I want to get my workout done before the beautiful bodies show up."

Sky covered her face with a piece of toast and laughed. "Oh, Daddy, you looked handsome in that Aloha shirt. I've seen some of the ladies checking you out."

Hank left for his bedroom and waved her off. "It's the Mustang."

Chapter Eighteen

Conner held the front door open for Sky and her father when they all hit Silver SEAL at the same moment. "Morning." Conner yawned hugely. "Mom woke me up with her phone call. She forgot we're six hours behind her. I think she drank a pot of coffee because she said she hadn't been up this early since she closed the diner."

Hank asked. "What time was it in Florida?"

Conner yawned. "She woke me at 2:30 and yapped until about 4:00. She's got a boyfriend. Oh, they go for motorcycle rides up and down the coast." He shook his head. "She's glad to hear I'm coming back home for school.

Sky jerked around at his comment. "What?"

Hank winked. "I'll see you kids."

Wearing state of the art exercise compression gear, Jordan approached Conner. "Lighting check in fifteen minutes, get your TV gear on."

Hank looked at Jordan. "What, do they just spray paint that stuff on?" He smacked his chest. "I've got a body for radio."

Conner exhaled heavily. "You mean, my porno wear?"

Hank's head swiveled around. "What?"

Conner shuffled off. "Oh, just wait, you'll see."

Jordan waved the comment away. "He looks wonderful in his tv gear, doesn't he, Sky?"

Sky's expression beamed. "Ah' hum."

****

While Conner and his Hawaiian family filmed in the mat room downstairs, Hank and Sky retreated to the exercise equipment area where he complimented her on her progress with the mural.

The filming of the TV segment was shown on the center's monitors. Every filming day, the center's attendance doubled with coeds elbowing each other to get closer to the monitors. As the show progressed, Sky noticed the wave of machines ceasing and the women ogling the Roman men. She leaned over to her dad on a treadmill. "Watch when they take a break." She bobbed her head toward the coeds. "They'll lean over the railing trying to get a look at them in the flesh."

Hank's guffaw drew heads all around what was becoming a sea of slack-jawed women staring at the monitors. Sky nodded toward the set. "Jax has been drawing the twenty-somethings. Since Conner showed up, they've been getting high schoolers and coeds."

A chunky guy in jams, tank top and slippers stood in the entryway and yelled. "Joy. You in there? Joy?"

Bonnie, at the front desk, waved at the guy. "Are you a member here, sir?"

The man swaggered over to the front desk. "I am not, I'm here to pick up my girlfriend, Joy O'Connell. She's here with a group of her bar friends." He turned from Bonnie. "Joy?"

A girl in teal spandex elbowed a thin girl wearing earphones tuned into the center's television. "Joy, Maximus Prick is here. Head's up."

Joy yanked out her earphones and waved. "Okay, okay, I'm, coming."

A giggling fan near the front desk sat on the bike, arms draped over the handlebars. "Joy, Conner will be on in a minute, can't he wait?" Joy's friend frowned in her boyfriend's direction.

He leaned on the counter and nodded his head at Joy. "You gals have given up happy hour for this? 10 AM at a gym?"

On the monitor, the show's producer clapped the board, and Kirk introduced Conner's segment. The room chittered until Conner stepped up and grinned before delivering his home run sales pitch. There he stood molded in compression gear, every ripple of his body emphasized by the gym uniform under the camera's light.

The guy hooked a thumb toward the monitor. "Is he why you're here?"

Joy wrung her towel. "The six of us meet here every Tuesday at 9:30. This show airs on Saturdays. I don't know what you mean." She buried her fascination with Conner.

He flexed an arm. "What? You think I could be in better shape?"

Bonnie eyed the guy's slightly swollen beer belly. "We do have an anytime drop-in rate. It lets you try the machines and the classes. Would you like to sign up?"

The guy looked up at Conner, who gestured toward a poster promoting the women's four-week self-defense class.

"It's a sad fact that many women, especially on campus, will need to protect themselves. Let us show you how to do that in a safe environment."

The coeds giggled and whispered among themselves, and the guy paid attention. He signaled to Bonnie, "Yeah, lemme see the classes." He scanned the brochure and laid it down, tapping the Beginner's Jiu Jitsu. "Four weeks, lemme see how that goes." He pulled out his wallet. "Joy, get your gear, we gotta go." He looked over at Bonnie. "My name is Agnew Nunamaker. Here's my credit card. When's the first class?"

Bonnie consulted the computer. "The next open class is in two weeks, you'll get a welcome email within twenty-four hours with that info."

Agnew pushed off the counter and winked as Joy joined him, her bag over her shoulder.

****

Wednesday at lunch, Conner put his hand over Sky's as she was pushing off to leave. "Angel, I want to talk to you about something."

The expression on Sky's face drained. "Please don't tell me you've decided against college."

Conner sat back and waved both hands. "Oh, good God, no. Nothing like that." He dipped his head closer to her. "Come sit next to me."

She gave him a curious look but came. "What is it, cowboy?"

"I was looking forward to tomorrow without any restrictions."

Sky squinted. "Restrictions?" She put her elbow on the table and put her hand to the side of her face to draw a wall between them and the world. "What kind?"

"Condoms."

Sky sighed in relief. "But, I'm on the pill."

Yeah, but, angel, when Tessa broke up with me, it was pretty clear she'd been knocking boots with another guy."

Sky's eyes widened. "Ahh."

"I know. I went to a clinic on Monday and got tested, but it will be next Monday before I know, so… condoms."

Sky rubbed his arm. "Oh, cowboy, it doesn't matter. You're trying to keep me safe, and I love that about you."

Conner caught her hand and kissed the back of it. "And I always will." The warmth in the gaze they shared floated with them the rest of the afternoon.

Chapter Nineteen

Sky waved an enthusiastic goodbye to her father very early Thursday morning. "You all have a wonderful time in Kauai. See you on Saturday! Can't wait for the dinner cruise that night!"

Hank waved a final time and disappeared around the corner.

The minute Hank was out of sight, Sky ran to her closet. What to wear? *Cute animal jammies? No. Silky slip gown? Trying too hard. Nothing but cologne? Trying way too hard.* The things she slept most comfortably in was her eyelet tap panties and matching camisole. *That wasn't trying too hard.*

She flew through the room, spritzing a spray she made herself called 'Happy Vibes', it contained tangerine, lavender, lime, and spearmint. The perfectly clean suite was too antiseptic for romance. This would do the trick. She placed bottled water on each nightstand and arranged the fruit she bought yesterday on a tray. When she returned from brushing her teeth, she opened the box of Honolulu cookies and artfully displayed them on the small table between the two chairs. Sky fluffed up the sheets and comforter, made them look neat, and then jumped in bed and made it look slept in. *Am I overthinking this?*

She dozed off to be awakened by the knock on the door. "Malasada delivery for Ms. Kingston."

Sky pulled the covers up to her nose, her wild hair framed her on the fluffy pillows. "But, I'm still in bed."

Conner's official tone went on. "Ms. Kingston, I've been empowered by the bedside malasada delivery union to bring these to you."

Sky heard his voice approaching. "Then who am I to stay you from the swift completion of your appointed rounds?"

"We appreciate your cooperation, miss." Conner stood in her doorway, holding the bakery bag in both hands. He looked delicious in his broken-in jeans, bare feet, and an open well-worn white striped dress shirt. Sky sighed. "You're late, Daddy left three hours ago."

Conner shrugged as he placed the bag on her night table. "The bakery didn't open until seven. These are still warm."

"Awe, you're so sweet."

"And I think of everything, I put the do not disturb sign on the door."

Sky began to slide up in the bed, holding the covers to her. "That you do. Are you staying tonight?"

"What? You think I need pajamas?" He sat on the bedside and leaned in for a good morning kiss.

She caught his face in her hands and peppered him with affectionate kisses. His chest pressed her back to the mountain of pillows. Her arms wrapped his torso under his shirt. "You are overdressed for this party."

Conner broke out of her embrace and sat up. His shirt became a puddle on the floor. "Let me look at you for a second." Sky pushed back the covers and sat demurely like a mermaid on her rock. "I want to remember this morning forever."

Sky rose to her knees on the side of the bed and wrapped her arms around his waist. She pulled him toward her and kissed his chest over his heart. He lowered his head and savored the scent of her hair and neck. With a deep breath, he stepped out of her embrace and removed a tin from his back pocket. Sky's gaze followed his movements curiously. Her attention returned to him as he began unbuttoning jeans that were beginning to tighten. "Let me crawl in there with you…" He sat on the side of the bed and kicked off his jeans. He was commando. Conner rolled under the covers and snuggled to her.

"Whoa, whoa… what's with hiding under the covers? I want to see what I've been drawing all this time." She lay on her side and lifted linens from his exceptionally sculpted body." Conner lay back, his muscular arms behind his head. "My isn't that a smug smile you're wearing?"

"No brag, just fact." He pointed one finger at her eyelet outfit. "Now ya know, you do look as fresh as a daisy in that frilly thing, but who's overdressed now? I can help you with that."

Sky sat back on her heels, threaded her fingers together behind her head, and sifted through the wealth of creamy blond hair hanging to the middle of her back.

Conner caught the hem of her camisole and raised it up her torso, stopping to kiss over her heart. They both rose to their knees, and his facile hands slid down between her waistband and her hips. Her tap pants were a memory. He rolled her over to her back, and she welcomed his weight. He devoured her with a possessive kiss.

Her fingers kneaded and massaged his back and moved slyly down to his hips as her knees rose in invitation. His lips moved to caress her cheek. Her fingertip traced the shell of his ear, and she gave his earlobe a tiny pinch. Conner shivered and growled. "What are you up to?"

"I just want to keep your attention, don't want to bore you." Her laugh was light but evil. Her hand traveled to his intriguing sex that stirred insistently at her belly. "Introduce your friend here. Does he have a name?" Her fingers curled around his girth. "It's not little, Conner."

His head dropped in forbearance. "His name is Desperate."

"Desperate? What a sad name. Can I make him happy?"

"You can make him any dwarf you want…" He levered his hips to move with her grasp.

"Yeah, this is no dwarf." They both collapsed in laughter and wrestled, kicking off the covers. So much tension dispersed with their tussling and pillow fighting that when they settled back in the bed, the nerves were gone. Panting with exertion, Sky's gaze met his. "Love me, Conner."

He reached for the tin on the bedside and yanked it open with one hand. Four condoms fell out. They both eyed the tin. "I have more in my backpack in the living room."

Sky nodded appreciatively. "Good to know."

Conner's body felt heavenly against hers. His muscles kindled heat of the most enticing kind. It was energy and exhilaration so new and fascinating she never wanted to leave his arms. Cocooned together, they rolled within a spell of breathless kissing. Their hands met, and their fingers entwined as they moaned with newfound joy.

"Oh, angel, I want to make this last all day." His lips ducked between her breasts as he held them. "If I died right now, I'd go happy."

She leaned back. "You better wipe that thought out of your head... if you die now, your daddy, my daddy, everyone will be after me." She caught his handsome face in her hands. "And we wouldn't have this time together." Conner rocked his body over hers, moving between her thighs.

"You've got a point there. I spoke too soon. This gets better every minute." He raised on his palms and arched his back. "Will you pass me one of those?" He inclined his head to the nightstand.

Sky slid sideways as Conner rolled to his back and groaned at the sight of her backside when she rolled over and reached for the nightstand. "I hope I'm the first one to tell you, you've got the sweetest heart-shaped butt in Hawaii." She brought the condom back as she stretched out alongside him. He watched her tear open the wrapper and went silent. His hand caught his erection, and his expression sobered.

Sky raised on her knees and held the condom by its tip. "We can make this fun." She stroked the head of his sex. He groaned. Sky's fingertips teased his sac as she rolled down the condom with one hand. When she held him fully encased, she kissed the tip of his length. "Fun, huh?"

****

Conner turned it on. If spending the extra attention to his boss's sister-in-law at the ranch taught him anything, he knew woman never got enough of the right strokes. It wasn't fun to come and run.

It was great fun to strike a balance with his tongue. No tongue at all felt like junior high, too much tongue felt like prom night. What's the right amount? If he had to ask, he wasn't doing it right.

He knew Sky was aching to get down to business. He also knew delayed pleasure was the best pleasure.

With a firm hand, Conner caught a thick length of Sky's blonde curls and wound them around his fist. He drew her slowly to his lips as her blue eyes widened in anticipation. He held her lips tightly to his and nibbled her bottom lip. Holding her this close, feeling her arms reflexively tightening around his torso, he moaned against her. The vibration shuddered through her and kept his latex covered erection bobbling. Her lips responded with the sweetest pucker. She suckled back, and they smiled into each other's kiss. "Mmm. Aren't you tasty?"

Sky's vibrant expression darkened to sexual hunger. He knew that look. His lips moved to the shell of her ear and still holding her in place, his open mouth skated the curve, and he inhaled.

"Ahhh." She huffed a deep gasp.

Almost biting her earlobe, he chuckled. "I could dine on you forever."

"Forever? I guess you got that patience back."

His teeth caught her earlobe, and he gently tugged. "You know, I can do this to other parts of you, too." She arched into him. His fingertips walked down her cleavage, tickling, and teasing her tight flesh. "I've been thinking about doing things to you all week, but now I seem to be stuck on just doing this." His palm covered her nest of dark blonde hair at her delta. With a gentle nip on her neck, his fingers stroked her anxious flesh. She bowed into his touch with a moan. He upped the ante, bit, and released her neck without leaving a mark. They shuddered together, him enjoying her responses.

His lips left her flesh to ask. "Do you know the rule of the nipple?" She shook her head. "Nipples are the key to everything. I've watched your nipples since our first kiss. They asked me if I'd like to kiss them. Did you get my psychic message?"

Sky's eyelids fluttered. "Who knew?"

His mouth devoured her taut pink peak as his thumb played lightly on her sex. "You are so beautiful like this." His tongue flicked at the rise he excited. "I'd like you to do this to me." He placed her hand on his chest and rolled to his back, still stroking her, bringing her along.

"You would? Ohh…"

"Angel, anything you do with those lips would please me… but let's not get ahead of ourselves."

Her hand ran to his sac as her lips sought his nipple. The sensations tied him in knots.

He moaned against her breasts. "Do you know how good that feels?"

Sky laughed gently against him and fell onto his broad muscled chest. "Unh, huh." Her lips never stopped their assault.

Conner sought her soft and magical gaze. "I need you, Sky." He smoothed back her wild tendrils of hair and held her forehead to his. He could smell her on his fingers, and before he pressed her back to the pillows, he licked them with a shiver. "You taste delicious." While her eyes widened at his declaration, he flipped over her, falling between her thighs.

****

Together, they anticipated each other's moves, responding with surprising joy. Raw joy, soulful joy, bodily joy. Each move became their horizontal ballet. This buff young man was her perfect partner in seeking and finding this deeply tuned affection. His mastery of her body stirred anarchy within her. With every stroke, they met in a poignant communion.

She rode the waves of his thrusts and parries, meeting him, challenging him to ride harder. With her strong legs wrapped high around his waist, she ached for this to never end. His lips covered hers briefly before he arched back, eyes closed, his chest covered with their mingled sweat and sweet anarchy overcame them.

She'd never experienced physical chaos unexplainable by words, simply uttered in breaths and moans. Her first full breath carried her release. A release that flung her into becoming his. Conner Jameson was everything she wanted. He was everything she never knew she needed. With the last gasp of their completion, Sky said a prayer for their happily ever after.

Chapter Twenty

Sky woke tangled in sheets and Conner's strong arms. She winked open one eye. It was 10:37 AM. Her stomach growled with rolling thunder. Conner's eyes flew open. "Who let the bear in?"

She nuzzled deeper into his embrace and sighed as his palm glided over her back. "By now, I usually have eaten a big breakfast." She rested her chin over his heart. "My dear cowboy, you are satisfying and filling... but this angel must be fed."

Conner threw a leg over her and caught her tightly. "Sorry about those donuts, they're probably cold by now."

Sky sat up with a lurch and leaned toward the bag. "I'd rather have cold donuts and warm Conner, than vice versa."

He sat up and passed the bag to her. "I got chocolate and coconut, which one do you want?"

She pouted. "Can we split them? Half of each?"

Conner dug into the bag and held the first malasada to her lips. Powdered sugar fell like snowflakes, and his eager tongue lapped up the sweet treat. Sky chewed and wiggled as his lips played havoc with her eating.

Once he fed her half of each, Sky crawled into his lap and wrapped her arms around his waist. "Hungry?" She rocked back, her sex dancing over his. She caught a donut in each hand, and alternately fed him as her steady motion woke up every part of him.

Chewing, Conner held up a finger. "These beat the hell out of power bars." Sky moved closer and licked the cream from the side of his mouth. "Oh, angel, you're not going to let me finish these, are you?" He fell back and grabbed for a condom.

Sky giggled lasciviously and shook the malasadas over his erect flesh. "Oh, look! This looks like one of those crème filled long Johns."

Conner narrowed his eyes and fell back on his pillow, his arms behind his head. "What are you going to do to me?"

Sky dropped the donuts to the flattened bag and crawled between his legs. "I've seen how those girls follow you around, and I think I need to give you something to remember."

His left hand skated from her waist down her hip to her thigh while his right hand caressed her breast. "Oh, trust me, angel, I remember you just fine."

It dawned on Sky, if he had to wear a condom for sex, she'd have to use one to pleasure him orally. *Plan B!* Sky caught him in a gentle grasp and lovingly kissed around the base of his sex. His hips rose to her, and she lightly tickled his sac as her lips traced his treasure trail. She dropped to his hip and rested her cheek on his thigh. Dancing her fingertips through the black bush at the base of his erection, she blew warm breath up and down. She followed the pattern of his groans and sighs, taking cues from his throbbing flesh. "This fellow is so pretty like this. I can't wait to meet him in the flesh." She held out her hand, and Conner had already ripped open the package. With a flourish, she was up on her knees over him, the condom in her mouth as she descended on him unmercifully. When the task was completed, she sat back on her heels. "Hey, cowboy, ready for a roundup?"

"What is it about you Florida girls?"

"What is that supposed to mean?"

"Isn't it the sunshine state?"

She weighed her next words. "Yeah…"

"Well, we're never gonna see sunshine staying inside doing this."

Sky climbed to straddle his hips. "The sun is overrated. Take me for a ride, cowboy."

And he did.

****

They dragged themselves to dress after a long bubble bath in the jacuzzi tub. Sky sat, drying her hair under Conner's watchful eyes. "Angel, you could do that all night, it is such a turn on when you move that hair over me. But…" He slapped his flat and tan belly. "You worked me like a ranch hand today, and I need considerable sustenance. You know, how about a big steak and maybe more steak?" He licked his fingertips and winked as he walked around the room, shedding his robe, and digging through his backpack for his dress clothes.

"Add a little lobster to that, and I'm game. I know just the place. There is a restaurant with a gorgeous white verandah around a huge banyan tree. A perfect way to cap the day."

"How would we get in? It's already six-thirty."

Her shoulders danced under the length of her dry hair. "I made reservations Monday."

"Oh, yeah. I like a woman who's prepared."

"Well, prepare to take your lady for an elegant evening, so we can come back and behave like animals."

"Animals?"

"Elegant and well-fed animals."

****

How did he feel walking through the most sophisticated hotel on the beach with the most beautiful girl in the world? He walked on air, that's how it felt. He couldn't let go of her hand, he wanted to feel her nimble fingers threaded with his because feeling this close reminded him how she plucked every sensual nerve. *Am I smiling too much?*

He looked down at the uncommonly stylish Aloha shirt Sky had waiting for him. Proms and big dances in Texas called for those damned monkey suits. How was it he felt so dressed up in khakis and the airplane Aloha shirt? It was from Sky. Sky had him in heaven.

As they waited for the maître de, he bent close and whispered. "Do you know how much I appreciate this shirt?"

Sky shyly looked up at him from under her lashes. "I could tell it was your favorite. The pale blue shirt flatters your dark features."

The man in the royal Hawaiian uniform smiled gently at them as he approached.

"Two for dinner at seven, the name is Jameson."

They were led to a railing side table on the verandah under the banyan tree. The man bowed, and within minutes their servers were there pouring water, delivering bread, and taking their order. The senior server bowed deeply. "Good evening, Mr. Jameson, is this your first visit dining with us?"

Conner grinned broadly. "Sure is, I'm from Texas."

Conner felt the older man's warm gaze. "Are we celebrating a honeymoon, perhaps?"

Sky dropped her left hand into her lap and grinned as Conner danced around the answer. "Tonight is a night of firsts." Conner nodded to Sky. "I have brought the most precious gal on the island out with me."

The server bowed, and before their next course arrived, he was back with a tray. "Compliments of the chef, to warm up your palate for the meal. She has prepared Scallops with Mango and Avocado." Once the server scurried off, Conner stared at the thing in the twisted won ton wrapper.

"Angel? Do I unwrap it and eat it, pick it up by it knot, and munch or cut it up?"

Sky flinched and looked around. "I think the scallop is inside with the chopped mango and avocado, and they've given us knives, so let's cut in." She wielded her utensils, and once cut open, fragrant steam escaped. "Umm, smells good." Conner followed her, and the two of them made small work of the treat.

Conner smoothed the napkin in his lap. "I'd need about two dozen of them, ya know? Ah, course, the chef doesn't know what you did to me all day."

She smacked his hand playfully and shook her head.

Chapter Twenty-One

As Sky dabbed at her lips after a heavenly meal, the music from the lobby began a dancing throb. The light in the lobby lounge dimmed, and more tourists congregated with fruity drinks and loud voices. "I know we can't drink, but do you think they'll have a slow dance anytime tonight?"

Conner reached across their small table. "Angel, if they don't, I'll find a place and hum…"

"Conner…. Jameson, it's him…" Joy's inebriated voice reverberated from the lobby lounge. Her date, who Sky recognized as Agnew from the fitness center, slammed down his beer bottle and shook his head.

Everyone turned to look for actors or athletes. When none were evident, they returned to their meals. Joy and her gym buddy Dreama skittered across the marble floors toward the verandah as their dates seethed in horrified jealousy. Agnew stood in front of Joy, but Dreama yanked her away with drunken laughter.

Dreama, phone in hand, pulled Joy close and turned their backs on Conner and Sky. "Photobomb selfie." Together they squealed at the image of a shocked Conner showing up between their heads. Dreama made a beeline for Sky and bent over, spilling considerable cleavage in Sky's face. "Sweetie, will you take a picture of us with Con?"

Joy checked her lipstick in her phone's camera and licked some off her tooth. She dropped her phone before Sky. "I have a better camera, be a darling and take one with my phone, too?"

Conner sat back as the two women framed him, and their hands skated down his back. Two battling perfume scents hovered like deadly gas clouds. Sky shot him a bewildered look. "Cheese." Then, with the other phone, she giggled. "Crackers." Sky thrust the phones back to the woman as their server appeared tableside.

"Now that you have your photos, may I ask you to return to the lounge. The verandah is reserved for our dining guests."

Joy and Dreama wiggled back to their scowling dates, still squealing, and looking at their photos.

Conner's face was ashen. "I'm sorry, sir... I don't..."

"No worries, Mr. Jameson. These things happen. Would you enjoy your dessert in our private dining area?"

Sky sighed with relief. "Oh, that would be perfect. Thank you so much."

The servers assembled around the area of their table as if performing general tasks, and Conner and Sky were led off without anyone noticing they were gone.

They were taken to an intimate dining area, surrounded on three sides by fluttering handkerchief linen draperies and circled by tall potted palms. They were nearly on the sandy beach. Soft music played from somewhere as they made their dessert choices and cuddled next to each other.

Conner ducked his head and looked around and whispered. "Private dining... wow, like rock stars."

Sky's blue eyes went round. "I didn't know I was dating a rock star."

He shrugged and grinned. "I'm a man of many talents..." The server rolled the dessert cart to their table. Two plates held tiny chocolate Bundt cakes. He scooped macadamia nut ice cream on top, sprinkled more chopped nuts, poured a liquor over all of it, letting it sluice in a puddle. With practiced flare, he torched the liquor, and blue flames danced on their plates.

Sky giggled. "Dinner and a show!" She watched the server squelch a grin at Conner's playful expression.

He pointed at the frolicking flames. "This will go out, right?"

"Ah, yes, sir. It's burning off the alcohol, leaving the rum flavor behind." And within seconds, the blue flames died. "May I get you coffee, tea, another punch?"

Sky nodded for the punch, and Conner agreed. Under the table, their feet tapped at the romantic music, and when their plates held nothing but smears of lava, their server approached. Conner smiled indulgently. "Would you mind if I dance with my lady? I promised her a slow dance."

The server bowed graciously. "No problem, Mr. Jameson. Let me know if I may be of further service." The man disappeared as Conner held out his hand to Sky.

"I'm no dancer, but I think you'll bring it out in me." They swayed toward the end of the patio as a sliver of the moon balanced against a blanket of stars. "The only thing more magnificent than you in my bed is you, right now, in my arms."

She ran her hand from the errant black hair falling over his forehead down his cheek to his chiseled jaw. "How lucky was I when I picked that seat on the airplane?" She nestled into his chest, and he tucked his chin on the top of her head.

"Ditto."

****

Damn, working really has me in the habit of waking early. Conner opened one eye, 0500. Sky's little whistle of a snore told him she was deep asleep. He slid artfully away from her, substituting his pillow for his body heat like Indiana Jones substituted the bag of whatever for the ruby idol.

He tiptoed into the living room and dialed up room service. *How could I be this hungry? Oh, yeah... they got to sleep around 2 AM. Maybe a nap will be in order by the pool?* Conner considered waiting for Sky to shower, bad idea. *We'd never get out of the room.* The light knock on the door told him it was time to put on the feedbag.

Holding the door open, wearing the hotel robe, his stomach rumbled mightily. He reminded himself to pay for breakfast, so it didn't show on the General's bill. He hung the robe up and strolled into the bedroom naked, a tea towel over his arm. When he saw Sky twist in awakening, he wore nothing but a grin. "Angel, are you hungry?"

She pushed her wealth of wavy hair out of her face. "I don't know, I'm still asleep."

119

"No, you aren't. I see those baby blues of yours, and I see what they're focused on." He leaned on the cart, one foot dropped over the other, one hand on his slim hip. "Focus, the food is on the tray." Purposefully, he walked in front of the cart and bent from the waist to remove the lids on the plates. He felt her admiration and heard the sheets crush as she crawled to him.

Sky's arms wrapped around his waist, and she sighed. "Am I in heaven? You keep me fed so well." She looked over his shoulder at the food. "Denver omelet? Waffle with strawberries and whipped cream? Ohh, whipped cream." She jumped off the bed and circled to the other side of the cart. "This is nice. Where's your food?"

He lifted the top off a steak and egg platter. "But there's also some guava turnovers for both of us." As he sat to eat, his brow rose. "Mom told me if there wasn't steak and eggs, I wouldn't be here."

"Awe." Sky plucked a warm pastry from the basket and danced around the room, nibbling. "With your our folks gone, maybe we need to put in an appearance at the fitness center?" Conner was already chewing a bite of steak when he nodded. "I had an idea in my dream last night about a technique I want to use on Jax's figure in the mural. It will take me about an hour. You could check in with Jax and Bonnie." He tore a piece of toast with his teeth and nodded.

Chapter Twenty-Two

Jax looked up in surprise when his brother and Sky hit the gym doors together. Sky's hair was a riot of waves held up with two pink chopsticks, her sundress swayed energetically around her, and she hummed an unrecognizable tune. Her shoulder bag hung casually on her shoulder. When she removed her sunglasses, her eyes were dilated and dreamy.

"Hey, guys. Didn't expect to see you two today." Jax arched a brow as he approached them for a once over. "What a coincidence, both here at the same time."

Conner fist-bumped his brother and turned to regard Sky. They exchanged silent looks with broad smiles. Sky's chin tucked and she blushed. Conner winked at her before he turned back to Jax. "I had to pick her up on the bike."

Jax nodded appreciatively. "Ahuh. Cause Hank is with Kirk and Jordan." He shook his head and bit his top lip. "Right. Good of you to think of her…"

Once Sky bounced down the stairs retrieving her art bag Jax thumped Conner on the back the head. "You started with thirty-six Altoids." He made air quotes. "How many have you got left?"

Conner scratched at the back of his neck, paused as if considering the number. "Let's see. That would be approximately, none of your damn business."

Jax grinned hugely. "I've never seen you this…" Jax waved his hand and conjured the word. "This relaxed."

Conner's grin went all the way through his body. "Ah, the world would be such a happy place…"

Jax chortled. "Yeah, that's what I tell Kameo when she gets home after a twelve-hour shift."

Conner eyed him sadly. "Sleep or relaxation? I know that must be a disappointment."

Jax turned away at the comment, pivoted, and grabbed Conner in a flat arm hold. He whispered in his brother's ear. "Yeah, but besting you is never a disappointment."

Sky entered the room in her painting smock, her art bag over her shoulder. "Jeez, guys, don't make me assign chairs." They dropped out of the hold and smacked each other on the back.

Jax waved. "I got Dad's mobility class in ten minutes. What are you up to?"

Conner waved at the machines. "I think I'll do a circuit up here while Sky paints your bod on the wall."

Jax waved and was gone. Sky referred to a website for a few moments as Conner began his sit-ups on the hyperextension bench to the far left.

****

The exercise machine room had two walls of mirrors, reflecting fitness clients into infinity. Conner tuned out the stares from the women and concentrated on his form. With each rise, he held the weight plate close to his chest and measured his breaths.

Within ten feet of each other, but involved in their own zones, somehow, Sky's strokes and movement before her art were in tune with Conner's controlled dips and rises. He moved to the lat pulldown machine. As he watched his posture in the mirror, he noticed over his shoulder, a densely built guy on the sit-up bench holding too heavy a weight. It required the man to jerk forward and back. *You're gonna hurt yourself doing that. Should I say something?* A challenging vibe rolled off the guy. *Nope.*

Conner finished his routine and strolled up behind Sky. She turned and blew him a kiss. He nuzzled her neck. "I'm all sweaty, I'm going to dad's office to shower. You about done?" Conner half stepped back. "Whattaya say we pick up Rainbow takeout on the way to checking on Dad's place?"

Sky turned and grinned. "I like that idea, then a dip in the pool?"

Conner raised his tee-shirt and scratched his belly. "Yeah, I need a nap." When he turned, the man from the sit-up bench swaggered past and clipped his shoulder into Conner's. *Well, that was intentional.*

Sky's gaze narrowed as she pulled Conner closer and whispered. "That was the guy from last night. I saw him..." She snapped her figures to conjure the day... "the day you filmed, all the women were here. He made a scene when he picked up his girl. She was Jane, Joey, it's Joy!"

Conner wiped at his neck with his towel and frowned. "I'll keep my eyes open for him."

****

Conner smelled great when he left his dad's shower. *I like that soap.* Toweling off, he strode into Kirk's office to grab his clothes and found Jax behind the desk. "You can shower all day, but you aren't going to wash that smile off your face." Jax shook his head and chuckled.

"Why would I want to? She deserves to know how happy I am." Conner ran his thumb over his bottom lip. All of his Hawaiian adventures were epic. His dad's easy but hardworking demeanor was unreal. Sky's zest for life and her talents for seeing beauty everywhere flavored his life with exactly what he didn't know he needed. Yet, in the middle of paradise was the dog hair on his sundae, the guy upstairs.

Jax sighed, and his head dropped back on the chair. "Young love." Conner pulled on his jeans, commando. "Hey, listen, bro. There's a guy out there, giving me the stink eye."

"Did he take your malasada money?" Jax comically brandished his fist. "Want me to beat him up?"

Conner pulled his shirt over his head and ran his fingers through his hair. "His beef is definitely with me. Something stupid about his girl taking a photo with me last night at the Verandah. You ever have any trouble like that?"

Jax fidgeted with a pen. "Oh, yeah. They always want a fight. Does he need to leave?"

Conner dropped into a chair. "No, that's not going to solve it. If something happens, I'd rather have it happen here." He bounced his knee. "Listen, I know you can't rush Jiu Jitsu training, but have you got some self-defense moves you can share with me?"

Jax frowned. "Sure, the only guy that beats up on you, is me."

Conner heard Sky's light steps toward the office. She swung into the doorway and grinned.

Jax winked at Conner and pointed to Sky. "You two have got to dial it back before the parents return."

Sky gaped. "Dial what back?"

Jax waved her question away. "He's on cloud nine, you're bouncing like an Easter bunny. When you're together, the pheromones you give off are causing international chubbies."

Sky turned bright red, and Conner stood to shield her. "Bro!"

Jax sniggered. "All I'm saying, if I see it, her dad will see it. You want her dad knowing, you know?"

Conner watched her pale. "Point taken." He accepted her art bag and stowed it in Kirk's bookcase. "We're getting out of here before you harsh my mellow."

Chapter Twenty-Three

Evan Silver's estate caressed the shore of Oahu from close to Lēʻahi Beach Park to nearly Diamondhead Lighthouse. The manicured green grass met a stacked stone wall and then a thin expanse of sugar soft sand. For about the past two decades, the pool house had been Kirk Roman's lonely residence. With his marrying Jordan, they waited to move into a larger condo they were renovating in her building overlooking the Ala Wai Canal. With Kirk and Jordan out of town with Hank, the mansion stood silent.

Conner no sooner turned off the bike when Sky bolted through the garden gate, dropped out of her clothes, and dove into the pool. Her long hair radiated around her as she floated on her back, gently stroking her arms out to the side. "I beat you!"

Briskly unbuttoning his 501s, he toed off his sneakers. "I have more complicated clothing, kiddo." By the time Sky did a kick turn and was at the center of the pool, Conner blocked her progress. Standing feet shoulder-width apart, his arms out to the side, he grinned at her barreling toward him.

Sky switched her stroke and caught Conner by the hips. She popped up and pressed her wet body to his.

In a sonorous cop-voice, he said. "I'm sorry, I am going to have to stop you here, ma' am."

"I'm sorry, officer. Who do you represent?"

"Fish and Game, there's been a report of a wayward mermaid in these waters."

Sky hopped and wrapped her legs around his waist, floating and grinning devilishly. "Haven't seen her, sir. It's just me here."

He turned his body right and left, swishing her through the water. "I'll have to take you in, give you an oral exam."

Sky jumped to her feet and blessed his neck with nibbling kisses. "Oral?"

Conner nodded. "You know mermaids are known to be extremely affectionate."

"You wouldn't want me to stifle my natural instincts?" Sky pouted prettily.

Conner scooped her up and carried her screaming with delight as he hoisted her to the side of the pool. "Just relax…" That only made her giggle more, and her knees drew together. He cupped her knees with his palms and, with a soul searching look, asked her, "Do you trust me?" She drew in a deep breath and nodded slowly. "Do you know what I'm going to do?"

"Maybe…"

"Have you ever experienced that?"

Her expression was expectantly eager. She relaxed into his grasp and sunk back on her palms. His fingertips danced up her thighs, dribbling pool water that sparkled in the bright afternoon sun. She sighed in surrender as he buried his nose at the apex of her thighs.

"Emm. So sweet."

Sky's head fell back as she bit her lip. "Oh…"

With his lips firmly over her flesh, he repeated her sound, sending vibrations through her.

She quivered out, "Ahhh…"

Conner turned his head to nuzzle the inside of her thigh, where her leg became that beautiful buttock. "Tell me what you like, angel. Let me know this is okay…"

She sunk both hands into his hair and moaned out a long, "Okay."

Taking his cues from her fingers and sighs, Conner dealt her a loving assault. He listened as her moans told him when to catch her between his lips and thrum a heartbeat with his tongue. It did not take long for her to melt into him, her legs over his shoulders as he held her sweet buttocks in his hands. As her soft fist beat a rhythm on his back, she let loose a thready wail and collapsed over his head, repeating his name over and over.

Conner drew her into the water and floated her in his arms. "I didn't hurt you, did I?"

She lay limp in the water, and her body blushed crimson. "I'm.. not... sure, you may have to do that again... in a while... to make sure?"

Conner lifted her to his lips. "You taste so fine, I might just have to."

Was it the noon sun? The Rainbow Drive-In pork plate or their tryst in the pool that drove them to nest under Sky's pāreu on the chaise in the shade. Wrapped around each other peaceful sleep overtook them.

****

Seeing Conner's bike in the driveway, Jax held a finger to his lips to hush Kameo as they approached the garden gate. In stealth mode, Kameo trailed Jax toward the sleeping couple on the chaise. "Jax..." In an atomic whisper, Kameo implored. "Stop shaking that bottle of sparkling water."

With a cocky expression, Jax shook his head and sprinted from his wife. When he stood behind the chaise, creating no shadow, he uncapped the chilled effervescent water and sprayed it over them.

Conner jumped with a yelp, saw Jax behind him and put a hand on Sky's back to keep her from jumping up.

Jax smirked and drawled. "This is the second time today I've seen your ass. Do you ever wear clothes?"

Kameo stood back twenty feet, her hand covering her eyes as Conner grabbed up his lavalava and wrapped it around his hips. "I'm in paradise. When in the islands, do as the natives do." He looked in Kameo's direction. "I'm covered, Kameo."

Sky's gaze wandered between Conner and Jax. "What just happened?" She held her pāreu over her and winced.

Kameo lifted her hand and approached the couple. "I apologize for my husband. Sometimes he's a dick."

Jax leveled her his best-crooked smile. "Them's fightin' words, baby." He sprinted toward Kameo, threw her over his shoulder, and ran for the deep end of the pool. He dropped them both in.

Sky used that time to stand and wrap up. When she sat back down, she shook her wet hair out and gestured to Jax. "How old is he?"

The following Wednesday, Sky completed Conner's figure on the mural. As much as her talent glorified the father and son fitness enthusiasts, Sky fought hard not to over-perfect the man she adored. Didn't she know his miracle of a body intimately? Her mind constantly wandered back to their playful connections. Wasn't he the best at everything he did? Those lips of his needed to come with a warning. His tongue was a secret weapon. She shook her head to snap out of her fantasizing.

Monday's news that he was healthy and clear found them dropping the remaining Trojans in a bowl in the hostel's bathroom. Sky wrote a sign in excited letters. 'Free to a good home'. She picked up her brush to begin stroking the paint on Conner's thigh, and she shivered with a broad smile. She was only too conscious of her father riding the recumbent bike behind her. Jax was right, she needed to tone it down a little.

She was immediately distracted by the arrival of Rando Kane. He sunk his hands in his pockets as he studied her artwork. "Oh, I've missed you, where have you been, Rando?" They shot each other a shaka.

"I've been in San Francisco, we had a show."

Sky nodded. "My dad is visiting on leave, may I introduce you?"

"Of course." Sky left to retrieve her father, and Rando studied her sketches laid in sequence next to the wall.

Pulling up next to him, Sky gestured to her father. After introductions were made, Rando motioned to the sketches.

"Sky, the inspiration to get fit lives in the anatomy of these figures. The muscles and the veins..." He acted out an explosion with his hands. "Everyone will want to be as vigorous as these three."

Hank wiped at his neck with his towel. "And every woman will want to be with one." His gaze slipped over to Sky, and she blushed.

Rando picked up Conner's sketch. "I'd like to matte and frame these studies of his pose." His hand hovered over the drawing. "The way Conner holds his weight on his right hand and left foot is deceptively graceful." He looked at Hank. "Have you ever tried to hold your body up like this and do those dips?"

Hank moved closer and winced in imaginary pain. "That's the damnedest plank I've ever seen." Hank pantomimed getting into the position. "I'd have to sit down, put my weight on my right hand, and flatten my left foot and then lift my lard ass off the ground using my core. Oh, I don't think so."

Rando chuckled. "And look at that nonchalant smile on his face, like it's nothing." He turned back to Sky. "I'd like to hang these in the gallery. I'm guessing they'll sell for about three each." He folded his arms over his chest and nodded.

Hank regarded the number of twenty-four by thirty-six-inch drawings. "That's a nice bit of walking around change, $2100.00."

Rando dipped his chin with a smile and approached Hank. "General, I meant three grand apiece. Of course, I'll take expenses and commission, but Sky will pocket the lion's share. We'd need a contract, and if you want to get legal advice, I suggest it."

Sky grew serious. "These seven are just Conner's sketches. I have at least seven or eight each of Kirk and Jax."

Rando's head inclined in contemplation. "Let me see them. I'm sure as one goes down, another can go up. We'll take a look at them to consider whether they go up as a family or as individual images."

Sky regarded her father, radiant with hope. "Daddy, if they all sell, that would be room and board for two years."

Hank smiled warmly. "Let me buy you a beverage, Mr. Kane." He hooked his thumb to the smoothie bar.

****

Rando buried a grin and followed Hank. When they stood out of Sky's sight, Hank turned to the gallery owner. "I appreciate your interest in my daughter's art. But as a father, I have to ask you, how do you appraise work like that? They're just studies in colored conte pencils. Why would you get her hopes up that they'd sell for three grand?"

The fitness center patrons moved around the men whispering at the end of the bar. Seeing the animation of one man's posture and the other man's peace, they gave them a wide berth.

Rando lowered his head, grinned, and itched a spot on his nose. "General, these sketches will be the least expensive original works in my

129

gallery. They'll sell quickly. If I shipped them all to my San Francisco gallery, they'd sell for twice as much." Hank thought for a moment, sucked hard on the straw, and Rando continued. "My son is a goldsmith. When he started, I had no contacts. He was fortunate to meet someone in a similar situation to ours, and now he has a thriving custom studio in Vegas."

"She's my baby, Mr. Kane."

Kane patted his back. "I have a daughter, too. Sky will make her way in art if she wants to. I'll be happy to show her work." He patted his shorts pocket. "I've got my business cards in the locker, I'll leave one with Jordan. Drop by and see what we do."

Chapter Twenty-Four

Sky was torn between delight that today was her birthday and the knowledge that her father would be flying out tomorrow to resume his command. So far, her day had been perfect. Everyone went out of their way to bring her favorite treats. All the clients at the gym offered 'happy birthdays', and she and Conner got off work early to get ready for the cruise and dinner show with her father.

As she twisted up her hair and walked through a cloud of her cologne, she thought the ultimate birthday present would be if Conner dropped this insanity of becoming a fighter pilot. It was too much to hope for. As usual, she had to say good-bye to her father for at least six months. It was the pattern of her life.

There was a knock on her bedroom door. "Peanut, are you ready yet?"

"Be right out, Daddy." She grabbed a pāreu to wrap around her shoulders if the boat got chilly, her purse, and found her dad in the living room. He strolled the room, hands in his pockets looking sharp in the Aloha shirt she picked out for him. "Oh, Daddy, you look so comfortable, are you sure you want to go back?"

Hank hugged her close and patted her head. "Peanut, it's just four more years, then I can dress like this for the rest of my life."

She came out of his hug and caught his shirt. "Four years is a lifetime!" He scoffed. "You look so darn handsome."

He touched the tip of her nose. "It's a curse, it's our family curse." He led her over to the sofa, and she scanned the room for a wrapped present. "Have a seat, I've got your present."

She sat and closed her eyes as she had done every birthday since she could remember. No sound of paper, no sound of rustling ribbons. *What is this?* She felt a slip of paper in her lap.

"This is a big girl present. Too big for a box. Sorry, we're not home for me to put a bow on it."

She opened her eyes and read the Florida Department of Motor Vehicles title. "You're giving me Tweety!" She jumped up and danced into his hug. "Oh, Daddy, you really trust me. Thank you, you know I'll take good care of her."

"While you're in school, I'll maintain the insurance." He bumped her hip with his. "You keep selling art like Rando says you will, you can buy me a car on my birthday."

****

Conner pulled up to the dinner cruise pier, parked, locked his bike, and pulled Sky's present from his saddlebag. He sure hoped she liked it. He didn't go extravagant, he'd already dropped half a week's wages on dinner at the Verandah. Hadn't that been well worth it? *What a night.* He wanted to win her smile with something more symbolic than a fancy dinner. This was the type of gift that symbolized them, where they met, and the time they spent together.

Conner stood at the pier with his gift bag behind his back. His heart did a flip when Hank and Sky arrived in the white convertible with the top down. Everyone in the parking lot watched his Sky as her daddy opened her door and escorted her to the gangway. They greeted each other. "Close your eyes."

Sky put her hands over her eyes and said. "The last time I did this, I got a car."

Conner dug into the bag for his first gift and stalled. "Well, this can ride in a car." He withdrew the colorful head wreath of white orchids and pink roses sewn with leaves into a Haku lei. "Bow your head."

"It's not a snake, is it?" Her voice quivered.

"I don't believe there are snakes in Hawaii." Conner placed the soft ring of flowers on her mass of twisted up wavy hair.

Hank nodded and winked at Conner in approval. The men said, "Open your eyes." She reached up and felt the velvet of the blossoms and drew in a deep breath. Conner dug out his phone and set it to selfie for her to see.

"Oh, my God, Conner." She looked up at her daddy. "I saw a wedding on the beach, and the bride wore one just like this, this is gorgeous, I've never had anything like this." She stepped into Conner's arms and kissed him on the cheek as her daddy looked away.

"Peanut, you wear it beautifully."

They took their place in line for their pre-boarding photo, and the three of them boarded the Oahu Star. As they were being led to their table, Hank and Conner blocked her immediate view so that when they entered the premier level, a chorus of their friends rose and shouted.

"Happy Birthday, Sky!"

In the corner, a round table was festooned by purple, gold, and magenta balloons, creating a backdrop resembling a throne for the birthday girl. Gift bags stood tall, with explosive amounts of tissue erupting from the tops. Sky gaped at the extravagance.

"You guys sure can keep a secret."

Jordan approached her with a lei that matched her crown and then draped leaf leis over Hank and Conner's shoulders.

Hank held out the garland. "We all match!"

Jordan kissed both her cheeks and led her to her chair, Hank on one side and Conner on the other.

Conner surreptitiously slipped in his second gift with the others for opening later. After the table toasted Sky with sparkling cider, they felt the ship move from its moorings. The gentle evening sea breeze carried the scents of the table's leis to everyone in the dining room.

When the scrumptious dinner was completed, and the dishes were carried away, Sky surveyed her embarrassment of riches. "Which one do I open first?"

Kirk winked at Hank. "Start with the biggest and work down." He passed a box to her. She sequentially opened box after box after box until she got to a gift card for Hawaiian Air. Kirk and Jordan smiled at her squeals. "That should be enough for you to come back at Christmas. Everyone should celebrate here at least once in their life."

Sky hugged each of them, making her way around the table, squealing, and catching her breath at their generosity.

Jax and Kameo made sure with their gift card that she would never be pinched to afford art supplies. Jax pointed to the bag. "According to your college's website, these folks carry your art textbooks, too. I hope this gets you to your next birthday."

Sky's eyes went round at the amount on the back of the card. "You guys! You guys are so sweet... I owe you all portraits." She turned to her family. "See what Conner gave me, this beautiful Haku lei." Kameo took a few photos. "Oh, I see one more gift." She reached for the phone-sized box clumsily wrapped in Little Mermaid paper. Sky held it to her heart and gave Conner side-eye. "Who could this be from?" She peeled back the over-taped paper. "Do we have time for this before the show starts?"

Conner spun his finger in the air. "If you hurry it up. You gonna use that paper again?"

She slowed down. "I might..." The box from a local Tahitian pearl dealer brought gasps from the women at the table.

Kameo craned her neck. "Jax, see that... your brother has taste."

Sky opened the box to reveal fat Tahitian pearls on rose gold lever back settings. She drew in a sharp breath. "Oh, Conner!"

He pointed to the box. "Keep diving." He buried his prideful grin.

The next layer of the box's tissue revealed a rose gold chain. Tiny rose gold beads flanked a plump Tahitian pearl slider in the center. Sky's eyes teared as she covered her mouth with her hand.

Conner put his arm around her and held up the box for her closer regard. "The pearls are considered a symbol of wisdom. Folklore teaches these were formed within a dragon's head. Once full-grown, the pearls were carried between the dragon's teeth." He posed like a dragon holding a pearl in his front teeth. "According to myth, I had to slay the dragon to gather the pearls. Actually, I paid the nice guy at the jewelry store to do that. The ancient Japanese believed that pearls were created from the tears of mythical creatures, like angels." He removed the necklace from the box and opened the clasp to put it on her. "So, angel, if you've cried to make pearls, you never have to cry again."

Sky raised her head to display her necklace and then changed her earrings. She beamed with the gifts and his intentions. This time, she caught his face in both hands and kissed him on the lips. "Thank you, Conner."

Jordan and Kameo exchanged sentimental looks, tears sparkling, but unshed in their eyes. Kirk poured from the champagne bottle in the table side cooler. "Conner, Sky, turn your coffee cups over." They obeyed with questioning looks, and Kirk poured the bubbly into each available flute and cup.

Hank raised his glass. "To my peanut."

"Oh, Daddy…"

"I can't believe it was nineteen years ago your mom gave me the best gift a man could have, a beautiful and healthy daughter."

The table became momentarily quiet at the idea that Sky's mom was not there, but they raised their glasses in joyous salute. As they sipped and chatted, a tuxedoed blond man with penetrating blue eyes silently approached. He was almost too beautiful. When he arrived, he stood between Kirk and Jordan.

Jordan looked up at the young man. "Des, you are incredibly formal tonight."

"I heard we had a special occasion, so I dressed for it." Introductions were made, and Des folded his arms over his chest and tapped his lip with his index finger. "Sky, I've been watching your art come to life at the fitness center. You possess an amazing energy, but I know people always tell you that." Sky smiled shyly. "I've been watching a woman behind you as you paint. Many times her hand hovers over yours. When you hesitate on a color, do you notice the brush gravitates to the one you use?"

Sky's chin fell, and she sobered. "It's more like a whisper…"

Des nodded to the balloons that bobbed behind Sky's chair. "She's always with you when it counts." Hank looked to Sky and put his hand over her hands, folded in front of her. "She was too young when she went to the other side. She did not want to leave you." Des nodded to Hank and Sky and then shook his head. "But her body could not sustain her. She loved the color pink. I see you do too." He nodded. "All the shades of pink."

Hank's face grew bittersweet. "If it was pink, she wanted it."

135

"Her face was as beautiful as yours. You resemble her, and you will more and more as you get older. She always said she could live in blue jeans."

Hank burst out laughing. "I had that song played at our wedding... "Forever in Blue Jeans". I was surprised she wore a white dress between the jeans and the color pink."

Des finished. "She toasts the two of you with her flute of champagne, and she says, Happy Birthday, peanut. You will have a long and wonderful life." He clapped his hands together and snapped out of the moment. "Showtime." Then he turned back to look at Hank. "Elle says, and I'm quoting, 'Would it hurt to go out on a real date'?"

Hank stared at Kirk. "You told me this was the guy who predicted Conner's arrival."

Conner looked askance. "What?"

Kirk picked up his glass. "Later, the show's starting."

Des stepped into the spotlight. He did some warm-up standard mentalist tricks predicting favorite numbers, home towns, ages. Then traveled to different tables with a deck of Tarot cards allowing those who wished to draw a card for a message.

He came to their table last and whispered to Conner. "I wanted to give you two extra time." He turned to the room. "Ladies and gentlemen, we have a birthday girl here with her beau and their families."

The crowd chorused. "Happy Birthday."

Des shuffled the cards with practiced thoroughness. "Okay, Birthday Girl, think of the coming year. Open your mind and be receptive. Choose the card with your heart."

Sky withdrew a card and handed it to him.

Des held up the card and announced. "Nine of Cups. Oh, this is a very special card. People sometimes refer to it as the miracle or wish fulfillment card." The crowd oh'd. "I don't see this card often. It tells us the rewards you work for are not all monetary. Happiness comes from providing good service to others, the support of one's family, as well as gratitude for talents and blessings."

"Well, I'll have to think about all that." Sky's eyes were round.

Des shuffled the cards again and turned to Conner. "Now, you, my friend. Pick a card, please."

Conner sat almost at attention to draw, with a serious demeanor, he hesitated and drew.

Des held up the card. "The Chariot!" He said with great import. "Things are about to happen very quickly for you."

Oh, yeah?" Conner's dark brows almost met as they rose in the center of his forehead.

"The Chariot is a card about overcoming conflicts and moving forward in a positive direction. It signifies victory, achievement, and spiritual evolution." Des held the card for the room to see. "The charioteer holds no reins – just a wand, like a magician." Des turned to Conner and pointed the card at him. "He controls through the strength of his will and mind."

The rest of the room's card choices were nowhere near as daunting as Conner and Sky's. The evening ended with a couple at the other end of the room announcing to their parents that Des was quite correct about a big change in the next year. The young couple announced to her parents they were expecting.

Conner raised his brow. "There are no mirrors in this room, are there?" He looked around to confirm and then nodded in satisfaction.

The ship's engines quieted as it approached the pier, and within the next fifteen minutes, they claimed their preboarding photo and were on to Kirk and Jordan's home for cake.

****

Sunday morning, Hank and Sky prepared to make their goodbyes in the lobby of their resort. Walking taller than usual in his operational camos, Sky knew her father was leaving 'dad' mode and assuming 'general' mode. She'd seen it too many times. Hank swung his pack around front to place the multi-page hotel bill into a pocket. He stacked the pack on top of his standing luggage and held out his arms to Sky. "Come in here, peanut, I need a huge hug to carry me back to base."

Within his arms, she was once again his little girl. Her face pressed to his chest, Sky ran her fingertip over the embroidered name on his pocket. She looked up at his loving smile and blinked back tears. He bopped her nose with a gentle finger and grinned. "You know, your young man is quite a guy."

She fawned over her father's approval. "Is that because he wants to fly Air Force?"

Hank stomped a foot and grinned. "Well, that's part of it. But it's his accountability I like."

Sky pulled back to look at his expression at the word accountability. "Yeah? How?"

Hank tapped the pocket with the hotel bill. "The morning he came by, you all ordered quite a breakfast. That boy has a hollow leg." Sky stiffened, still in her father's embrace. "What I like is that he came down within an hour or two and paid cash and left a nice tip. You can tell a lot about that kind of behavior."

Her voice pushed its way out. "You can?"

"Peanut, you're nineteen. I'm proud of the fact that you have taken precautions." A grimace spread across Sky's face. Hank shook his head. "I get the insurance bills. If you hadn't done that, I probably would have discussed it with your aunt. Remember, I deal with men and women your age every day." Now Sky buried her smile into his uniform and hugged him harder. "They've got a room key there for you. I've deposited more money into your debit account. My card will cover your room and expenses."

He let go and stepped back to look at her. "I'm sorry you can't keep the rental car, but you have plenty of Lyft money. Be safe." He turned to walk away and spun on his heel. He gestured toward the gift shop and the restaurant. "Just don't buy the place, okay?" He clipped out in full military walk, people nodding at him as he cut through the crowd.

Sky sighed, this was the first time she felt infused with freedom. She was sad he had to go back to command, but he left trusting and empowering her to become an adult. *Wow.*

Chapter Twenty-Five

Sky checked around the suite one last time to make sure she had everything. She called bell services to move her luggage, and then, she called Conner.

"Hi, angel, did your dad get out okay?"

"Yup. He's fighting traffic to the airport as we speak. I'm moving to my new room, it's quite a bit smaller, but it has a beach view if you stand on the balcony and look to the right. And... it has a king-size bed."

"Tell me it has closet space for two, and I am so there. The youth hostel management just realized I've been there for three weeks. They hung a note on my door. I couldn't miss it. I've lost my lease. Everything must go."

"Did everything fit in those saddlebags?"

Conner chuckled. "That's what bungee cords are for."

Sky walked toward her purse as the bell staff placed her luggage and art cases in the dressing room. She pulled out some cash, and they gratefully accepted their tip and disappeared. "I have a key card for you, I'll bring it, I have to come in and paint. I'll be there by lunch."

"Great, you can watch me kick Jax's SEAL ass."

"Oh, yeah, that's going to happen."

"He could afford to let me win once."

"He might think it will go on his permanent record. See you around noon."

****

Conner did not, however, kick Jax's SEAL ass. But he did more than hold his own. Sky guessed that most attackers would not be SEAL trained. Jax threw his arm around Conner's neck, and this time, Conner did the evasive maneuver and ran as he'd been instructed. Jax came in with a high five. "Smooth move, bro." He tossed him a towel, and they stood grinning at each other, both feeling triumphant.

"You've got a beginner's Jiu Jitsu class starting Wednesday night, okay if I join?" Conner wiped the sweat off his neck and looked up at his brother.

Jax pulled himself up to his full height and smirked. "If you think your cowboy-chaps-wearing ass can handle it."

Conner shook his head and pointed at Jax. "Those chaps turn girls on." He spun to leave the room and, at the doorway, looked back. "Of course, here in Hawaii, I didn't need 'em. I found a fine filly all by myself."

****

Wednesday, mural unveiling day, Jordan stood fussing over the bottled effervescent spring water and fresh fruit for the reception at three o'clock. "Sky, your work has a life of its own, no matter where you walk or sit, they seem to watch you. The poses are inspiring."

Sky laughed. "I made fun of Conner's pose, and then he made me duplicate it. No way I can hold myself up on my right hand and left foot and do those dips."

Jordan waved at the impossible pose and nodded. "That's what youth and fitness can do."

Jax walked up in his compression gear, shiny and fresh. "The kid was just showing off, knuckle pushups really improve your wrist strength." He pointed to his pose that accentuated the muscles of his upper chest and arms.

Conner slid in behind Jordan and tapped Jax on the shoulder. "Oh, wrist strength. Gotta have that." Conner pantomimed, jacking off with a thoroughly bored expression.

Jax smacked at Conner's head. "You little …"

Jordan stepped in to separate them. "Gentlemen."

****

Once the lobby filled with gym members invited for the unveiling, Kirk, Jax, and Conner filed in to meet Melly Adler from the local evening news. Their local PBS show had whipped their viewers into an adoring horde. Kirk extolled the virtues of fitness, martial arts, and proper nutrition, as the camera operator focused on the new mural. Rando invited the public to view sketches by the 'Guest Artist' at his North Shore gallery.

Jax took the mic and cleared his throat to quell the shrieks. "Sky Kingston has generously donated this preliminary sketch for a silent auction to benefit The Oahu Free Clinic, where my beautiful wife, Dr. Kameo Alana-Roman practices. Please visit the website and bid until it hurts."

The crowd applauded, and Jordan heard Joy whisper to Dreama. "If it were Conner's sketch, I'd clear out my bank account."

The students for the beginner's Jiu Jitsu class began to filter in, looking puzzled by the news team and commotion. Agnew Nunamaker stood off from the rest of the class holding his gym bag close to his beer belly as he cut through the crowd to stand within an arm's length of Joy and Dreama.

Conner accepted the mic from Jax and nodded at the squeals. He pressed his hands down in a quieting gesture. "Hello, members. Just a reminder, this Saturday, moms, daughters, and friends, sign up for the women's self-defense class that also benefits the free clinic." He consulted a tablet. "We've got six spaces left, don't delay."

Dreama fanned herself. "Why would I want to defend myself against him?" The two girls fell against each other, giggling. Dreama pouted. "But I can't afford four hundred dollars for a self-defense class. I don't care how cute he is."

Joy smirked. "Next month is my birthday, and I told Agnew I wanted an Apple watch, he gave me four hundred dollars. I'm going to that class."

Kirk took back the mic. "Folks, feel free to wander by and enjoy the new mural. Our guest artist, Sky Kingston, is a portrait artist accepting commissions. My lovely wife, Jordan, has set out refreshments. Help yourself. Anyone interested in signing up for new classes, Jordan has listings for September. It will be here before you know it. I see by the clock on the wall, Jax's class begins in ten minutes so, I'll say thank you and goodbye."

****

Jax had everyone remove their shoes and kneel along the mat's perimeter. He watched them watch each other in the mirrors. Combining humor and instruction for their first lesson, Jax joked. "My name is Jax Roman. I've been studying Jiu Jitsu for nine years, and I have a purple belt. A lot of people have asked what to call me." Jax paced the length of the mat, his fingers tented before him, and a wry smile grew across his face as he spoke. "I'm retired military, so you no longer have to call me sir." He paused for a laugh. "Call me Jax or teacher."

The class murmured. Jax introduced Bonnie, his blue-belt assistant instructor. She covered the basics of cleanliness, wearing the gi, and respecting the group by being on time. This allowed Jax to watch each of the twelve students as they absorbed the instruction.

Jax took over and covered safety and general respect for other class members. "What you are studying is considered a martial art, a sport, a way of promoting physical fitness and building character. It is not beat-up-on-people time. I did not accept you in this class so you could go to Coconut Joe's and wipe the bar with an opponent. Martial arts are for defense only. Any questions about that?"

Most shook their heads, some visibly juggled mental debate about Jax's comment. Jax and Bonnie demonstrated some basic moves and positions. He broke the class into partners for them to replicate the moves. Whether they were male or female, Jax and Bonnie paired up students according to their weight and size. This left a fairly chunky ex-high school footballer to spar with Conner.

Chapter Twenty-Six

A few exercises in, Jax did not appreciate the ex-footballer's vibe of chained aggression. He walked up to Conner and the guy on the mat. "Hey, buddy, what's your name again?"

The guy turned slightly, releasing most of the pressure his knee inflicted on Conner's belly. "Agnew." The guy almost snarled.

Jax nodded. "Agnew, that's right." Jax physically pushed his knee off Conner. "So, Agnew, if you were really in a fight, that kind of pressure would be warranted. In practice, especially your first class, take it easy, man."

Conner's gaze met Jax's, and they exchanged subtle nods. Agnew watched them and shook his head. Under his breath, he whispered. "Baby brother."

Conner halted mid-move as he heard Agnew's sneer. The two men stared each other down for a beat.

Jax clapped to move the class to the next set of instructions, and Conner defended himself against a few guard moves. Conner and Agnew cooperated to accomplish the bridge moves, although Bonnie watched Agnew with a sharp eye for the rest of the class.

The room's temperature rose with class excitement and participation. As the second hand moved toward ten, Jax and Bonnie stepped into the center of the mat. "We've got another ten minutes. Each of you try the movement you had the most problem with, then we'll wrap it up."

Conner and Agnew stood opposite each other. Agnew complained. "I can't get that falling thing right."

Conner nodded. "For me? It's the shrimp crawl."

Agnew shrugged. "Yeah, that's awkward…"

With Agnew's comment, Conner dropped to the mat and began his shrimp crawl, his right shoulder on the mat, and his left foot propelling him away. Simultaneously, Agnew dropped to his back, his arms outstretched in an 'A' configuration. The bully's heel thrust directly into Conner's armpit with tremendous force.

The yelp heard around the room, froze all activity. Jax spun and was down on his knees beside his brother in seconds. "Don't move, Conner. I know it hurts. Don't move." Conner moaned and tried to take the pressure off his dislocated shoulder. "I said don't move." Jax signaled to Bonnie.

She nodded and caught up her phone. "Calling the squad now. Conner, they are close. Stay cool."

Jax looked up at a nonchalant Agnew straightening his gi. "What the hell happened here?"

In a calmly practiced tone of voice, Agnew gestured to Conner. "He said what he had a problem with, and I said I had trouble falling. He must have thought he was going first. I didn't see him when I fell."

Bonnie's face flamed, she cleansed her expression and addressed the class. "We're going to excuse you a minute or so early. See you next Wednesday." She bowed to them, and the class scattered like crabs, including Agnew.

The paramedics with a gurney hurried through the garage entrance. Jordan, followed by Sky, came down to see the commotion. When they saw Conner down on the mat, face white and grim with agony, Sky hurried to his side and was intercepted by Jax. He put a gentle restraining arm around her waist. "Sky, let the paramedics do their work." He looked over her head at Jordan. "Want to get the car? You and Sky can follow us to King's ER."

Conner moaned as they lifted him the few inches onto the gurney. Tucking his arm across his waist seemed to be even more painful. Jax winced for his brother when they tightened the gurney's straps and pulled it to its rolling height. "Hang in there, kid."

By the time Sky and Jordan got to the hospital, Conner had been medicated with the first of several pain killers. None knocked him out completely, but he was plenty goofy. "Angel, I'm so happy to see you. I'd hug you if I could. Can we go home? I want to float in the pool."

The nurse winked at Sky and turned to Conner. "We'll have you floating soon." He addressed the newcomers. "I'm his nurse, Bob. Dr. Māhoe is writing orders for Conner right now. We know that shoulder is dislocated, but the doctor wants an x-ray before we try to reduce it. It's an ugly dislocation." He gestured at apparatus with tubing that ran from a canister on a low table to a pad over Conner's shoulder. "That's circulating ice water to try to decrease swelling. We're going to keep him comfortable till we know more. Dr. Māhoe is calling in an orthopedic surgeon."

Jordan caught the nurse's arm before he could leave the curtained area. "This sounds serious. Should I call his father to come?"

The man nodded. "Never a bad idea."

Conner startled awake, moaned from the movement, and looked over at Sky, who gently resettled him. "We're not at the pool yet? Where's your suit?" His stage whisper was slurred. "No skinny dipping."

In time, Kirk slid around the curtain. "What the hell? Kid, are you giving me every parental experience this summer?"

Conner looked up, unfocused, and grinning. "Hi, Dad. I have a bum wing."

Kirk grimaced, reached out to pat Conner's foot, and withdrew his hand. He saluted the boy. "Yes, indeed, you are my son." He turned to Jax and Jordan while Sky comforted the poor kid. "Bonnie called me. She says she saw the whole thing, and she doesn't believe it was an accident."

Jordan gasped. "That jerk kicked him on purpose?"

Kirk, hands on hips, nodded once. "That's what she said."

Jax hissed. "Son of a bitch."

Jordan looked back at Sky and Conner and whispered, "We have the videos, watch them later."

"Jax, help me up, I wanna swim." Conner reached out with his good arm.

Jax scratched at the back of his neck. "Maybe later, buddy. Stay put." Jax's deep blue eyes flared. "I'm making copies of the class tape, and we'll consult counsel as the next step."

****

Conner was mercifully medicated and asleep when they took him down for the MRI. Dr. Māhoe stopped in to talk to the family. "I'm getting the MRI at the request of the orthopedic surgeon. From what I saw on the X-rays, we're not going to be able to reduce that shoulder outside of surgery. All I'll do is risk further damage if I try. We suspect he has a complete tear of his labrum. The labrum is an extremely important part of the shoulder. That will have to be surgically repaired in any case. We'll do both surgeries at the same time."

Jax picked up a text from Kameo. "Kami will be here in a few minutes. I guess Conner won't be doing martial arts for a while."

Kirk rubbed at his face. "Man, I hate to send him back to his momma with a busted wing." He looked over at Jordan. "We need to get the guest room ready. He won't be able to return to the hostel."

Sky sat in the bedside chair and winced sheepishly. "About the hostel? He was only supposed to stay for two weeks. He moved into my hotel room Sunday."

Kirk and Jordan buried a smile, Jax was the first one to find his tongue. "From hostel to Waikiki resort, nice bounce."

Kirk spoke reasonably. "He's still going to need more help than you can give him, Sky. You're welcome to the pool house for the rest of your time here. That way, you can be close to him."

****

Conner was rolled back from the MRI as the pain medication was wearing off. The hot rush of pain and nausea returned with a vengeance. With his good hand, he grabbed for the emesis basin. "I'm gonna be…."

He spewed, filling the small pink basin and then some on his bed linens and the floor.

Sky jumped and gagged at the same time. She ran for the bathroom. Jordan pressed the call light and began winding up the soiled linens. As she tried to clean up Conner, Kirk and Jax retreated to the other side of the curtain. Kirk cupped his mouth to Jax. "You guys want kids? I've had this kid what, three weeks, what more can happen?"

Jax shook his head. "Don't say that."

Kameo strolled up and looked at the two of them outside the curtain. "What's going on?" The retching continued from the other side. "Oh, dear. Is that his nurse at the station?" The men nodded, and she approached Bob. "Hi, there. I'm Dr. Alano-Roman, your patient in curtain three needs something for nausea, a change of linens, and a bucket."

The medication worked, and in short order between Bob and Kameo, Conner was clean, on new linens, and back to sleep. Dr. Māhoe approached with the radiology report, and after introductions, confirmed their worst suspicions. Dr. Bond is ordering an OR and scrubbing up now."

Kameo made a face and nodded. "At least his stomach is empty."

Dr. Māhoe grinned. "They'll be in to get him in a few minutes. Mr. Roman, I'll send the surgical consents in for your signature. We'll get him patched up. He'll be sore, but not the kind of pain he came in with."

Sky returned, swabbing her face with wet paper towels. "How long will he be in the hospital?"

"If everything goes fine, he'll be released tomorrow morning."

Chapter Twenty-Seven

Sky lay in an X in the queen-sized bed, alone and half awake. If the rollercoaster of the last week told her anything, it was not to guess what was on her summer's Bingo card. Meeting Conner, arguing till all hours with him about the Air Force, and making up for the rest of those hours. *My, isn't he an unexpected adventure?*

She covered her face with a pillow, wanting to go back to sleep. One eye half open and she saw it was only six-forty-five. Rolling over and digging into the duvet, Sky concentrated on finding her lazy place.

This was the first time in the last three days she'd begun to relax. Her entire body ached with the tension. First, it was the happy expectation of unveiling the mural. She was waiting for a wisecrack or two. None came. The rest of Wednesday made up for that. She had never seen anyone close to her injured intentionally. Conner suffered so much, and she wasn't sure how much pain he was in when they parted last night. She sighed and fell into the clouds.

With a delighted shiver, Sky rolled over, and when her eyes fluttered open, there was Conner's muscled tight belly with his jams riding low on his hips. She blinked. *Am I dreaming? I love his treasure trail of black hair that disappears to his fun parts.*

She looked, and there he was, standing next to her bed. Shirtless, shoeless, and pitiful with his sling across his handsome chest. "Hi."

****

"I was lonely, I couldn't sleep."

"What are you seven?" She giggled and rolled to her stomach across the bed. She rested her chin on her hands and grinned. "You don't look seven. You look all grown up to me." Her hand slipped out from under her chin and skittered up the inside of his jams. He shivered.

"Now, I'll definitely not sleep." His back bowed into her grasp.

"I miss you next to me in bed, too." With her free hand, she mounted her assault on his fly. As his britches slithered down his thighs to his ankles, she reared back on her hands, her pink-tipped breasts swaying with her movement.

"Nope, I'm awake now." He stared down at his jams and stepped out of them.

"Oh, no, no, no… stay right there."

Conner narrowed his gaze and whistled. "Hatching a plan, are you?"

Without words, she moved in for a frontal attack on Mr. Desperate. With a supple grasp, she looked up at him. "Is he still Mr. Desperate, or is he, Mr. Happy?"

Her lips curled around his crown, and he swayed closer to her. "Mr. Happy, he's here right now." He braced his stance and let her have her way with him. With every other stroke of her tongue, he measured whether he would fall. *How in the name of sweet Pete can such a precious pair of lips be so savage?* He moved to her rhythm as she coddled and stroked with both hands. Her tongue followed with gentle swipes up his length. His knees bounced against the mattress as he watched her whole body engaged in his pleasure. That heart-shaped ass of hers, those dimples, and when she put her heart and soul into the tempo of her strokes, her toes curled, and he grinned at her coral toenails.

"Sky, ahh…ehhhh…" Her name elongated on his lips into a series of wordless moans. He panted along with her suckling. "Oh, there… there… right…" The only part of his body that spoke to him now was in her mouth. Whenever she laughed or sighed or moaned his name, it was like a repetitive strike of a piano key. The tone played through his body, releasing every happy endorphin he thought had abandoned him. *Pain? I feel no pain. I need her every four hours.*

When the perfect storm of her comfort met his exact level of need, he sagged toward the bed and let out a low guttural cry. His half-lidded expression of gratitude met her happy, wide-eyed expression of 'look what I just did to you'.

With great care, Sky released him and carefully pulled his body into the bed. "I recommend bed rest. I'll be right back." Recovering from ecstasy, he watched her bounce from the bed, and when she returned, she had a warm washcloth and towel to refresh him. "Can you sleep now?" She tossed the linens into the hamper and returned to cuddle along his good side. They did sleep.

****

That morning Conner had an appointment with the surgeon. Sky drove Jordan's car so they could enjoy some top-down sun on the ride. As they entered the medical office's parking lot, Sky pointed out Kane Gallery. "When we're done, let's have lunch, my treat."

Conner grinned in his Percocet infused happiness. "Sure."

Sky got him settled and checked in at the doctor's office and made sure he had his phone. "While you're here, I'm going to visit Rando at the gallery and see how sales are going. You text me when you're ready, and I'll pick you up out front."

Conner blew her a kiss, and she was almost airborne, curious to see what the gallery was hearing about her work.

Rando greeted her with quick hug. He drew her to the mid gallery with one arm around her shoulder. "Notice how we've had to regroup them?"

Sky bit her lip. "You took down the unpopular ones?"

Rando let go of her shoulder and swung to face her. "Sweetheart, you are such a virgin. Sky, they're gone because they've sold. You're a hit."

Sky floundered for words. "Well, the guys are, I mean... who ...."

Rando belly laughed. "We've sold ten so far. I know you're going home tomorrow, so I cut a nice little check for you." He winked at her. "Are you sure you don't want to send that hand study sketch to your dad? I'll be happy to wrap and ship it. He did like that one. If you don't pluck it out before the weekend, it will be gone."

Sky considered. "He has a favorite spot at sunset, I snapped a photo to paint it for him. You sell those." She pointed to the remaining sketches. "Each one of those means fewer school loans I'll have to take."

Rando nodded, his hands clasped behind his back, and led her to the office. "Let's get your check." Before he entered the office, he turned. "Have you seen the reviews?"

"No, when was there a review?"

"It was in the Arts section yesterday under Showings this Weekend. I saved a copy for you." He handed her the folded paper with the show review and a photo from the mural unveiling.

> With inspired strokes, this young artist has reminded us what a piece of work is man. Most gyms feature steroid pumped pitchmen, Silver SEAL Fitness Center capitalizes on two generations of fit men.
> Emerging artist, Skyler Kingston, captured athletic energy and unleashed it on the thirty-foot wall in the fitness center's exercise machine room. While these three poses are meant to inspire people to sweat their best, the art reminds us that perfection is within each of us if we work for it. Become a member at the fitness center to see this art daily or visit The Kane Gallery while preliminary pose sketches of the mural are available on a limited basis.
> We'll be watching Ms. Kingston's career with interest.

Sky read the review twice and squealed. "They liked it!"

Rando chuckled. "Of course they did." He handed her an open envelope.

She gave him a smirk. "I've always been paid cash."

He shook his head. "You don't want to carry this much cash around."

She peeked inside at the check and paled. "Good golly, Miss Molly."

"Of course, we'll 1099 you, so put some back for taxes. You're a working artist now."

Sky nodded numbly. "Seriously, I want you to consider coming back next year and participating in the street art fair. Buildings are submitting their availability now, and artists are planning their works.

Don't let that opportunity slide. Tourists from all over the world follow these artists, it's great exposure."

"I'm going to miss you so much. Thank you for helping me."

"Discover yourself at art school, let yourself go." He walked her to the door, and she wandered the arts center, wondering if she'd ever be as big as these artists.

When Conner's text came, she was there within minutes to retrieve him. "I'm going to take you to lunch in style." Conner yawned and tried to look bright. She could tell he was wearing down. "On the other hand, we could pick up takeout from the Rainbow and lay around like slugs by the pool. It's my last full day here." She pouted. Conner played with the seat control all the while he gazed at her. When he was half reclined and drowsy, Sky figured, *Rainbow takeout it is.*

****

Sky made one more pass through the pool house to make sure she was packed. When she woke up this morning, she thought, why couldn't it be two weeks ago? When they were both on the journey of discovery. How could they have pivoted to avoid Agnew Nunamaker? *Where is that damn butterfly in the rainforest that flits its wings and changes everything?*

Sky entered the kitchen, where Conner sat reading his tablet at the breakfast table. "Hey, angel, Jordan made fruit cups and waffles. All you have to do is warm up the waffles." He nodded to the fridge. "Kirk and Jordan will stop back at lunch to say good-bye."

Sky poured coffee and juice and brought it to the table. While she warmed the waffles and the fruit compote, she nodded to the calendar on the wall. "Want to plan our weekends together in Florida?"

"I'm not sure when they'll let me go home." Conner's expression turned glum.

"Didn't they say six weeks?"

Conner nodded and scrolled through his phone calendar. "I won't be back in Florida until the end of August, but then you'll be getting settled at school."

Sky leaned across the breakfast table. "I wish I didn't have to go home, I hate that I have to start school so soon. I want to stay here with you."

Conner trailed his fingertips over her hand and caught it. "I want you here, too. But don't you have a scholarship you have to honor?"

Sky walked around the table to hug his good side. "I do." She kissed the top of his head and held on for dear life until the oven dinged. "I'll be right back."

Sitting over waffles and fruit, Conner discussed the duplex his mom purchased. "She's got a three-bedroom, but I'm not sure how it's furnished. I wish I could see you every other weekend."

Sky scrunched up her nose. "It's a two hundred mile drive that puts the driver going through Orlando at the worst possible times. What do you think about Halloween weekend and a long Thanksgiving weekend?"

"With lots of facetime in between." Conner agreed.

With the breakfast dishes washed, Sky followed Conner into the media room. They stretched out in the dual recliners, turned on movies, and necked until Conner dozed from the pain medication. Sky watched him sleep. *He's beautiful.* She dreaded getting into the rideshare at 7 PM to be at the airport for her flight.

Chapter Twenty-Eight

Her first days at the art institute were filled with excitement. She felt guilty that Conner was back in Hawaii, recovering from surgery and doing physical therapy. When he wasn't doing that, he was the guy sitting on the stool at the reception desk. He told her, "If I hear one more person say, are you going to be able to do that move when you're out of the sling? I'll hang a sheet over my part of the mural."

Sky blanched at the thought and went back to coordinating her class schedule. She and her roommate, Ali, met up before the semester and bought a second-hand loft bed from some sophomores moving off-campus. The contraption built with 2" x 4"s allowed Ali to work at her bank of computers under Sky's elevated twin bed. Ali slept in the twin that tucked up next to her computer desk. It was great, Ali was all geek, and she was paper and paint. No competition but great comradery. *Life is good.*

The arrangement allowed space for two beanbag chairs and a table between them. Sky could envision Conner sitting there with his wicked smile. She cut-out paper seashells inspired by her time on Oahu and hung them from the ceiling. Ali added the constellations in glow-in-the-dark stickers.

Jordan sent two framed pictures the week she moved into the dorm. One was a snapshot of the news crew filming the mural unveiling, the other was Hank, Conner, and Sky before her birthday cruise. She missed Jordan. Most of all, she missed Conner.

****

Most of all, Conner missed Sky. Sweating, hot bods surrounded him, eager to soothe his pain. He feigned taking pain killers or having therapy to avoid meeting people at the beach after work. As much as his libido admired all the spandex encased flesh, they lacked Sky's heart.

Physical therapy was great. He felt command of his arm returning.

They still insisted he allow the PT to exercise his arm with passive movement. The exercise helped with the soreness unless he tried to cheat the system and overwork.

The college application process was more painful than his therapy. With his late application, he was forced to wait for classes in the second semester. He began researching the CLEP process, at least he could test out of a semester's worth of work.

Conner was beginning to know his mother as a human being via long-distance telephone chats at her convenience. But hell, she'd never had this time for him before. Tammy wasn't working eighteen-hour days. Living in Daytona, she picked up a part-time job at a beachfront motorcycle store. No bikes, all tee-shirts, and an endless stream of guys asking her if she was single. *Go, Mom.*

Every night Conner sat outside at the fire pit with his father. Pieces and parts of Kirk's life unfolded in stories. Some nights they ended silently, each going their separate ways, Conner wondering why life was sometimes so unfair. Strange to think that if his father had not been sent to prison for a crime he didn't commit, Conner would not exist. Some nights they laughed until it hurt. Kirk assured him there was no growth in your comfort zone and no comfort in your growth zone. He was blown away that this guy was his dad.

****

Sky woke up to a video message from Conner. He blew her a good luck kiss and reminded her, "You're my world." Powered by his message, she nearly levitated into the studio on her first day of drawing class. She found a seat with the light over her right shoulder and waited for the class to fill up. Sky was not the only one with a new portfolio and supplies. Looking around the class, it appeared they'd all cleaned out the book store art department. The ceiling fans whirred above them with an irritating rotational creak. Popping a stick of peppermint gum into her mouth for concentration, Sky waited with the eleven other students.

****

The hippy type guy in a tie-dye tee-shirt and ragged cargo shorts drummed his fingertips on the shoulder bag he cradled. As the instructor paced the perimeter of the room and stared at the backs of his class, the tie-dye guy raised his hand. "Sir?" The kid's voice cracked. "Why are you wearing that maroon tie in September in Florida?"

Seeming to ignore the kid, the instructor carefully and methodically opened his portfolio and removed a fountain pen and automatic pencil from his sport coat pocket. Rolling the fountain pen between his finger and thumb, he glared at the kid. "This is not maroon." He gestured to his tie. "This is my alma mater's tie, Harvard's colors are crimson and grey." He surveyed his twelve students. "This is drawing class, you are artists. What's the difference between crimson and maroon?"

None of the students wanted to bite. Sky slid down a half a head in her seat, thinking of color theory and mixing paint. The instructor tapped the butt of the ink pen on the blotter. "The difference between crimson and maroon is that crimson is a strong, bright, deep reddish-purple color and maroon is a color."

It's going to be a long four years. Sky nodded appreciatively and waited for more zingers.

"My name is Eric Page. I am your instructor for Drawing I. Your syllabus will be unlocked when you log in to the class cloud. All written assignments should be uploaded directly, keep your confirmation numbers. Drawn assignments will be collected in class only. I do not accept work at my office."

There was a universal tremor throughout the room.

"For those of you who wish an office appointment, they can be made online and only online. Instructors are not gifted with secretarial help."

Now the room's energy shifted to dread.

"As I mentioned earlier, my alma mater is Harvard. I'm a graduate of the Department of Art, Film, and Visual Studies. Now that you know about me, let me share something about each of you."

He spread photocopies across his desk. "Michael Alston," he stared down tie-dye guy, "won a Juror's Choice Award at last summer's Ohio State Fair for his watercolor entitled Solstice Barn? Okay..." The class suffered through his discoveries peppered with snide editorial tones. "Last, but never least, Skyler Kingston. Not just a muralist, she has sold pieces in a swanky Oahu gallery. And she's also been selected to paint in next summer's urban street art celebration in that same city.

157

Congratulations, Miss Kingston." He reassembled his dossiers on his students and slid them into a Harvard portfolio.

"Very well, now that we know the players, let me introduce our model, Francie Rice." The model entered, nodded to everyone, dropped her robe, and assumed a cliched pose. "Since I've been chatty, I'll request a contour drawing. Nothing ornate, just down, and dirty. Move wherever you like. You have twenty-five minutes. When you're finished, sign the bottom right corner with your first initial and last name and leave it on this desk. " He tapped the blotter with the fountain pen.

He slid earphones on, adjusted his phone, and paced the room with no particular focus. Once the sinuous lines began appearing on the twenty-four by thirty-six-inch sketch pads, he hovered from student to student. Sky finished first, and self-consciously carried the paper to his desk and turned to leave. Page ambled to his desk and picked up her contour drawing. In a stage whisper, he proclaimed. "Amazing, incredible how you transfer images from your mind to the paper. Very nice."

Sky accepted the compliment humbly, they nodded at each other, and she took off like a scalded dog. The minute she vacated that room, her energy shifted positively. *Jordan, I am eating chocolate immediately. He's a Dementor.* She bought a bar from the machine of nutritional death and found a seat right in the quad outside the building door.

Her classmates assembled one by one, with tie-dye guy arriving last. He looked up at a friend. "Oh, Page had to stop me and accuse me of being color blind." One girl did a spit take with a machine latte. "He may think that's a Harvard crimson and grey tie, but Google says it should be an OSU Scarlett and Grey tie." He belly laughed as Eric Page strolled out of the building, their drawings rolled into a tube. Tie-dye guy raised his voice to be sure he was heard. "Google tells me that's an OSU necktie, and Page is an OSU graduate." He returned Page's glare.

Chapter Twenty-Nine

Sky winced. *This will not end well for tie-dye-guy.* Sky sent Conner a message as soon as she got back to her room. Her first day of college was a roller coaster. Conner's message began the day sweetly, but she walked into a buzz saw in her art class, and that was supposed to be her favorite class. All her core classes were an extension of high school. she breezed through those. How could she tell Conner the class she'd been looking forward to for weeks was taught by a snobbish tyrant. She sighed and composed what she hoped he would read as a great day because of his message.

What a way to wake up, your message made my
day.
College is high school on steroids.
I have a beanbag chair waiting for your fine ass.
Always, your angel.

She snapped a photo of the chair and sent it off with a kiss emoji.

****

Wednesday night, Sky and her roommate stood in line for their dinner, chatting about excessive carbs and the freshman fifteen. Tie-dye-guy cruised by with a tray, and Sky waved. "Where were you today?"

The kid shrugged. "Miss Kingston, are you meeting anyone for dinner?"

She grinned. "You can call me Sky." Sky and Ali looked at each other. "My roommate and I just came to eat." She faltered. "I'm sorry, do you go by Michael?"

He chuckled. "Only when I'm in trouble. Call me, Mick."

Sky looked at the line ahead and nodded. "Mick, I'd like you to meet Ali. She listens to me snore."

After they made brief roommate jokes, Mick told them he'd reserve a table in the far corner. He had to vent.

Ali grimaced. "Venting, the first week? Yikes."

Sky licked her lips at the food. "Oh, you shoulda been there. It was a Monday like no other."

Spreading cafeteria comfort food between them, Ali and Sky sat with Mick, mostly eating, and making general observations. When it came down to drink refills and ice cream sundaes, Mick gestured them to move closer to him at the round table. He surveyed the rest of the room suspiciously. Bug-eyed, both girls sat stirring fudge into their vanilla ice cream.

Mick nodded with cagey caution. "Guess who suggested I drop Drawing 1?"

Sky's mouth was full of ice cream, and she shook her head.

"Mr. Harvard suggested I walk my Buckeye ass to the registrar's office and drop the class while I could get a full refund. That was after he called me a talentless hack."

Sky swallowed hard. "No shit?"

Ali looked askance at Sky's comment. "No shit, that's all you've got?"

Sky waved a hand. "Mr. Harvard is a Dementor, plain and simple. If there was room in any other class, I'd be gone. He gives me the creeps."

Mick inclined his head and dragged his spoon through the chocolate jimmies on his ice cream. "Great assessment. Anyway, I don't recommend you stay either. Move heaven and earth to get the fuck out of Dodge."

Ali sighed. "Don't you need that class?"

Mick, generally a source of endless energy and constant movement, abruptly stopped and softly recounted past accomplishments. Sky immediately realized his achievements had accumulated since middle school and soared once he began competing in juried competitions in high school. Although he was here to study Game Design, fine arts were another arrow in his quiver. "I'm not hanging there to let him abuse my talent or me." He leaned into their personal space. "I did a little digging, and yeah, he went to Harvard, but he didn't graduate, he ended up down the street from me at The Ohio State University. Rumor has it, he hates talent."

Sky sighed hard and bit her lip. "So whattaya going do?"

Mick returned to his perpetual motion. "My folks are both artists and they're loaded. I can take a different elective, no skin off me. I know people joke about OSU being in Cow-lumbus, but at least I know bullshit when I see it."

"I've got to have this class for my major, I can't advance next semester without it. Now we're down to eleven, and that means he has more time to pick on the rest of us."

Mick sat back in the chair and pushed his bowl forward. "Anytime you want to vent, let me know. Sorry, it sucks to be you."

****

Slogging through the first week of school, Sky woke Friday morning, girding her loins for Drawing 1 and her next encounter with Eric Page. The class was down to eight people. Six coeds sat together in some unknown solidarity, the two guys sat on the other side of the dais. They rarely associated in class, the energy was forbidding.

By Friday, Sky realized Page probably had a closet of khakis, white dress shirts, and a selection of Harvard neckties. His loafers squeaked when he walked. It was like belling the cat and kept her alert as he roamed the room while they drew.

"Today's exercise is Value Drawing."

Of course, it is. The table in the center of the dais sat stacked with textured items. Grouped were fruits, plants, and assorted fabrics balled up. Sky pulled out her perfunctory collection of pencils and worked on obeying Wednesday's admonition to look more at what she was drawing while she continued to draw. Halfway through the class, when she felt she was hitting the high notes, she felt Page's presence behind her. Her gut went cold, and she consciously worked on relaxing her breathing.

With a jabbing index finger, Page whispered. "You have the essence of the assignment, but you're working with stone-age tools. That crap they sell at the bookstore…" He shook his head. "For an artist of your caliber, you need better tools."

161

Thank God, that's all he had to say. Please, walk away. And he did. She turned in the assignment at the end of class and ran back to her dorm for a shower before her afternoon classes.

****

"Hey, angel, guess who misses you?"

Sky sat under a spreading palm tree in the shade of the quad. She ducked her head. "Mr. Happy?"

She heard his familiar chuckle, and her tummy did flip-flops. "I miss you so bad. When are you coming back to Florida?"

She heard the background noise diminish and a door close. "In another three weeks, I'll be released and referred to a local place for rehab."

"How does your arm feel?"

"Still in a sling, I'm feeling with the other arm. I'm learning to be a lefty."

"Does it still hurt?"

"The thing is, it's not the pain, it's anticipating the pain. In the shower, I go to move a certain way…"

"Is that when Mr. Desperate is talking to you?"

Conner snorted. "No, not Mr. Desperate." He laughed and then continued. "Anyway, I get a warning, stop it, or it's going to hurt. I listen to those warnings."

"We are going to have to plan on getting together – Is Halloween weekend still on?"

"Yeah, so how're your classes? Are you the star?"

Sky stretched out on the grass and winced. "Well, most of it is great. One class is a bugaboo. I need to spend more of that gift card for better pencils. I have no idea how much that will set me back."

Conner soothed. "It's nice you have that gift card. Use it, you deserve the best."

She rolled over on the warm grass and sighed. "But what if there's some sort of art emergency?"

Conner tutted at her. "Ah, I'm the only art emergency, you know that."

"Yeah, I do… oh Con, I want your good arm around me and my head on your chest."

Conner groaned. "That would require much longer arms at this point. But come October, I'll treat you for the whole weekend."

"Can't wait to trick or treat with you."

"Till then, remember, angel, you've got a big guy in your corner."

"Get yourself back to Florida, ASAP." When Sky closed the call, she didn't know if it made her feel better or worse. They hadn't named their feelings. *Is it presumptive to close a call with 'I love you, Conner'? He'd feel forced to return the reply, and then our easy relationship would run off the rails.*

****

Conner, Kirk, and Jax sat on the other side of the conference table with their attorney Kalea Hale. Native Hawaiian art depicting sharks graced the four walls of her brightly lit office. Conner nodded at the images. "You've got a thing for sharks." He let out a low whistle.

Although petite and feminine, Ms. Hale nodded. "When I was born, my auntie looked at me and said, "Sharks are born swimming, you need to watch this one." Her diplomas were flanked with certificates of merit. "In the world of law, what could be better to protect you than an apex predator?"

"Okay, manō, what do we do with my son's situation?"

"First, Conner, I'm sorry for your pain and what you've been through." She spread out her hands at the reports. "I know Bonnie was an eye witness, and she's convinced Mr. Nunamaker caused the injury intentionally. Unfortunately, because of the angle of the cameras, we cannot prove intent. I could depose Bonnie, but even Conner didn't know what happened." The four of them sat in silence for a beat. "My investigation of Nunamaker reveals he owns no property, he has no appreciable assets, and although he has a juvenile record, it's sealed. I would not pursue this past a restraining order, and the fitness center could bar him."

Conner sat back with a mix of relief and disappointment.

Kirk wiped at his face and sat taller. "It's being swept under a rug?"

Jax drummed his fingers on the table. "Yeah, but Conner has enough with rehab and getting to one hundred percent. Do we want to prolong this by going through a lawsuit, too?"

Conner shrugged. "That guy did his worst, he has to live with knowing what he did."

Kirk drew in a deep breath. "That's pretty mature of you to recognize that." He nodded to Hale. "Let's get the restraining order filed and take life from there."

Hale capped her pen and nodded. "My office will keep you in the loop. You'll know when it's done."

Chapter Thirty

Sunday afternoon, Sky lay on her tummy, highlighting the finer points of grammar in bright pink. Her cell chirped a text.

You have a package at the reception desk.

Did I buy something from Amazon? Nope. She climbed down the loft bed ladder and grabbed her student ID and key fob. *In one week, I've learned, I need these at all times.* The package was not large. Sky sat on the lobby sofa and peeled it open. The gift note was signed,

Enjoy these, your guardian angel.

The bubble wrap came off the box of a full set of graphite pencils, erasers, charcoals, sharpener, and a stomper. It was too beautiful to use. The box was imprinted with a prestigious brand she never had the money to buy. *Oh, Conner. He must have asked Rando for a recommendation. What a true guardian angel.* She looked at the time, and it was still early on Sunday morning in Hawaii, she'd call to thank him later.

****

Sky shivered when she looked at the syllabus for today's drawing. Gesture drawing had to be the least enjoyable exercise in art. There was nothing better than to linger and perfect each part of an image. Gesture drawing was like speed painting. It went against every one of her artistic instincts. *What sadist dreamed this up, and what benefit is it?*

Making sure she had plenty of paper, today's class would drill through at least half a sketchbook, she trudged out of her dorm room and toward the classroom.

Page enjoyed being a taskmaster. "The first drawings you only have 20 seconds to complete. Yes, 20 seconds!" Sky saw the inevitable coming when he arched a brow and said. "You are doing this nine more times." The class groaned, and they did it nine more times, each time they dropped the sheets with the bell and at the next bell began again.

Sky watched the wall clock run backward. She blinked. Page developed a little bobble of his head and announced. "The next series, you have 40 seconds. You want to be bold with these drawings and forget about the mistakes. Oh, brother, will you all make mistakes. You have to keep drawing like you were when you only had 20 seconds."

The universal energy flagged as the eight students labored between bells. The stack of papers at Sky's feet looked like a pressroom after a bad run. Black lines on nearly crumpled newsprint. It was frustration illustrated.

As the class ended, Page stood at the door with a garbage bag. "Bring today's work up and toss it here."

"What?" Sky's brows knit tightly. "All that work in the trash?"

"Oh, Miss Kingston, I know you consider everything you do golden. This was an exercise to improve line quality and your confidence."

The class left sweaty, their faces smudged with pencil, their hands, and fingers black with charcoal, each of them shaking their heads, some grinding their jaws.

Page maneuvered her so that she was the last student out of the classroom. Lingering in the doorway, his arm high, he blocked her way. He flashed her an amiable grin. "Was the exercise a little easier with your beautiful new pencil set?"

Sky frowned and cocked her head. "First, no. And second, how did you know I have a new pencil set?"

He settled his stance in the center of the doorway, now totally blocking her. "Everyone needs a guardian angel from time to time."

Sky gasped. "They… came from you?" She stuttered. "Oh, Mr. Page, I'm sorry. These are extremely expensive. I can't accept a gift like that."

He smiled expansively. "Of course you can, my dear. You are on scholarship, I know your money is dear. And you needn't worry about the expense. Actually, this was a regift. I already had a set."

Sky put her hand up. "No, these came from Amazon."

"Well," Page stammered. "Ah… They were sent to me. I had a set because these were a gift… it would be awkward… I had them sent to you."

All the while, he verbally tap-danced Sky nodded slightly. "But they are still very expensive."

"You can thank me by gracing me with your company for coffee."

Sky glanced back at the clock. "My Mondays, Wednesdays, and Fridays are booked solid. I've got to run right now for my next class."

He sniffed, and his voice panned. "Admirable. Tomorrow? How about lunch after your math class?"

Sky swallowed hard as needles flashed up her spine. *Public place.* "Starbucks? The one between Everson Hall and Bexley?"

"I would have preferred Italian, maybe next time."

Sky drew in a deep breath, hoping to propel herself through him. He moved aside, and she swore she felt his hand glance at the end of her hair.

****

The next day, Sky starred in her own Mission Impossible. She scurried behind palm trees and into doorways on her way from the math department on the far side of the campus back to her dorm's lunchroom. She skirted the area around Starbucks to avoid any possible sighting by Page.

She came out of the lunch line and had chosen a discreet corner in the back when she saw him. Generally, a tied-up priggish instructor, today, Eric Page was a fashion-forward guy. His coal-black hair, usually slicked into newscaster's hair, was dry loose waves that fell boyishly over his forehead. He wore the collar of his bright white dress shirt open, his rep tie pulled down to reveal a hint of tee-shirt with ebony curls escaping the neckline. His often rigid posture was softened with a less threatening stance, almost a slouch at least until he spotted Sky.

Sky cringed, and as he advanced toward her, she recalled the scene from The Terminator, where the destroyed cyborg emerged from molten metal and formed more fully as he drew closer to Sarah Conner. Sky stood, not wanting him to tower over her. "Mr. Page." She gasped, her gaze dropped from his blazing blue eyes. "We had an appointment for coffee, and I forgot, didn't I?"

"But, you didn't forget to eat." He clipped.

"Oh, yes, I ah… I was late this morning and didn't catch breakfast. I'm sorry, I forgot. I had a call from my boyfriend in Hawaii, and they're so far behind us, and…" She began to falter, and she felt sweat run down the center of her back."

"I do not appreciate you wasting my time, nor do I appreciate your discourtesy."

"I'm sorry. I can see why you feel that way. It was not intentional."

"You truly do need to put your studies ahead of your love life. Unless your boyfriend is the gallery owner."

Sky's shoulders shook. "Oh, my God, Rando Kane, is twice my age, I'd never date somebody that old." She watched his face flush red.

"I wanted to assist your development, but I may have misjudged your maturity and ability to form relationships."

Sky thought she must really have a guardian angel when Mick, the tie-dye guy, suddenly appeared at her side.

"Did you ask Bud about the Hawaiian fabric we need for that thing?" Mick stood, his bushy head of dark blond hair maintaining movement long after he spoke. He put his tray down between Page and Sky and pulled out the chair. "Hey, Page, how's it hanging? You're looking business casual today, or is this relaxed stalker?"

Page took a step back, and Mick kissed two fingers and shot Page a peace sign. Page dug his hands deep into his pockets and walked around the other side of the table. He bent to Sky's ear. "We'll talk after class tomorrow." He turned on his heel and measured his steps.

Mick opened a carton of milk and shook his head. "What a douche." He sipped. "I take that back, douches have a purpose." Sky all but collapsed in her chair. Mick gave her a sharp look. "That asshole really got to you, didn't he?"

Her eyes wide, Sky confessed, "I don't know how I'll sidestep him for an entire semester. The class is down to eight people."

"Look, Sky, if you need help, you come to me. I know people here."

Chapter Thirty-One

Before Sky put her phone on the charger for the night, she checked her messages. The text message from an unknown number said:

Twinkle, twinkle, little star,

How I wonder WHERE you are.

She deleted the text and rolled over to sleep.

****

Mid-October Sky looked at the calendar on the wall. It was finally less than six weeks until she'd see Conner. He was home, the time difference was no longer a problem. He wasn't in school, he could drive over. The problem was, the last time they talked, he explained he was going to CLEP out of four basic classes. So he had some study and testing to complete.

Plus, he said his mom needed some four-handed repair help around the duplex. He was pursuing aggressive physical conditioning. Their first chance to see each other would be over Thanksgiving break.

He asked her if she was doing any painting yet, and when she said no, he bragged he had painted three bathrooms and a kitchen. She found her phone and dialed, she wanted to hear his voice.

"Deakins Duplexes double your fun…"

Sky held her phone away from her ear and stared. "Conner?"

"This is your maintenance man, need maintenance?"

"If you only knew…"

"Drive that little yeller bug over, and I got the tools to fix anything."

Sky sighed with agony. "Oh, gawd. I wish I could. I've got a huge art project due on Monday. It's got to be perfect."

"You do everything perfectly, you missed all the great comments on the mural. Dad's reshooting commercials with that in the background."

"Oh, that makes me feel invincible. Thank you for telling me that."

Conner's voice was concerned. "You okay, angel?"

Sky ruthlessly smothered her emotion. "It could only be better if you were with me." She swallowed hard. "How are things in Daytona? Jeeze, it's been years since I've driven on the beach. I remember one summer, Aunt Sherry let me drive her Jeep. It was so cool."

"I wouldn't know, I'm living la vida home repair. You wouldn't believe what they call turn-key." Sky caught a hint of sadness in his voice as he rushed to talk about the family that moved next door and their two-year-old twins who shrieked all day.

She almost got lost in his voice, imagining him holding her. "If you're doing all that home repair, it sounds like you have good use of your arm. Are you still going to the gym?"

Conner paused a beat too long. "Oh, yeah. Strict orders from Dad and Jax to keep up the peak physical fitness, I'll need it for ROTC and my pilot exam."

"Is the gym there very different from your dad's?"

****

Conner rubbed at his shoulder and turned away from the bedroom mirror. "It's not as refined, but they have the equipment the NFL uses. I can personalize every setting."

"I'd love to see you sweat."

He laughed. "I know the kind of sweat you want."

"Have you made any new friends at the gym?"

He chuckled. "There's about five of us who work out at the same time…"

"And you're the best…"

"About 90% of the time. I got a lot of personal instruction over the summer."

"What about that 10%?"

Conner struggled to minimize his horror. "The arm still needs some work." *Jeez, Jameson, can't you do three pullups? You big baby. Why are you*

170

nursing that arm? Go for it. So I tried for five and dropped off at the third when I felt the burn and not in a good way. In his mind's eye, he visualized the two guys who started their workouts by running to the bar and ripping out twenty kipping pullups. Lots of show, but that move is a no-go for the military.

"Hello, Conner, did I lose you?"

"… Ah, no angel. I'm here. These phones are wonky. Hey, how about this Sunday, if you aren't too busy with your project, we can Zoom at dinner, and you can chat with my mom and me?"

"Ooh, that's cool. Yeah. Do you think she likes me?"

Conner hemmed a second. "Angel, she doesn't know you. But we're gonna change that. If Brewer, my mom's boyfriend, shows up, you can meet him. Wow, is he different from dad."

"Yeah? Do you guys get along?" He heard the concern in her voice.

"Yah, know… He's a big guy, he's a biker but not the crazy kind. I don't know a man in my family who has a head of thick white hair and a bushy mustache like Brewer. He's nice enough, he treats mom good. But I gotta say, I don't know enough about him."

"Perhaps I can give you a woman's perspective?"

"Oh, yeah? Am I going to have to ride over on my new bike to satisfy your biker fantasies?"

"When did that happen?"

"Yesterday. I've never been near a new bike. It's not as big as dad's, but it's cool. I get to break this one in." Conner looked out the window at the bike and wished he could ride it for more than a few miles at a time without the vibration pinging his shoulder. "Maybe one day, you can paint the tank." He heard music in her background but no comment.

Sky giggled. "Is that code for something?"

"No, it's paint, you know, the gas tank, maybe the fenders? Just a thought. Hey, angel, I gotta go. Mom's waving the paintbrush at me. Keep smiling, we'll talk on Sunday."

Conner closed his eyes tight and winced. The doctor in Hawaii kept talking about mind over matter. When was his mind going to matter? It had been two weeks since he'd been released to work on rebuilding his pull-up game actively. Why was that particular exercise so damn important to the military? He could exceed everywhere else. He shook his head in the duplex's silence and hit the radio to hear noise other than the condemnation that was in his head.

****

When she hung up the phone, Sky's mind wandered. *If only I was perfect.* Her shoulders shook with the memory of anger over her last Drawing 1 class. Once she returned to her dorm room, she swore, *I'll never let Page see me sweat.* Page had held up her class assignment and shaken his head. He tsked in that derisive tone of his. "Class, this is an image woefully done by an artist deconstructing weekly." He had dropped the assignment in her lap. "Every week, you hit a new low." The other six students stared at their hands. *No wonder another girl dropped the class.*

Sky refocused and stared at the box of six Conte pencils. Her mission impossible was to breathe life into three envelopes of varying shades of cream, ivory, and white. It was her assignment to arrange the envelopes artistically and draw the hell out of them.

She wished she could have seen Page's face when he finally noticed his 'gift' of the high-end drawing set she left on his desk after he eviscerated her in front of the entire class.

This assignment has to be perfect. Yes, all of Sky's other classes were going swimmingly. She managed to maintain a solid B+ average in her first semester. She had to be doing things right. *Page is a sonnofabitch, Mick is right.* She needed to finish *Native Son* for English by Monday. She sighed, feeling so exhausted. All she wanted to do was hide under the covers and sleep.

How could she hold a brilliant conversation and look like the girl Conner fell for when she looked like a wraith? Her complexion was sallow, her hair was a mop, and her pill pack told her she was due to bleed for seven days and not die. She was bound to have a zit the size of a pencil eraser by noon Sunday. *Kill me now. I can smear mayo on the camera lens.*

She gave up fighting sleep. She plugged in her phone, and there was another message from an unknown number.

Head, shoulders, knees, and toes,

172

Knees and toes.

Head, shoulders, knees, and toes,

Tits and toes.

Well, that's creepy. Sky erased it, rolled over, and tried to go to sleep.

****

The emotional boost from having dinner with Conner and his mom via Zoom on Sunday night didn't last longer than walking through Page's classroom door. Seven of the most miserable students sat, each with their own annoying nervous tell. If that mousy girl doesn't take that pencil out of her mouth, *I'm going to feed it to her like an electric sharpener. Oh, crap on a cracker, what do I do that makes people crazy? Probably in this class, just exist.*

Page entered and began his ritual degradations of this week's assignment. He was back to his usual priggish uniform, complete with a sports coat and the ever-present Harvard Crimson and grey tie. His ebony hair shone like it was Simonized. Not one hair out of place. So different from when he was on the hunt. *Where did that guy go?*

Sky looked around and caught glimpses of her classmates' works. What the hell can you do with envelopes, paper clips, razor blades, pens, and cups other than these ridiculous groupings? *Five items, seven class members, who else went crazy stacking envelopes?*

Sky turned off her mind and watched the class like a bad movie. He started with 'mousy girl'. *How horrible that I don't know her name. Does she know mine? Does anyone know anyone else in this class?*

Page picked up the four-inch square piece of Bristol board. He held it up like he was shaking a spider off the surface. "Oh, yeah. This is reality in black and white." Page licked his top lip and pumped one arm. "I'd swear this razor blade could cut. Incredible. Very nice." That was the best in the class. As Page worked the room, his enthusiasm dwindled.

The second razor blade rendering was dull. No highs, no lows, just a few sorry shades of grey. Sky drew in every available liter of oxygen in the room as his shadow darkened her desk.

He stood over her, arms clasped behind his back, tapping a loafer as he cocked his head right and left to see the drawn envelopes in her eighteen by twelve sketchbook. "Are you brave that you're the only one who drew envelopes, or was it just another poor choice? The composition is static." He pursed his lower lip, his nostrils flared as he squinted both eyes. "It's a shame. What, you're only working with six pencils again?" He swiped a red china marker in an X across her work. "Do it again. Next time, do it right."

The universal energy in the room evaporated. Glances darted from student to student, ending with them contemplating their navels.

Sky felt the floor start to heave and spin. She broke into a sweat. The room was way too hot. The stress of holding back tears tore her heart in two.

"Class, I have a unit meeting to attend. I think I've seen enough of your efforts today. If you wish to free draw, there are items you can pose and submit for extra credit."

Chapter Thirty-Two

Seconds after he strode from the room, Sky made her escape. She saw Page exiting to the north, and she chose the south exit.

Clouds hung low over the quad today, dribbling spurts of rain. *Good,* she thought. *Maybe people will think these tears are raindrops. I don't know why I'm wasting them on that Dementor.* It popped into her head unbidden, *there's good times and bad times, and then there is bullshit.*

She plopped herself on a concrete bench under a covered patio and watched the fountain dance with the raindrops. Sky studied her sketchbook. Underneath the waxy red X was hours of work. How many times did she change the layout of the paper, or the direction of the lamp? Ali loved it. Conner and his mom said they'd never seen anything like it. Were they patronizing her? She knew what this was. Repayment for declining, coffee, the pencil set, and a night out off-campus with Eric Page.

It began to rain in earnest, Mick skidded under the overhang on rain-slick concrete. "I was just thinking about you."

"Cut that out." He flashed a smile. "Your boyfriend is too big."

"I wish my boyfriend was here. I'd ask him to Jiu Jitsu Page."

Mick put a foot on the bench and leaned closer. "What was today's bloodletting?"

She flipped her book open to her vandalized sketch. "I want your honest opinion. Honest, Mick."

Mick leaned back and raised his right hand. "Okay, okay, honest."

"Do you think this composition is static? I'm quoting now."

Mick raised a blond brow. "Aside from the large red X in the center, I plainly see the source of the light. You have black blacks and definite highlights. Although you've only used basic pencils, the envelopes are clearly different colors. " He looked closer and pointed.

"That deckled edge is feathery, you nailed it." He sat down next to her and gave her a friendly nudge with his elbow. "My mom's been bugging me for a letter, can I borrow these?"

Sky took a deep breath and shook her head. "I don't know how much more I can take, thanks for the good words. I know that X is retaliation."

Mick shook his head. "How did it wind up on this sketch, anyway?"

"After he called it static, Page drew the X through it and told me to do it right next time."

"Will you trust me with this for a day?"

Her gaze searched his. "Why? What are you going to do?

"Will you trust me?" His usually active body was still, his large grey eyes focused.

She answered slowly. "Oh... kay. Don't get me into more trouble."

"How can you be in any trouble? You're the innocent one here."

****

Conner worked himself up to a fine dither by the time he got into the ortho's office. He tried for a month now to get above three pullups. He finally made it to five, and that required three days of recuperation and all the ice his mom's freezer could make.

Dr. Woodbury was tall, grey, and even featured with a pleasant bedside manner. He glanced down at Conner's chart, frowned, and looked his patient in the eyes. "Blood pressure, 140/90? No. Are you in pain, son?"

Conner shook his head. "No, sir."

The doctor nodded and called for a blood pressure cuff. As he took the pressure himself, he chatted in a relaxed way. "So, Conner, this injury's about three months old? You been under some stress?" He frowned at the reading.

Conner looked around the old fashioned doctor's office and winced. With a nod and a shrug, he replied, "All my life, I've wanted to be a pilot. I've been told by men who should know I have the skills. I'm in college right now, well, I'm testing out because this injury kept me in Oahu for the start of the semester. But I'm told I have to do a minimum of twenty pull-ups for the military physical. Anything less, and I'm nothing but a civilian."

The doctor watched him kindly. "Would civilian life be so bad?"

"I wouldn't be a fighter pilot."

Again, the doctor's eyes were kind. "Conner, I'm going to tell you straight. This injury was so severe, you're never going to do twenty pull-ups. I don't care how hard you try."

Conner's face turned red. "But, the guy in Hawaii said it was mind over matter. He said I could do it if I focused."

"Dammit. I hate it when these young hotshots make such unrealistic promises." The doctor looked at the letterhead from the referring surgeon. "These practices move sports injuries through like cattle through a turnstile. Conner, I know what I'm saying is a terrible disappointment. He rolled his stool closer. "You already knew that, didn't you? You've been giving it your all, and you can't do the impossible, isn't that right?"

Conner sat, his knees spread, and his hands clenched between his legs. The tension in his body was palpable. "I don't want it to be right, I want to do it."

The doctor patted his knee. "You can still fly, it's not like you were robbed of sight or hearing. You're not crippled. You can make a good living flying. But not as a fighter pilot, and I'd be a lying sonofabitch if I told you otherwise."

Conner said all the right things, made a new appointment as directed, but he didn't absorb another word that was said. Everything was clamoring white noise. When he finally got downstairs to his mom's car, he sat, key in the ignition, going nowhere. He watched older people struggling with walkers, high school kids on crutches, and they all looked impaired. They grappled visibly with their infirmities. *Why do I look okay when I'm not?*

Conner sat as the color drained from the sky, and indigo overtook the pink sunset. Car lights turned on, the fast-food restaurant signs throbbed, and he figured he'd better go home. What would he do after that? He didn't know.

****

Christopher Hilliard, Dean, and Chairman of the Visual Studies Department was only months from retirement. Yes, after the current seniors graduated in May, he would hang up his tenure and move to Marco Island. His wife currently spent her days decorating their new luxury cottage. He was going to do nothing but paint, swim and relax. It had been his dream all his life, and no troublesome instructor would interfere with his dream. Not when it was this close.

His secretary alerted him. "Mr. Page is here."

Hilliard stalked toward his office door and flung it open. "Come in, Page." The door closed with a firm click as Page entered. Hilliard made a point of mounting the excellent sketch of three envelopes on a large bulletin board beside his desk. He pointed at it after snapping, "Sit." Page dropped into the chair like a trained poodle. "Does this work look at all familiar to you, Page? I believe that's your red 'X' decorating the center."

Page cleared his throat and obsessively straightened the pretentious Harvard tie he insisted on wearing whenever he was on campus. "I believe that was done by a young woman in my Drawing 1 class. How did you come by it, Dean Hilliard?"

"If you think Ms. Kingston ran to me with it, you'd be wrong. It was brought to me by Michael Coe-Alston. Do you know Michael?" Page frowned in concentration. Hilliard could see the name was a millimeter away from his grasp. "Michael is a Freshman in the Game Design program. He enrolled in your Drawing 1 class because he's a gifted artist as well, as are his parents. Might you have heard of them? Angela Coe and David Alston?"

Page looked gobsmacked. "I...I... never knew he came from such illustrious stock. I mean, he won a prize at the Ohio fair for barn art..."

Hilliard cut through the intended insult. "That painting was just one of many in a career of award-winning juried pieces Michael has done. I understand you encouraged him to drop your class, calling him..." he looked over his desk for his note pad, "...ah, yes...a talentless hack?" Page fidgeted, his color rising. "However, Michael Coe-Alston is not the reason for your visit today." Hilliard turned away to study the envelope drawing, and then turned back to Page. "Though it may interest you to know Michael is my God Son."

Page went pale. "I'm sorry, sir. If I had known…"

"If you had known that he wouldn't have been a talentless hack?" Hilliard waved away the excuse on Page's lips. "Michael is the one who brought me this sketch." He tapped beside Sky's drawing. "He tells me Ms. Kingston was in tears after the class in which you described this work as 'static' and told her to do it again. I believe that was just before you decorated it with the big red 'X'." He stabbed the 'X' with a long forefinger. "Would you care to explain yourself?"

Page shifted in his chair to sit ramrod straight. "Well, sir, as you know, I went to Harvard. And at Harvard, when there is a promising student, that student is put under more pressure than most to live up to their highest potential…"

Hillard shut his eyes, searching for patience and drew in a deep breath. "Please, spare me your Harvard pretensions. You attended for one year before leaving. I have no idea what transpired. But I assure you, I have a BFA, MFA, and a Doctorate in Modern and Contemporary Art from Princeton, so please don't tell me how artists are trained in the Ivy League schools."

Page kept mute, his gaze wide and blinking. "Michael went on to say he witnessed an interaction between you and Ms. Kingston, which he felt was entirely inappropriate for a student/teacher relationship, and he accuses you of degrading Ms. Kingston because she rebuffed your attentions."

Page leapt dramatically to his feet. "Dean Hilliard, you can't…"

Hilliard stared him into silence. "Mr. Page, I've been a college-level educator for forty years. I assure you, I can and do believe the accusation. Do you know what I want, Mr. Page?"

Page swallowed convulsively. "No, sir."

Hilliard skewered him with a look. "I want a peaceful retirement. I do not want to be dragged into testimony on a sexual harassment suit by a student against a faculty member. I do not want to testify before a board of inquiry about the need to fire an instructor."

179

Page paled to a pasty white. "I can understand that, sir. What can I do to help?"

Hilliard shook his head and looked toward heaven as if beseeching divine intervention. "Oh, I'll tell you exactly what you'll do…"

Chapter Thirty-Three

Sky came in from a study group and found stacks of pizza boxes in the dorm's common area. A girl she never remembered meeting waved at her. "That was incredibly kind of you, I'm broke, and if you hadn't bought salads and pizza for the floor tonight, I'd be hungry right now. Gawd, what a guardian angel you are!" The girl snapped up another small salad and headed for her dorm room.

Sky mentally calculated the number of pizzas and salads and reached for her phone. Checking her bank app, she didn't find a hack. Who paid for this in her name? She read the name on the box and called Gordo's Pizza.

"This is Sky Kingston, may I speak with the person who took my order earlier tonight?"

The late-night sounds of a pizza shop clamored in the background as someone picked up the phone. "Hello? This is Gordo, thanks, Ms. Kingston for the order, we'll have it out every week just like he ordered."

"He? Who did this?"

The shop owner fell silent for a beat. "Your uncle." It sounded like he accessed a keyboard. "Jack Anderson, I've got a PayPal account on file."

"I didn't ask for this." Sky protested.

"Yeah... but your uncle thought it was a good idea since you're shy, and you don't make friends easily."

Sky counted to ten. Goose flesh spread everywhere. "You know, I'm doing better, so can you deliver that food to the Women's Shelter for the remainder of the order?"

Gordo's smile came through the phone. "You know you're a good kid. I don't care what your uncle says. Yeah, I can do that."

Sky almost reached for a slice of pizza, and then her stomach churned. *Nope.* She sped to her dorm room, throwing the locks on as she leaned into the door. Her phone dinged a message, another from the unknown number. Looking at it, she thought. *I'm getting a new phone.*

Rich Man, Poor Man, Beggar, Cheat,
Doctor, Lawyer, Charlatan, Thief.

****

Sky didn't want to go to the dean's office. In fact, in her entire life, she couldn't think of anything she wanted to do less – well, maybe the Air Force Academy. She gave her sketch to Mick, and now what had he gotten her into? She guessed she had no choice. When the dean called, you went. She sat, trying not to fidget in his secretary's office. *She asked if I wanted something the drink. Is that a good sign, or was she suggesting hemlock?*

"Ms. Kingston." Dean Hilliard stood at his open door, welcoming her with a big smile. Sky stood and hesitated by her chair, uncertain. "Don't look so stricken, my dear, I'm sure everything will be fine. Please, come in."

Sky glanced at his secretary as if another woman might rescue her from a sinister unknown. The woman smiled reassuringly. Sky commanded her feet to move, and after another awkward moment, they did. She nearly stopped dead again when she saw Eric Page sitting in a chair in front of the dean's desk. She might have turned and run, but the dean was behind her, so she stiffened her spine and waited for some direction. "What…" Page still did not deign to look her way.

"Please, have a seat." The dean suggested genially, gesturing to the seat opposite Page and choosing the seat facing them for himself. As she sat, Page did look her way with an acknowledging smile that was the creepiest she'd ever seen. *How does he make his lips do that?* She looked away and saw her sketch laying on the dean's desk. She closed her eyes. *What next?*

"Ms. Kingston, you must be wondering why I asked you to visit me today," Hilliard began. "I'm sure you're surprised to see Mr. Page here as well. Let me explain."

Page leap-frogged over him. "Ms. Kingston, please forgive me if I gave you the idea I didn't care for your sketch. Perhaps my criticism was a bit harsh. It's just that I know you have enormous talent, and I want to see you live up to your potential."

Sky didn't speak, but she was alert on all cylinders.

"I know Mr. Page regrets that 'X' he placed on your work." Hilliard prodded.

"Yes. I…I…do regret that. I had some personal aggravations that day, and it's no excuse, but instructors are people too, you know…"

Sky knew Page was full of it. She couldn't quite read Hilliard except for his understandably intense desire to smooth over the situation. "The two of you have a class together in about thirty minutes." He glanced at his watch. "I hope a little apology and forgiveness will smooth the way. Both of your attitudes will go a long way toward improving this situation. No one here wants a referral to the Dean of Students, do we?"

Page looked shocked. "Of course not. This was a simple misunderstanding."

Sky's internal alarms went off. *Page is acting. He doesn't mean a word of this.* She waited, saying nothing. The ticking of Hilliard's watch was ridiculously loud. *Is he wearing a bomb?*

Finally, Hilliard turned to her. "What do you say, Ms. Kingston? Will you accept Mr. Page's apology and let bygones be bygones?"

Sky did not change her rigid posture. She did not sigh deeply nor bite her lip as she wanted to. She refused to give them any 'tells'. "I do accept your apology, Mr. Page." She said in what she hoped was a calm and firm voice. "Anyone can have a bad day. However, I ask you never to speak to me in that way, especially in front of the class, ever again."

She saw a flame of arrogance spark in Page's eyes, but he contained it. "Of course, Ms. Kingston. I agree. Again, please accept my apology." He stood. "Now, if our discussion is concluded, I must go and prepare for class." He turned toward Hilliard.

"Have a pleasant day, Mr. Page. Thank you for taking care of this matter. I'm going to ask Ms. Kingston to stay behind and speak with me for a few minutes…"

Page bowed rather formally and left.

If Sky hoped for further discussion or clarification from Hilliard, she was disappointed. He handed her sketch pad back to her. "I believe your envelope sketch shows a good deal of talent, Ms. Kingston. I'm glad you made friends with Mr. Coe-Alston. I'm very fond of him."

Sky left, asking herself what that was all about.

Chapter Thirty-Four

Conner bounced his fist off his thigh as his heel bobbed, he could not sit still. Dr. Woodbury had his opinions, but he was an old guy. Maybe there was a younger guy with better ideas and miracle cures... The recruiter clipped into the tiny office, throwing Conner into silence.

The young man with the extreme grooming of a poster boy searched the tablet, his guest, then the tablet again. "Mr. Jameson. I am Master Sergeant South, Sergeant Williams has brought me up to speed on your situation."

Conner nodded. "And?"

"Your post-surgical consult was with Dr. Daniel Woodbury?"

Conner shrugged. "The report's right there, I didn't catch his first name, sir."

The spit-shined Master Sergeant's lips drew straight, and he nodded. "This report says Daniel Woodbury." The senior recruiter sat back in his chair and effected a less formal conversation. "Do you know anything about this doctor?"

"No, sir."

South dropped the tablet softly to his desk and sat with his hands folded in front of him. "He was a leading flight surgeon for over thirty years. In fact, you might have heard of his brother, he's one of our more famous test pilots. Andrew Woodbury?"

Conner's jaw dropped. "I didn't connect the name. Everyone knows Andrew Woodbury."

"Anyone who flies does."

Conner nodded. "Sir, I'm sure Dr. Woodbury is wonderful, but I'm seeking the kind of treatment that will enable me to do those twenty pull-ups."

Sergeant South stood and extended his hand. "I wish you luck, Mr. Jameson. I want to express, if Dr. Woodbury says there's nothing to be done, there is nothing to be done. I'm sorry for this news. Your country appreciates the efforts you've made to join the military."

Conner went numb. This was it. This was the end. Next stop, the friendly skies of pulling a suitcase through random airports all hours of the day and night. *The airborne taxi-driver.*

****

The sun set, and Sky sat with Tweety's top-down at the beach. She seethed at her grades in the last three weeks of assignments. Big, fat, red Ds on each of her drawings. *Asshole.* The clouds crawled across a radiant late afternoon horizon. She should be inspired to paint this work of the Creator's hand. *Not today, not here.* How can this artistic dictator quantify her talent? She would work on her other classes, she yawned heavily. She wasn't sleeping. She'd lost seven pounds, and her clothes hung on her. The shadows under her eyes were cavernous, and she ached all over. *Maybe there is something wrong with me. Should I see a doctor?*

****

On the first Sunday in November, Conner parked his bike at Ponce Preserve, almost detouring to walk through the conservation area. But he needed to run even though he felt like crap. *Maybe a run will improve my mood.* He stretched, leaning into a fence. The trail was great training for keeping up his two miles in less than seventeen minutes. His path stretched down the area's eastern shoreline from the southern outskirts of Daytona Beach and through the quiet coastal town of Ponce Inlet.

At Major Street, he huffed out a breath. *Do I feel like doing this? In a minute, I will.* He followed South Atlantic Avenue through quaint neighborhoods and an array of nature's beauty. When he wound his way through the ocean dunes, his head pounded with the rhythm of the swaying sea oats. The sound of his heartbeat muffled the noise of tiny wild things scurrying in the palmettos. His ears ached, and so did his throat. He fought the temptation to sit in Winterhaven Park. The picnic tables were full of tourists anyway.

There must be a storm moving in. Conner felt a sudden chill of the breeze. The trail ended at the very tip of the peninsula, a place called

Lighthouse Point Park. This was where he usually cooled off with a dip in the ocean, but not today. The brief chill had become a major onslaught, and his body shook. He fought to reach the jetty's railing, and the two old fishermen turned and stared at him as he hit the concrete.

Conner returned to awareness with the feel of a hornet's sting in his hand. He meant to jerk his hand away from the IV but was stopped by a stronger grasp. "Welcome back, young man." Conner watched, fascinated by the bushy Sam Elliott style mustache on the paramedic.

"What happened?" He blinked and looked around.

The EMT pointed to his Air Force tee-shirt. "Training a little hard in this heat, Airman?"

"I don't feel so good."

"What's your name, young fella?"

"Conner Jameson."

"Have you taken any drugs, Conner?"

Conner stared incredulously. "No."

The paramedic nodded. "How long since you've eaten?"

"I had chicken ramen at lunch. My throat's kind of sore."

The EMT aimed the thermometer at his forehead. "Yeah, you've got a pretty high temp, you know that? We're going to take you to the hospital."

"Awe, do I have to?"

"Yeah, you really have to. You can call your family from the ER."

****

The ER doc was a pretty blonde, who reminded him of Sky. "Have you had any headaches, Conner? Any stiffness in your neck?"

"No, ma'am. My throat's real sore, though."

She pulled out a tongue depressor and a penlight. "Let's take a look." She nodded. "I'm going to have the nurse get a swab. We're going to give you fluids, but I'm betting you have a good case of strep throat."

Conner closed his eyes and dozed. When he awoke, his mother was at his bedside, along with the doctor. The nurse hung another bag on his IV stand. "Yep, the swab test confirms strep throat. We'll give you a bag of antibiotics and send you home with oral medicine." She glanced at his mom. "However, I have some concerns with your bloodwork.

You are anemic, your mom tells me you've lost weight. Your immune system is down. What's going on with you, Conner?"

Conner rubbed his forearm across his forehead and pinched the bridge of his nose. "Nothing's going the way it's supposed to."

"Your mom says you've training for the Air Force."

"Yeah, but it's not gonna work." His voice trailed off.

Tammy turned to Conner. "What do you mean, that surgery was just a setback, you'll bounce right back."

Conner's face paled. "No, mom, no bouncing this time. I'm a washout. They won't take me. That guy messed me up worse than I thought."

Tammy abruptly stood and paced the length of the gurney. "When did you find this out?"

"A couple of weeks ago. Then I started that trash diet of leftovers and pier chili dogs."

The young woman doctor winced, and Tammy shook her head. "Why didn't you tell me?"

"I was trying to train through it. But, now, I see the doctor's right. Nothing I can do is gonna make a difference. I have to rethink my whole life."

The doctor's smile was sympathetic. "The antibiotics will take care of your throat. But you have to take care of the rest of you. We have counseling resources if you'd like a referral…"

"How are they going to talk me out of a lifetime of what I wanted to do?" He slid further down the gurney.

"They might surprise you with how they could help. I'm going to write your discharge papers, and when this little IV bag is through, your mom can take you home."

"Mom, I've got to pick up my bike at Ponce Reserve."

"No, you don't. Brewer will get it. I'll drop him down there once I get you home."

Chapter Thirty-Five

The second Monday in November, Sky folded and unfolded the letter from her doctor'.

> Skyler Kingston has been seen in my office. She has been diagnosed with an illness that prevents her from attending campus classes for the remainder of this semester.
>
> I recommend she complete this semester online.

Who knew depression and anxiety felt like this? Her core classes accommodated her with online links. She wasn't ready to face Page. She could muster the courage to see Dean Hilliard. She waited in his office, holding the doctor's letter in her lap. His greeting was funereal. In their conversation, they stepped around each other like mating porcupines. When she felt there was no more to say, she pulled her portfolio out and opened it on Dean Hilliard's desk. "With all these Ds, what's the point of me completing a final project?"

With his hands folded before him, he watched her flip page after page of excellent composition and technique.

He nodded. "These are very dark images, although they are the generic items from Drawing 1, you have imbued them with an almost Addams Family style." His brow arched, and his lips straightened. "If I thought that was your mode, I'd say kudos. However, I've seen your work, and this is a grave departure from your art's initial message."

"Could Page stalking me have effected that?" She met his serious expression and raised him a furrowed brow. "He's been at the pharmacy when I pick up my medication. He's at the bank when I go to the ATM. I'd swear he's tagged my car."

The dean closed the portfolio. "May I have these?" Sky nodded. "I understand your desire to cut and run. But I want to encourage you to complete the final project." He consulted his computer monitor. "You are on the path for making the Dean's List in your first semester of college."

Sky's head dropped, and she mumbled. "Until Page, now my GPA is garbage."

"I'm encouraging you to prepare a final project that illustrates your craftmanship, your technical ability, but I want you to portray a subject of complex composition that connects on a personal level. Do your best. Isn't that what our parents told us?" The dean sat back and nodded. "I'm old, but I remember my mother telling me that."

"May I bring my project to you? I won't do it if I have to face him. I'd be afraid of what he'd do to it."

"But of course. I won't allow him to harass you further." Dean Hilliard nodded and rose, walking around his desk to see Sky out.

At the door, Sky shook the dean's hand. "I wish this could have ended differently."

On the walk back to the dorm, Sky stopped at Tweety and brought the five empty duffle bags to her room. Ali was in fencing class and wouldn't be back until around 10 PM. She always stopped with her fencing partner for sandwiches.

Sky peeled all the posters off her walls, balled up the blue putty adhesive, and left it on the desk. She packed her clothes and art supplies. She left an assortment of Ali's favorite snacks with a gracious letter asking forgiveness for leaving like this.

If she drove home tonight, it would be late, but she'd have the house to herself. Her Aunt and Uncle were on a cruise.

I have not heard from Conner in over a week. I've called, not gotten through. I've messaged him and only gotten short text responses. His phone goes straight to voice mail. I've left my new number three times. Has he gotten a job? She glanced in the rearview mirror and asked herself the most threatening question. *Has he met someone else?*

As she pulled into the garage and the door closed behind her, her first thought was physical safety. On her phone, she resumed the security system. *What if Page followed me home? All these times he's magically appeared, I've never seen his car. How will I protect myself?*

Once she was inside the home, she walked the perimeter, checked the security cameras, and double-checked the window and door locks. She scrambled into the kitchen pantry and found the security system keypad, where the portable key fob hung. Pocketing it, she felt more protected. Her uncle's golf clubs stood in the garage, and she pulled out the golf club Uncle Dan was so proud of. The head was the largest legally allowed on a golf course. The titanium and carbon fiber made it easy to swing. The flexible shaft made a mean whistle when she swung it. If she hit someone with it, it was bound to sting.

She thought about the Hawaiian Air gift card burning a hole in her wallet. Page wouldn't be able to follow her, surely he'd find another victim. She hadn't touched a dime of her gallery money. She brewed a cup of tea and sat at the computer. *I want to be at the last place I was happy.*

Starting her search, there were a few extended-stay hotels to consider. Bingo, right off Ala Wai, was a nifty little place with a Murphy bed and all the comforts of a dorm without a roommate. She booked a flight for late tomorrow afternoon, booked a room, and began doing laundry. She was going to Hawaii, thanks to Jordan and Kirk's gift card.

As her head hit the pillow, she wondered, *Am I going into the belly of the beast? If Conner is seeing someone else, I might as well forge a stronger relationship with Rando and the gallery. I'll need that. I'm not going back to Central Coast, even if they serve Page's head on a platter.*

✳✳✳✳

Dean Hillard waited with the Institute's HR representative. He'd already filled Ms. Eckert in on Page's behaviors. His secretary spoke into the intercom. "Here he comes."

With a significant look at Ms. Eckert, Hilliard stood at the door. "Come in, Page. I believe you know Ms. Eckert." They nodded to each other, and Page took a chair at the conference table. "Mr. Page, we had a brief, but what I believed to be an effective meeting regarding Skyler Kingston." Page nodded silently. "In our meeting, I believe I made myself clear that Ms. Kingston was to receive unprejudiced grading in your class, and your relationship was to be purely instructor/student."

"You made that crystal clear, and that's how it has been."

Hilliard slid the class portfolio across the table. "This is unprejudiced? Were these images the assignment? Before you answer, remember I have access to your syllabus." Page's shoulders rose and slumped, his complexion went florid. "It may interest you to know, Ms. Kingston has left school under doctor's orders. She has not... yet... filed a harassment complaint against you, though from what she tells me, she has grounds to go to the police over your stalking her off-campus. She has two witnesses."

"Stalking? That's absurd. This is a small town. The closest shopping center is within walking distance. I live on the other side of that shopping center. Because of her, I'm supposed to drive to the next community?"

Hilliard raised a quelling hand. "The stores can be compelled to surrender their security videos. Don't push it that far, Mr. Page. I'm not putting this institute in the position to defend you. You are terminated for cause. You forfeit all benefits, effective immediately. Security will escort you to your office and then off-campus."

Page sought Ms. Eckert's input. "I have no say in this?"

Ms. Eckert's face was pinched. "From the witness's statements, you should consider yourself fortunate you're not walking out in handcuffs."

Chapter Thirty-Six

Days and nights bled into one another. Conner stuck to the leather sofa in the den. *How many episodes of King's Kustom Kars can I watch?* When he raised the remote, he caught a whiff of himself. *When did I shower last?* He looked at the pill bottle, one more dose of antibiotics, and he was done. He heard Brewer's bike pull up outside. Conner shook his head and took off for the bathroom.

The front door opened, and it was Brewer, his mom's boyfriend. "Con, I need you. Got a minute?"

Conner shrugged, acutely aware that at this moment, a guy who worked on motorcycles all day was cleaner than he was. He leaned against the doorframe, shirtless, his basketball shorts hanging by a miracle. "What's up, Brewer?"

The tall, wiry biker removed his sunglasses and hung them in his shirt collar. "I got a guy who needs a yard attendant for a small marina. Have you found a job yet?"

Conner's gaze narrowed. *Job? Was I looking for one?* He rubbed his shoulder, a gesture he'd fallen into recently. "No, I haven't been looking. I've been sick."

Brewer's bushy mustache flinched. "Yeah, I know. Remember, I brought back your bike. What's it been, nine, ten days? You're better now, aren't you?"

Conner shook his pill bottle at Brewer. "One more dose…" Brewer paced, and Conner realized his sofa surfing days were over. "Yard attendant?" He scratched at his shaggy hair.

Brewer slipped a business card out of his vest pocket. "Call Freddy, we go way back, he understands you're a student. He's flexible."

Conner accepted the card and read about the business. "I don't know a thing about boats."

Brewer laughed. "It's a storage facility. You check their ID, and they drive off with their boat, easy peasy."

Just the beginning of a lifetime of crap jobs, sure. Conner frowned. "If I'm gonna get a job, I'd really like something where I have more contact with people…"

Brewer nodded. "I think you'll find a lot of good jobs over the holidays have already been filled. You might have to take what you can get. But your mom mentioned she was concerned about you finding something, I thought this would help." He raised both hands at Conner in surrender, walked to the front door, and turned. "Yah know, there are two kinds of people in this world."

Conner stared blankly and shook his head.

"The ones that drop their bike, pick it up, and get back on it and those who just walk off. Which one are you, Conner?"

Wonderful. Biker Philosophy 101. Sure, Brewer. Conner didn't answer but turned into the bathroom and started the shower full blast. *Who the hell does this guy think he is? He's known my mom five months, and now he thinks he's my stepdad? Big bad biker grease monkey, owns a shop. Doesn't drink, doesn't smoke. Thinks he's all that because he did four years in the Army. Big deal, he drove a truck in the Grenada conflict. I'll get a job when I find something I want to do. He didn't offer me a job at his place.*

Conner had to admit he felt better after a shower. Looking at the wreck of a kitchen, he realized, *I'm a pig. I'd never do this at my dad's house.* He tied on his barbecue apron and started cleaning up his mess. *I've got to call Sky, she's probably thinking I'm an asshole.*

From the looks of the kitchen, that could be true. While the frying pan soaked, he dialed her cell. It went straight to voicemail. He hung up. He tried again in a half-hour, voicemail. When the kitchen floor was drying, he got voicemail a third time. He looked at the clock. *She never has classes on Tuesday night, where is she?*

Conner scrolled through his voicemails and messages. If the emojis didn't send a message, the tone of her voice in the last three voicemails ranged from concerned to aggravated to plain pissed off. *How did I miss these messages?* He paced a circle in the family room, righting the couch cushions and folding the throw over the sofa back. While he vacuumed, he thought about her last voicemail.

"Conner, what is wrong with you? I've texted I've called.
I'm over here going through hell, and to add to it, I can't
find you. Are you done with me, or what?"

She was mad. He'd never heard Sky talk like that. *Is this a dose of my own medicine?*

****

His mom worked late on Tuesdays, she'd get home about ten and probably appreciate the ribs, potato salad, and coleslaw he'd made for her. After he cooked, he cleaned the grill out back and made a plate for the fridge. He looked around the house. The smoky barbecue smelled better than the gym sock odor from earlier today. He sat on his end of the sofa, dressed in a clean tee-shirt and shorts. After not shaving for ten days, he looked like a new man.

The front door opened cautiously, and Tammy stuck her head in before she threw open the door. "Did we have fairies drop in? Maybe forest animals straight from Snow White?"

Conner stood up and smiled. "I've been grumpy, sleepy, and sneezy, I might as well be Cinderfella, too."

Tammy walked through the cleared room, saw the magazines spread on the coffee table, plants watered, tabletops dusted. "Awe, you feeling better?" She hung her purse on the rack in the kitchen and headed to the fridge.

"I made a plate for you." Conner heard the foil, and he followed her into the kitchen. "I hope I did the potatoes right."

Tammy's face brightened at the food. "Have a seat with me while I eat?" Conner got sodas for them and sat with her while the ribs heated in the microwave. "Son, I know you've had a huge disappointment. Sitting around at home where you don't know anyone is not going to make it better…"

Conner held up a hand and ducked his head in guilt. "I was a jerk to Brewer today when he came by about a job offer."

Tammy got the ribs from the microwave and sat down, popped open her soda, and shook her head. "Don't take that job. You need to

195

be around people you know, doing things you enjoy." She began pulling the rib bones apart and gestured with one before she bit. "You have two choices."

Conner winced. "I do?"

"Yup, you do. You can go home to Dolly and work at the Rocking Horse, or you can go back to your dad in Hawaii and work for him."

"But…"

"You can't stay here. You have no friends, and you haven't made a life here with college or a job. You can transfer those test scores anywhere. I can tell you're not happy. I don't like living with unhappy men."

"Won't you be lonely? You didn't want me to go into the Air Force because you wanted me…"

"I don't want an unhappy you. You can go until school starts in January, or you can check out college there." She chewed and let him think. Waving another rib bone, she arched her brow. "Is that thing over with that girl? You don't talk about her?"

Conner wiped his face with a hand. "I probably screwed that up. I didn't answer her messages while I was sick, now she thinks I'm done with her."

Tammy shook her head. "That quick? I guess you two didn't mean a whole lot to each other."

Conner's elbow rested on the table, and he covered his mouth with his hand. "That's not true, Mom."

Tammy caught her son's gaze. "Don't let a lack of communication end a good thing. I know how that happens, personally." She tapped his hand on the table. "How different would our lives have been if I'd kept in touch with Kirk Roman?"

"I've been trying to call her tonight. She's not picking up."

"You don't know why. You keep calling until she does pick up. Even if it's to tell you to take a hike."

Conner shook his head as his finger traced a pattern on the tablecloth. "Dolly, Texas is too damn cold. Why should I go back there? Hawaii is nice all year long. I'm old enough to know which one to pick. Maybe, Sky will meet me in Hawaii for Thanksgiving?"

196

Tammy pointed to the kitchen calendar. "You better book that flight now if you want to be on that plane. Call Sky."

****

As Sky left the baggage claim area, she turned on her phone, and a series of blips announced calls, text messages, and voice mails. All from Conner. Did she dare open them while she stood waiting for her Lyft? Sure, might as well. If they were over, she needed to ride by Leonard's and buy a dozen support malasadas to eat in one sitting.

The texts seemed to have one theme: Call me. That didn't seem too ominous. After the drought, the flood of contact concerned her. Where had he been? In a coma?

Sitting in the Lyft, watching the sun come over the mountains, she closed her eyes for a second. *This has got to work out.* She pressed play on the first message. His voice was casual, "Hey, angel, I'm sorry I missed your calls. I had strep, and I was down. Call me."

Oh, my poor baby, strep?

The next message was a hang-up, not even a huff. By the seventh message, she could hear him sweat. "Angel, I'm a doof. I got sick, and I wasn't paying attention to my phone. I'm sorry, how can I make this up to you?"

She bit her bottom lip and listened to the last message. "Sky, you know who this is. I was thinking I really screwed us up. I had a talk with my mom, and she told me how lives can change with just a phone call. I think you understand what she means. No matter what time you get this, please, call me…"

Sky closed her eyes and drew the phone to her heart. *This is the best phone message ever.* She dialed his number, and he answered before the second ring.

"Sky?"

"Conner? How are you? Are you better now? Can you fly?"

"Yeah, I can fly. Fly where?"

"Hawaii."

"You must be reading my mind. My mom and dad put their wallets together and got me a ticket for Thursday, but you're still at school…"

"It's too much to go into right now. I'm in Honolulu, I found an extended stay hotel. It's small, but the murphy bed is a queen."

"Wow, I'll be there on Thursday. The flight arrives around 6 AM."

Sky blinked, her eyes moist. "I thought you gave up on us. I was so worried."

"Angel, you mean too much to me to disappear. I'm sorry I upset you. Glad my strep throat is all gone, I need one of your kisses."

"Just one?"

"Well, you know… one long session of your kisses…"

"I forgive you. I'll text the address of my hotel as soon as I get inside. Oh, Conner…I…."

"Angel, you are my world."

Chapter Thirty-Seven

Sky dropped her bags at her hotel, texted the address to Conner with kiss emojis, and then headed to Rando's gallery.

The pre-holiday traffic in the art gallery ebbed and flowed with tourists and locals as Sky entered. She saw Rando at the back of the deep gallery, he was head to head with another artist in front of a colorful triptych depicting dolphins. As Sky meandered, scoping out all the new art, she overheard Rando's encouragement. "This guy is a huge collector, he has five properties, and he's entertaining the idea of using this in a new hotel."

By the artist's expression, Sky didn't think Rando was convincing him. "You told him this is the only one, there are no prints."

Rando nodded. "How do you feel about seventy-eight?"

The artist bobbed his head, weighing the figure. Sky thought, *Seventy-eight hundred dollars for those three, I'd take it.*

"Okay, if you truly believe this guy is in the market, I'll sacrifice it for seventy-eight thousand, but he better load up on the rest of the series. Does he like sharks?"

Sky rocked back on her heels and counted seventy-eight thousand reasons to keep painting. Rando shook his hand and pointed him in the direction of his gallery manager. With a nod, an assistant came from the back and placed sold signs on the work. When Rando turned, Sky grinned and waved. "How are you doing? Are you too busy to spare a minute?"

He welcomed her with a fatherly hug. "What are you doing here now?"

Sky looked around the gallery, no one paid them any attention, so she drew him to her last remaining sketch on the wall. She pointed to the lone framed work and winced. "Runt of the litter? No one loves it?"

The picture was Conner's back, his left arm raised and bent at the elbow, the fingers of both hands threaded, hovering over his right shoulder. The image was searingly erotic. The pose accentuated Conner's lively ripples of musculature. His bike shorts were nearly invisible, their luster highlighting the defined muscle tone of his hips and glutes. It was the most controversial sketch she'd done with people thinking she'd drawn him nude.

Rando's wild head of hair danced with his laughter. "Oh, dear, child… The reason it hasn't sold as yet is that it's in the middle of a bidding war. The last bid was fourteen thousand."

Sky's jaw dropped.. She mouthed, "Fourteen thousand dollars?" She shook her head and paced a small circle, her hand wiped her eyes. "You don't know how encouraging this is."

He shrugged nonchalantly. "Encouraging? I'd expect nothing less from your work." He looked at his watch. "Have you eaten? We need to talk."

Sky's world plummeted from elation to the Marianas Trench. "We do? Can you give me a hint?"

"I've got a high school artist expedition going up to Turtle Beach at sunset. I can't keep turtle art in stock. You brought your art equipment?" She nodded numbly. "You don't like painting turtles?"

She waved that question off. "Chalk it up to jet lag, sure I'll paint turtles. Glad that's all we need to talk about."

He leveled her with a look of fatherly concern. "Now, Sky, what's troubling you? We'll have a little breakfast, and you can tell me about it."

****

There was nothing like having a huge breakfast and then crawling between clean sheets for a nap. Sky set her alarm for three in the afternoon. That would give her time to wake, shower, and meet Rando at the gallery for the Turtle Beach trip. She thought about splurging on an odd-sized canvas, depending on the photos she'd capture tonight. *Only good vibes. Turtle vibes.*

****

As Sky rode back up to the gallery, she wondered how Rando processed her info dump this morning at breakfast, but that was washed away when he met her outside the gallery. "Everything that jealous prick did to you? Forget it, flush it. You are already a commercially successful artist. Never let that bad experience cast doubt on your potential." His hands cupped her shoulders, and he gave her a little shake. "Now, quit drawing those macabre masterpieces, and let's go draw happy turtles."

Sky brightened and grinned widely. "Happy turtles, swimming in the sunset."

In all her visits, she'd never made it to Turtle Beach. The location was fairly hidden, and that was a bonus for the turtles. Laniakea Beach was within the 7-Mile Miracle, an area in the North Shore prime for big surfing waves during the wintertime. Today, Sky wore a swimsuit under her sundress. She slipped out of it and packed her phone into a waterproof holder. She wanted to capture the effect of the setting sun coming through the water. Hopefully, a few turtles would swim by her.

****

Early Thursday morning, when his flight arrived, Conner called his dad as he waited for the ride-share to pick him up at the airport. The last time he was here, he hadn't known his father. He'd been standing next to the most adorable girl on the planet and wondering whether his biological father would toss him out on his ear. How his world had changed!

Now, he explained as he spoke to his Dad and Jordan, he was on his way to Sky's hotel and would bring her to their new condo for lunch. First, he was headed for a private reunion with his lady love.

Conner wanted to warn her about his new look. That spit and polish military haircut had grown out to chocolate waves that tumbled over his ears and plaid collar. He didn't want her to wonder who he was when he stood in front of her door's peephole.

I'm heading upstairs now! Kiss emoji.

She must have been standing behind the door, watching for my shadow. When he knocked, Sky ripped the door open, squealed, and jumped into his arms, her legs around his waist. "Hey, angel." Her lips muffled his words.

"Hey, cowboy. Toss those reins over the hitching post and come on in."

For the first five minutes, they scarcely came up for air. Conner barely got inside the door before he pressed her up against the wall and reacquainted himself with her dangerous curves. "Oh, angel, you feel like…. Ahhh." Another resident walked down the hallway and shoved his duffle inside the door. The hint taken, he broke off the kiss and nodded to the stranger. "Much obliged."

Sky caught his face in her hands. "Close the door, lock it, and come to bed."

"You're tired? Want to sleep?" He teased. "There's something about landing in Honolulu that keeps me alert and buzzing."

Sky caught him by his fancy belt buckle. "Let me fix that buzzing. I know the perfect relaxation techniques."

Clothes went airborne. Sky turned on music to buffer any sounds. The murphy bed was open and waiting. She winked at him. "How's your desperate friend?"

Conner raised his right elbow and flexed his damaged arm. "You know…" He wiggled the fingers of his left hand. "I've had to retrain my technique for being a lefty."

Sky ran her palm down the front of his jeans. "Your left hand might be retrained, but Mr. Happy still hangs to the right."

"He's Mr. Happy because he's finally home."

They rolled in the queen size bed, still kissing, and celebrating the fact that their flesh was together in the same city. Sky pinned him on his back and swept her long hair back and forth across his chest. She teased him, his breathing quickened. "No more phone sex!"

Conner's fingertips danced lightly down her arms to tickle her hips. "Nope, if I have anything to do with it, we'll never be apart again."

Sky leaned forward and kissed him to punctuate that statement. "I agree."

****

As they shared the shower in the oddly shaped tub, Conner whistled. "Boy, howdy, weren't you the insatiable filly?" He soaped her back as she held up her loose tendrils of hair.

"The last time I saw you was July. It's November. What the hell were we doing staying apart from each other when we could have been together on weekends?" His gentle scrubbing halted, and she looked over her shoulder at his sober expression. "What was going on?"

Conner took the shower wand and rinsed away the bubbles, his chin to his chest. "I don't want to talk about it. Later..." *Why didn't he just wave a red flag at her?* "You were the one with the car. Why didn't you come to visit me?" He arched a serious brow.

"It wasn't because I didn't want to. I was slammed. I had incredible assignments every weekend. You know I'm on track for the Dean's List?"

"But you're not in school, what happened, Sky?"

She ripped back the shower curtain, grabbed a towel, and darted to the furthest point in the three hundred square foot apartment. Her long hair dripped as she frantically dried herself with the thin towel.

She heard the water turn off and felt his gaze as he stood in the bathroom, drying off. *Did she want to do this now? Better now than later.*

Sky watched his reflection in the mirror as he strode from the bathroom, his towel wrapped low on his hips, his shoulder scar bright pink from the hot water. His chest hair was darker and thicker, his burning gaze more intense when framed by his coal-black lashes. His exquisite face was accented by his rough morning stubble and wild curly hair. He was almost feral. As he walked, water dripped from his much longer hairstyle and recognizing the droplets on his chest, he pulled the towel from his hips and dried his curls, watching her, out of her reach. He stood naked, every part of him moving as he ruffled his locks dry.

Standing by the window, drawing a wide-tooth comb through her hair, his stance mesmerized her. She held out the comb. "Need this?"

"I think I need an explanation."

She gestured him to fold the bed into the wall. "Have a seat, hold on." She walked to the kitchenette and put two bowls and bananas on the bar. She quickly brewed a small pot of coffee and then put the milk and cereal box on the counter. "Want to hunker on the barstools or eat on the sofa?"

Still naked, save for the towel over his shoulder, Conner made himself a bowl of cereal and ate the banana while the coffee brewed. "Let's sit over there." He took a seat and waited until she returned with a tray bearing the coffee mugs and her breakfast. "No rush, eat first." But his gaze weighed heavily as he watched her eat. The silence unnerved her.

When their bowls were empty, Sky swallowed hard and began. "There was an instructor…"

****

Conner and Sky stood on the curb, waiting for their ride. He crushed her close and tucked her under his chin. "Oh, I swear to all that's holy, if I knew you were in that situation, I would have handled it. I would have swooped in and given that mother fucker a Texas tornado of a beat down."

She wrapped her arms around his torso. "No, cowboy, you would have been the one in jail. I'm just glad it's over."

Chapter Thirty-Eight

They walked into the condo foyer and showed their IDs to security. Once they were verified, they rode the elevator to the thirtieth floor. Conner raised a brow. "Back home, this is what we call tall cotton. But I won't say the rest of the phrase."

Sky narrowed her gaze and giggled. "Well, now you have to tell me the whole thing."

Conner ducked his head, and with a bad boy smirk, he replied, "It's a Texas thing, shitting in tall cotton. Life is good."

She giggled. "I better learn Texan. They can certainly turn a phrase."

The penthouse door opened, and Jordan welcomed them in a huge hug. "Get in here, it's been so boring without you two." She led them down a hall where they kicked off their shoes and dropped Conner's duffle. "Kirk is on the lanai, come out and tell us what's happening."

Kirk met them in the living room and hugged them each, visibly thrilled with their arrival. "Okay, fill us in. Howzit with you kids?"

Sky and Conner exchanged nods. Conner stood, his hands splayed on his hips, his head nodding before he spoke. He blurted out, "Sky's been evading a psycho stalker." His fingers combed through his long hair. "This head will never wear a military haircut. How are you, folks?"

The four of them stood stunned. Kirk gestured to Jordan. "Why don't we have some iced tea out there?" He led them to the wraparound lanai that afforded them views from Diamondhead to the Hilton Resort towers. The kids stood stunned at the view. Jordan followed with a pitcher of tea and gestured them to sit.

Once they were sipping, Kirk twirled his index finger. "Give that to us again, this time with details."

Sky turned to Conner, with a seriously furrowed brow. Her voice was barely over a whisper. "What did you mean about the military haircut?"

Conner sighed and gulped tea. When he put the glass down, his finger trailed the sweat on the glass. "Thanks to good old Agnew, I've been declared 4-F. The doc says I'll never pass the physical required for military service." His audience sat stunned, and then everyone spoke at once.

Sky's hand covered his. "Oh, Conner…"

Jordan shook her head. "You must be heartbroken…"

Kirk let out a held breath. "I'm sorry, son."

Conner's left palm pressed hard over his incision. It was a habit he developed as soon as the surgery healed. When he pressed the heel of his hand there, he headed off a deeper and broader ache, replacing it with a momentary white-hot burst than calmed to nothing. He drew in a deep breath. "Yeah, it's taken some adjustment. I don't know what I'm going to do now."

Sky looked at him from under her eyelashes. "But you can still fly, right?"

Conner shrugged. "You know how I feel about that."

Kirk leaned toward his son. "Have you truly explored all the opportunities? Don't settle without knowing all the prospects."

Conner's dark brow shot up. "Yeah, right now, I'm cruising through grief, hitting all the stages, a couple of them many times over. I'm not sure when I'm going to arrive at acceptance and find what I'm looking for."

There was silence between the four of them. A tourist helicopter buzzed by almost even with the condo. They all followed its flight until it disappeared behind a building. No one spoke.

After an uncomfortable silence, Jordan turned to Sky. "Did he say you had a psycho stalker?"

Sky raised her glass like a toast. "Why, yes, he did. You have no idea how relieved I've felt since I arrived yesterday morning. I'm completing my semester online…" At Kirk and Jordan's nods, she ran the story of her harassment out in even greater detail than she'd given Conner.

Kirk stood in agitation and walked to the lanai railing. He turned. "I'm going to assume a fatherly duty here since your dad is unavailable, if that's okay with you, Sky?"

Sky shrugged. "Sure, what are you going to do?"

"I'm calling the dean. I want to know where that creep is and what they intend to do about him."

Jordan nodded. "He has no place in any classroom."

Sky huffed out a breath. "They won't admit anything. They called a problem-solving meeting, but it was a farce. Luckily, I know a guy and his parents are pretty important." She found her phone and forwarded Mick's contact information. "Mick got more done behind the scenes than I did through proper channels."

Kirk held his phone. "Let's call him now." He set his phone in speaker mode in the middle of the table.

Mick answered in a few rings. "I don't know who you are, but I recognize that area code. Who is this?"

Kirk lowered his voice. "This is General Hank Kingston, I understand I owe you a debt of gratitude for helping my daughter?"

Sky blushed at Kirk's spot-on impersonation.

"No thanks needed. I was happy to skewer that rat. General, sir, Sky's gone, do you know how I can reach her?"

Sky spoke up. "I'm here, Mick, we're on speaker. I'm sorry I left without giving you my new number. I got a new phone, and those wacko messages stopped."

"They may have stopped because that Page has been ripped from the annals of Central Coast Art Institute."

Kirk interrupted. "You mean he was fired?"

Mick offered, "Of course, they won't say, but the little mouse Page was grooming as his next victim burst into tears when a teaching assistant walked in Wednesday morning and announced Page was no longer teaching the class."

Kirk shut his eyes with a frown. "I don't suppose anyone knows where he is?"

"I could skateboard past his bungalow, see if he's still there."

Kirk nodded actively. "How soon?"

Mick hedged. "Is tomorrow on my way into school, okay? I could leave some sand on his doorstep and see if it has footprints when I go back later."

Kirk's brows tented high. "What's your major, Mick?"

"Gaming technology, why, sir?"

"Oh, no reason. Keep my number and call me with your observations."

Mick's chuckle covered the miles. "Your number is a Hawaiian area code."

Sky agreed. "That's true, but mum's the word, okay?"

"Exactomundo. General, sir, I'll text you. I'll photograph his car if it's there. Tie-dye-guy is on the case."

When Mick and Kirk closed the call, Sky was red-faced. "I had no idea he heard me call him that."

Jordan stood, all motherly efficiency, her arms crossed over her chest. "There are four bedrooms here." She pointed to Sky. "You are moving into one of them, and you," she pointed to Conner, "are going to move into the bedroom on the other side of the bathroom." She put her fingers in her ears. "I do not want to hear a peep of argument out of you two. Got that?" She nodded at Kirk, and he shook his head in surrender. "Good."

Chapter Thirty-Nine

Kirk shook his car keys. "I don't know about you kids, but I'll feel better with both of you under this roof. Conner, you get comfortable in your room, Sky and I are going to move her over." He kissed Jordan and nodded to Conner but pulled his wife down the hall. "Take the kid grocery shopping, we're not prepared for his appetite."

Sky giggled at the thought of the four of them under one roof as they walked to the garage beneath the condo. "You know, Kirk, before Conner was injured, we..."

Kirk looked at her as he slid into the driver's seat. "Yeah, you were honeymooning."

"That's a nice word for it."

Kirk glanced at her. "You two have had a whirlwind love affair, but it seems to be working. I'm not the morality police, and let's not pretend you aren't sleeping together."

Sky blushed and backed to the passenger door, nodding. "I just want you to know, Conner has always been a gentleman." Kirk nodded, keeping his eye on traffic. "But, I've been responsible, too. We have always been very conscientious."

Kirk sat at the light, head nodding with the music. "There are two bedrooms there, a bathroom in between, you two work it out. I don't want to hear about the toilet seat, got it?"

Sky worked to keep the mortification out of her voice. "I'm sure it will be fine. We're grateful for your help."

Kirk's momentum picked up. "Now, about other protection. I want you in the women's self-defense class and see how your schedule jives with the martial arts classes. With Page being a free-bird at least for now, I want you prepared."

"I can understand that. I feel safe here in Hawaii."

"You are safe. Trust, but verify."

"I don't think he'll bother with me anymore. Out of sight, out of mind. He was hitting on a girl in class who just ate that up with a spoon. Why would he come after me?"

"You're probably right, but you did cost him his job. Humor me." As Kirk pulled into hotel parking, he added, "Does your Aunt Sherry's neighborhood have a watch program? You might want to call and alert them to possible prowlers."

****

Jordan and Conner cruised the grocery aisles. "Conner, what do you like to eat?"

Conner winced. "There at the end, I was on a steady diet of leftover nachos and pier chili dogs."

Jordan stopped in the aisle. "Pier chili dogs? I guess I haven't been on the mainland in a while. Do you miss them?"

Conner tossed three bags of pretzels and a barrel of cheese balls into the cart. "I know you guys eat healthy but break me in easy, okay? I promise to eat better, Sky manages to coerce me. I am trainable."

Jordan put back the barrel of cheese balls and nodded. "I know. I'm going to start now. If you like cheese, let's get cheese. Have you ever had cashew cheese?"

Conner gave her a doubtful look. "Is that something people slip by you?"

"No, it's used in vegan cooking. I won't trick you. I promise. Now about tofu…" She led him away from the junk toward the fresh foods. "Let's talk about tofu."

****

Sunday at noon, Sky got a phone call from Aunt Sherry. "How was your cruise? Did you enjoy working on the tall ship?"

Her aunt chuckled. "I'm not ready to join the Navy yet, Uncle Dan enjoyed the daily rum. Me? I like deck chairs. By the way, what's with the new number, and why aren't you in school?"

Sky cringed. "You know about that? Funny story…"

"I'm not laughing yet, but I do have a letter from the college, it was with our held mail. Tell me what's up?"

Sky told her an abbreviated version of the ordeal but laid heavy on the fact that she alerted the neighborhood watch because this incident got the instructor fired.

"That explains the torn screens in the back of the house."

"Did he get in?"

"The window wasn't broken. Thor, the Rottweiler next door must have scared him off."

"I wish Thor had gotten him."

Sherry dismissed it. "It didn't even register on our security system, so no harm. The watch group did keep an eye on the house after your call."

"Oh, Aunt Sherry, I am so sorry. But the good news is, I'm keeping up my classes online. I'm on track for the Dean's List if I get this drawing class straightened out."

"By the tone of your voice, you make me wonder if you are coming home."

"No. I had decided not to return to Central Coast in any case. Daddy was right, it's expensive and look what I got. My art has been requested for a show here in December. They are throwing together six young artists, and Rando is renting a warehouse for it. I wish you and Uncle Dan could come."

"Oh, Sky, we just got back to work, maybe when it's just your show, we'll come out. So what about college? Hank is going to dance me around for twenty questions, so spill."

"I've applied to the university here, and I'm pursuing business management at the gallery owner's advice. It's far cheaper and has a broader reputation."

"As long as you're back in school, your father will approve. I'm sorry you had such a bad experience with that instructor. College should not be frightening."

*****

Thanksgiving morning, Conner sat with a stack of aviation textbooks. He started flight school next Wednesday. It couldn't be soon enough. With the thickest book open on his lap, the aromas wafting from the kitchen distracted him from thoughts of flying. Today was going to be great. His first Thanksgiving with his family and then Jax was treating everyone to a helicopter flight around Oahu at sunset.

He looked at the clock and realized his mom and Brewer were probably already done with their meal. He figured he'd better give her a call before the tryptophan took over, and everyone fell asleep.

He video called her. It rang once, and a dark-haired little girl with curly ribbons and missing teeth grinned over her shoulder. "Missus Tammy, it's Conner…"

Brewer approached and extended his hand for the phone. "What did I tell you about picking up phones? You only pick up Daddy's phone."

"But it was ringing, and Missus Tammy's hands are wet, and I wanted to meet Conner."

Brewer held out his hand for the phone. "Did you get all that? I was drying the dishes your mom washed. Zoe has heard so much about you, she had to see you first."

Conner got a laugh out of that. "Zoe?"

Brewer tucked the phone up close to his face and walked away from the kitchen. "Zoe's going to be living with me from now on. My ex decided she was done being a mom, and I'm great with that. But before your mom gets here, since you were the man of the house…" Brewer lowered his voice. "I'd like to propose to your mom at Christmas, and I wanted your approval."

Conner fell back in his chair. "Wow, I guess I'm not the only one in love. Good for you, man. And I've got some news that might make it more peaceful. I'm staying in Hawaii, transferring to Embry Riddle out here in Honolulu."

Conner watched Brewer's expression brighten seconds before Tammy took the phone. "Did I hear you say you're staying in Hawaii?"

"How would you feel about that, Mom?" He paused, and before she could answer, went on. "Sky's business is here. She's going to the University of Hawaii, and I'll be at Embry Riddle."

Her forehead relaxed, and her shoulders softened with her broad smile. "You made that phone call to Sky in time, didn't you?"

Conner grinned effusively. "Everything is working out better than I expected."

"I have to apologize to you, Conner. When we first moved here, I know I said I wasn't ready to let you go yet. That was wrong of me. You were right. I raised you to be independent, and you have to live a life that makes you happy. I spent half my life for my dad, the diner, and you. You're grown, dad and the diner are gone, and Kirk was right, I can do a lot of things."

Conner watched Brewer with his daughter on his hip as he came up behind Tammy. The mechanic's muscled arm wrapped around her shoulder. "I promise your momma will stay busy. One day you can fly us somewhere."

Zoe's face went cross. "I want to fly!"

Conner grinned. "That's the way I started, Zoe, keep your eyes on the prize."

Once the call was closed, Sky slipped behind Conner and wrapped her arms around his neck. She nuzzled him behind the ear and ran her fingers through his curls. "I like this hair," she whispered. "Have you ever had tofurky?"

Conner looked appalled. "I've never had athlete's foot."

"It's not a disease, it a vegan turkey replacement. Thankfully, Kameo brought an actual turkey."

Conner raised a brow and pulled her into his lap. He whispered, "Why, what does it taste like?"

"It should be called Not Turkey. But be polite, they're putting a roof over our heads."

****

Seated around the large oval dining table, Kirk and Jordan stood to raise a toast. Jax and Kameo sat across from Conner and Sky.

"We're starting a new tradition. Everyone have their wine?" The folks at the table lifted their glasses. Kirk raised his. "We're all going to say what we are thankful for and drink a toast. We'll be grinning before we take the first bite. I'll start." Jordan sat down and nodded to him. "This time last year, I was a guy eating tofurky in a pool house by myself. This year, I have two sons and a wife."

The table toasted and Jax quipped. "Okay, what's the good part about two sons?"

Kirk gestured his glass to Jax. "Well, If I only had one, think of all the crap I'd heap on you."

Jax nodded to Conner. "Good point."

As the junior son, Conner waited for Jordan, Jax, and Kameo. He stood, raised his glass, and cleared his throat. "I want to thank Hawaiian Air for bringing me to my new family. Sorry, Jax, about the pony." He smiled down at Sky. "I'm grateful for seats thirty-four A and B."

There was a chorus of 'Awwes'."

Sky stood and blushed. "I have an embarrassment of gratitude. I'm grateful for a cowboy who flew to Hawaii, and his family who took me in as one of theirs. I'm grateful Daddy is safe, although we aren't together. And lastly, for that fitness center that needed a mural."

As bowls circulated the table and biscuits were buried under gravy and mashed potatoes, family chatter ended, and serious eating began. When Kameo and Jax took the task of clearing the table, Jordan brought pies and whipped cream back.

Once everyone had a dessert in front of them, Kirk raised a hand. "One more bit of sweet news…" Everyone paid close attention. "Evan asked me if I knew someone who could move into the pool house as a caretaker. I told him about a young college couple, and he thought that was dandy. So Saturday you two are getting the boot."

Conner and Sky shared explosive grins. "No kidding?

"He wants us to watch that fabulous house?"

Kirk raised a staying hand. "You guys get the pool house, and the main house stays move-in ready for Evan at all times. The gardeners, housekeepers, and security folks will report to you. Sounds better than a dorm, doesn't it?"

"Sounds wonderful!" Conner caught Sky's hand and kissed it. "Great start, isn't it?"

Chapter Forty

Sky decided to let Tweety stay parked in St. Petersburg and bought a more practical Toyota hatchback to carry art. Kirk signed his Harley over to Conner, and now they both had dependable transportation.

By the second week in December, Conner divided his time between flight school, the fitness center, and getting acquainted with the house staff. His halfhearted mood didn't begin to lift until he attended the seminar discussing the different opportunities open to pilots. "You know they have special medivac planes?" He told Sky as they sat at the kitchen bar.

She passed the ketchup. "Sure, I thought they were mostly helicopters."

Conner dipped a French fry. "Yeah, they have helicopters. But they also have jets that carry critical cases from here to the mainland for care."

Sky nodded. "If you worked for a company like that, you'd get to fly different types of aircraft."

"Yeah, depending on the destination. I'd feel like I was helping people, too."

"I see how you'd find helping people appealing."

Conner began clearing away the fast-food sacks. "They also have specialty pilots who fly fighting forest and brush fires. Those terrible fires in California are a good example."

Sky stared at him. "That's about as safe as being a fighter pilot."

His voice was light. "That's why they need the best pilots to do it…"

"How far away are you from that decision?"

Conner tossed out the trash and wiped the bar counter. "I'm a few licenses away."

"Good." Sky sighed.

"It's not full time, anyway. I'd mostly do medical transport."

"That would be my vote. If you want hot, stay at home."

****

Sky finished her online classes ahead of schedule and took extra care to pack her final drawing project. It was far happier than the mournful subjects she drew in class. This piece was a joyous celebration of new life.

"How long were you underwater to catch that photo?" Conner walked up behind her to join in admiring the translucent colors.

"Off and on about an hour. But the time I spent paid off." She gestured to the perfect sunbeam flowing into the ocean as two baby turtles took their maiden swim. "Did you ever hear the island legend of a mystical sea turtle named Kauila?"

Conner gave her a squeeze with his hug. "I am painfully low on island lore.

Sky pointed to the ethereal figure. "When she was in her turtle form, Kauila's air bubbles rose to the top of the pond delighting the children of Ka'u. She loved children and would sometimes change herself into a little girl so that she could play and watch over the children on the black sandy shores."

Conner raised a brow. "You did such a great job, it looks like you're seeing her from underwater."

Sky was especially proud of how Kauila looked, drawn as a child spirit. Her posture and gesture portrayed her giving her blessings for these new lives entering the vast ocean.

"As much as I like this drawing, the colors would be fantastic in oils. I have to get that big canvas and start painting."

"Are you shipping this today?"

"Yes. As soon as I hear confirmation that Dean Hilliard receives this? I am done with Sarasota."

Conner kissed her temple. "They didn't deserve you."

****

Sky chose four of the most popular mural studies and had them made into high-quality prints, producing only ten of each. She would sell signed and numbered prints at the show in December. Her centerpiece work would be the Spirit of Kauila. She worked locally with a sea turtle charity to pledge a portion of the sale to their conservation work. She looked at the calendar. *December 22nd will be here fast, get painting.*

One morning as Conner prepared to leave for flight school, he hung over her shoulder as she flipped through her iPad, searching for his image. "What are you looking for?"

"I'm going to do a pastel of you, nude."

"I beg your pardon?"

"Just from the back, remember that bidding war that bought me the car? That was you." She laughed at the look on his face. "Don't worry, nothing graphic. It's a picture I took of you on your tummy in bed."

"I feel so cheap."

"Oh, no, they're going to have to pay for your backside." Sky set up her easel under the pool house's covered lanai and hugged him as he slipped from their embrace. She called out to him as he walked toward the garage. "That butt of yours is a moneymaker."

He called over his shoulder. "Then, I guess I feel expensive."

She watched him get on his motorcycle and ride off. For a few moments she sat with her morning tea, looking at the different photos she'd snapped of him.

He is so expressive. She giggled at his image with the tip of his tongue escaping his barely parted lips. *In many ways he is my muse. What am I to him? We've been together off and on for six months. Did we start living together too soon? Are friends with benefits all we'll ever be?* She looked at the charm bracelet he bought her. At the most unexpected times, he would bring home a charm. Last week it was the turkey for their first Thanksgiving. *He says such sweet things, but never, I love you.* She fingered the charm. We talk about the future like we're there together, but how? She sighed, locked the screen, and began blocking the pastel image.

****

The Friday before Christmas was also the day before her first show. Sky's nerves were shot. Between transporting her art to the gallery for setup and the show's preparations, she wished Rando wasn't in San Francisco. Lara, his assistant, was alright, but she wasn't Rando.

The dress Sky bought did not fit the way she wanted. She needed a better bra. *Where am I going to find the right bra the weekend before Christmas?* Her latest haircut was just 'meh'. She had to go to the nail salon tomorrow morning, she just broke a nail, and her toes were terrible.

She stared at the oven, waiting for it to reach 350 degrees. Tonight was lasagna, salad, and garlic knots. Hopefully, Conner would take care of her nerves. He did that very well.

The front door flew open, Conner cradled a bag to his chest and bolted through the living room into the bedroom. Sky heard his nightstand drawer slam closed. He yelled as he jumped into the shower. "Sorry I'm late, I stink. We were at the airfield inspecting planes. I'm grungy, dirty."

Sky tiptoed through the bedroom and seeing the shower door obscured by steam, she peeked into his nightstand drawer. There was a black jeweler bag. A very small bag. She slid the drawer shut and headed back to the kitchen. Once the lasagna was in the oven, Conner was out of the shower and dressing.

Sky set the plates on the breakfast bar and poured Conner's favorite Arnold Palmer with extra lemon. Then she waited. Conner wandered out of the bedroom, slipping on a polo shirt.

"What made you so dirty?"

His smiling face appeared through the neck of the polo, and he shook out his damp hair. "We were crawling around the hangar."

"Wow, exciting."

"Your day was more exciting. How does the show look?"

Sky held up her right hand. "I broke a nail." Her expression was not amused. "My dress doesn't fit right, I need a different bra, I could go on, but I'm too frustrated." She turned and looked at the oven timer.

"If you ask me, you don't need a bra. They are perky on their own. I could walk around behind you and hold them up."

"That's not how the dress is designed. Sky sighed in exasperation. She poured a fruit juice and added Seven-Up to make a spritzer. "So, since I have to pretend I like the way the dress looks, I'll pretend I'm drinking."

"Hey, I've got something that should improve your mood. Close your eyes. I'll be right back." He went into the bedroom, and Sky's heart began to pound.

With the uncertainty in their relationship, was this what she wanted? She took her seat at the bar with her hands over her eyes.

"Don't open them yet." She heard him sit beside her. "Skyler Kingston... open your eyes."

Her heart plummeted, and she felt the color drain from her face. It was a Christmas tree charm. She looked at the blank space in the corner of the living room where she wanted a tree and back to Conner. "Wow."

"Here's our first tree. How do you like it?" He was buzzing, he was so happy.

"It's definitely our first tree." She nodded and began removing her bracelet to add the charm.

Conner's grin evaporated. "Don't you like it?"

"We've been so busy, but I was hoping we'd pick up a tree and get some decorations this weekend." She nodded to the clear floor space.

"Do you want to bother with that? I never grew up with a tree..." Sky's expression stopped him. "My grandparents lived next door, they put up a tree. Mom and I were too busy for that stuff."

"I... I... did, but you don't want a tree? I think the traditions of Christmas make the season. This is the first year daddy and I didn't meet in some insane location to celebrate."

"Well, what happened this year?" Conner missed all six cylinders of her appreciation of Christmas.

Sky held the boxed charm and offered a weak smile. "What happened this Christmas is I'm living with you. We're playing house, and every day I cook and do your laundry, and I paint and..." She ran a hand through her hair and propped her elbow on the bar, her forehead hit her palm. "Take the pan out of the oven when the timer rings. I've lost my appetite."

Sky pulled a hoodie off the wall rack and quietly left for the beach.

****

219

Conner watched astounded as she let the door close behind her. *What the hell just happened? Is she not happy with me? What did I do? I don't have the money to fly her to Disneyland Paris.*

Conner looked at the enameled charm and then the open space. *Am I double dumb?* Conner debated running after her. *Or should I run to the store for a tree? Where should I run?* Honestly, Christmas wasn't a big deal. His family business eclipsed two days of celebration. The holiday was hot, exhaustive work in a diner.

The timer rang, and he brought out a tray of the most fragrant lasagna he'd ever smelled. *She'd probably think I'm a heel if I sat down and ate this right now.*

He turned off the oven, covered the lasagna, and left a note on the bar, saying that he was running an errand. He made sure the porch lights were on.

Sky wanted a holiday tree. The best he could do after the third stop was a grocery store potted eighteen-inch tree with red and gold balls. *It will have to do.*

As he carried it back into the house, he hoped she understood it was the best he could do. He took a shoebox and covered it with a red hand towel and elevated the tiny tree a few inches. Moving the flameless candles off the mantle, he arranged them on either side. It looked bare without gifts. Conner sat in the feeble candlelight and waited.

Chapter Forty-One

A little after nine, Sky walked in, sucking on a milkshake. She flipped on the light at the front door and found Conner sitting next to the tiny tree. His stomach rumbled loudly. "Didn't you eat?" She slipped out of the hoodie and hung up her keys. The night air was breezy, but no match for the emotions.

"No, I was waiting for you." His words did not match the tone of his voice.

Here reply was smooth and even. "I told you I lost my appetite."

Conner turned away from her as he fought his facial expression. "Obviously, not completely."

She shrugged and prowled around the kitchen island and threw her cup in the trash. "Do you want me to heat some for you?" She made a step toward the kitchen.

He waved her back. "I can heat my own food." Conner rose and dusted off his hands on his bottom, went to the kitchen, and cut a slab to heat. While it turned in the microwave, he dished salad and dressed it.

Sky stood over the tree, her fists on her hips. "Where did you find the plant?"

Conner silently seethed as he removed the heated plate. "It seems the tree lots are sold out unless we want a designer tree. This little guy," he pointed with his fork, "seemed about the right size until I got it home."

Nonchalantly, she flipped her head in the direction of the property line. "You can always plant it outside, and perhaps in a few years, it will do." She turned on her heel. "I'm going to get a shower and turn in. You're at the fitness center early tomorrow, right?"

Nodding, Conner stood chewing molten food. It hurt to swallow. "I guess I can't make you happy tonight."

"I think I need to be clearer about my holiday expectations."

Conner ate red-hot cheese and shook his head. "When did we cover that subject?"

Sky leaned in the bedroom doorway and crossed one foot over the other, her arms folded over her chest. "I've always talked about how Christmas was a big holiday. I've talked about how Christmas was special in my childhood."

Conner spoke so low, she had to listen closely. "See, that's the thing. I thought we were adults now."

"There's a difference between child-like and childish, look it up." She turned abruptly and headed to the shower.

Conner let his food cool to semi-warm before he finished eating. He nursed the burnt roof of his mouth with a glass of milk, and then Monday morning quarterbacked their fight. *What is she expecting? Diamonds? Not diamonds, a diamond.* He pressed the heel of his hand into his forehead, trying to push some sensitivity into his skull. *Oh, God. How could I hold up a box that size and call her by name?* He'd seen enough rom-coms to know what women expected.

Yes, her family did holidays big. Yes, they went to bizarre resorts. Hank invested the money and concentrated effort on those two weeks to be together because of his Air Force career.

Yes, he had not spent enough time with Kirk to learn what he and Jordan were doing for each other besides dinner at the penthouse around three. Jax and Kameo would be satisfied staying in bed till noon.

Conner washed his dishes and grabbed his headphones for the PlayStation. He resumed his place in Combat Ace Elite Pilot. Hunkering into the comfy leather sectional, he decided at least he could win something this evening. He slipped on the headset and flew into synthesized warfare.

****

Within the hour Sky emerged from the bedroom to find the great room illuminated by seventy-five inches of airborne warfare. Flashing explosions shattered light in different directions. She got a bottle of juice and made sure the lasagna was put up. The light reflected off Conner's concentrated gaze, and his hands moved rapidly in response to some attack.

She stood there for a series of gun bursts, and when her shadow did not register with Conner, she turned out the kitchen light and went to bed with a book. *Are vampires any smarter than mortal men? Jeesh.*

Around 3 AM, Sky rolled over on the Kindle and woke. Conner still wasn't in bed. She checked the great room. The screen was frozen with the question, "Are you still playing?" He was asleep, the controller in his hands and his body in a contorted pose. *He's going to hurt when he wakes up.*

Slowly, Sky touched his shoulder. "Conner, are you coming to bed?"

He startled. "Huh?"

"It's after three, don't you want some comfortable sleep?"

He whipped off the headset and peered at her seriously. "I thought you were mad at me."

She sat on the back of the sofa and reached out her hand. "Aunt Sherry and Uncle Dan have been married thirty years, do you know why?"

"I don't know how to make you happy, how can I know the secret to thirty years of marriage?"

Sky looked to the vaulted ceiling and shook her head with a slip of a grin. "They never go to bed mad. We can pick this up when we're both rested. Trust me, I will. But right now, come to bed, please?"

When Conner slipped out of his polo and shorts, Sky slipped out of her nightgown, and they clung to each other as if their skin could transmit the understanding their brains and mouths misfired.

****

Sky sat next to Jordan at the nail
spa, their purchases in bags between them. Once the foot spas were at a low rumble, Sky leaned to Jordan and looked from under her eyelashes. "Why are men so incredibly thick?"

Jordan narrowed her gaze. "Are you speaking about them in general or one in particular? Remember, it took Kirk eighteen years to ask me out."

Sky shook her head. "I would have killed him. I'm going to kill his son."

Jordan nodded and drew breath through her teeth. "First fight?"

"Oh, yeah." Sky shook her head. "We have no Christmas tree, and it wasn't until I mentioned it that he went to the grocery store and bought a potted one." She gestured its size.

Jordan looked skeptical. "And that's what you fought about, a tree?"

"Uh-hum."

Jordan arched a brow. "Why do I feel there's more to this story?"

Sky huffed. "Well." She held up her arm with the bracelet. "When he's thinking of me, he stops and buys a charm that recognizes something we've done. It's not a birthday gift, not a holiday, it's what he does."

Jordon nodded. "So, he's not a flower guy?"

Sky shook her head. "No, so when I was dancing on a shred of a nerve last night, he thinks he's going to make all my anxieties about this weekend go away with a Christmas tree charm…"

Jordon nodded. "Uhum."

"Every time he buys one, he comes home and asks for the bracelet, and he arranges them and makes a big deal about putting it on me."

Jordon's brows formed a high V. "Go on."

"Well, this time, I was talking about being stressed, and he tells me he has something to cheer me up. He tells me to close my eyes. He disappears to get a small jewelry box, then he says my name, Skyler Kingston, and what do you think I'm expecting?"

Jordan covered her face in her hand. "He's been watching too many holiday jewelry commercials, and he used …"

"Yeah, Aunt Jordan. He used the engagement ring presentation. Well, you should have seen my face when it was this charm." She pointed to the green enameled tree.

"Oh, dear."

"He told me Christmas was for children, and I told him there was a difference between childlike and childish. Then he enlisted in a video game war until I found him asleep at 3 AM."

"Did you ever make up?"

"I know enough not to go to bed mad, but I didn't go to bed happy. He came back to bed, and we held each other, but it was like two porcupines…"

"Let's be clear, this fight is not about Christmas or a tree. This fight is because you want a commitment. Does he want to give it?"

Sky stared at her toes. "I don't know. I came back to Hawaii, ready for him to dump me because he hadn't returned my calls for a week. I can make a life if he doesn't need me."

Jordan weighed Sky's words. "Need you or want you?"

Sky looked at her manicure. "Aunt Sherry raised me to understand, a man has to love and need a woman more than she needs or loves him. If you love each other equally, they don't need you enough."

Jordan's expression reflected what she thought about that logic. "While there may be some truth in that philosophy, I've always thought a woman must always be ready to take care of herself. Whether through death or separation, what seems like perfection at first may have some cracks in that foundation."

Sky nodded. "You were alone for a long time. Frankly, I was preparing myself for the worst until I heard from Conner. Aunt Jordan, should I not have moved in with him? Should I move out and see if he wants to pursue something with me?"

"I wouldn't be honest if I didn't tell you that would be your strongest position. But can you get there from here? If you move out, will he understand why? Or, will his trust be broken?"

Sky drew in a deep breath. "You're telling me I have to deal with this uncertainty of not knowing if he cares enough to marry me."

"You don't have to. The two of you must sit down and figure out why you're together. Was it love at first sight, and it's cooled? Are your goals allied to build a life together?" Jordan reached for Sky's arm and patted her. "You two are figuring out the toilet seat and who eats what, but that's putting the cart before the horse. Have you figured out if you're committed to each other?"

Sky shook her head. "The romance was so heady, it didn't cross my mind."

Jordan's smile spread across her face. "Honey, you were raised in a home with a husband and wife who shared responsibilities equally. That's where your comfort lies. Life is not a rom-com."

Sky pressed both hands to her temples. "I knew it, I really did. Jeeze." She threw up her hands, and the nail tech looked up from his work on her feet. She waved him on. "I'm fine. That feels wonderful." She turned to Jordan. "I just have to get through tonight."

Chapter Forty-Two

It was six o'clock when Sky got into her hatchback. Waving away any tagalongs, she humorously ground her heel into the floor when Kameo and Jax offered to skate the perimeter to inflate the bids. She drove out to the Hale'iwa show with a promise to check in later tonight before she began her long ride home

Sky stood consumed by her first professional gallery show. There was so much to see in the other five artists' works that she buzzed from station to station, taking in the variety of mediums and schools of expression.

Aficionados from as far away as Kyoto circulated within three feet of her painting, Spirit of Kauila, as well as her other work.

While they honeymooned in the pool house, Sky's stolen moments translated sensually into pastels, portraying a sleeping Conner like a god in repose. This image had the cougars leaning into the art.

****

Conner pushed the bin of soiled towels to the pickup point for the laundry service while Kirk sanitized exercise machines. Kirk called his name twice before Conner looked up from whatever private preoccupation he was thinking.

"Conner."

Conner looked at his dad in confusion. "What, did I forget something?"

"You've been in a fog all day. Something bothering you?"

Conner's brows knit, and he shook his head. "I've been stepping in it for the last twenty-four hours. Dad, do you ever feel like you're fishing with the wrong bait?"

Kirk narrowed his gaze. "Well, what are you fishing for?"

"I just want to make Sky happy, and I keep screwing it up. I can't read her mind."

Kirk stopped what he was doing and grabbed two bottles of water. "Have a seat, son. We're going to talk about what you're trying to catch."

"I already caught her. It just doesn't look like I'm any good at keepin' her." Conner accepted the water and shook his head. "I piss her off just doin' stuff. By tomorrow my breathing should annoy her."

Kirk's head dropped back in a silent laugh. "Wait until the sounds of her eating makes you want to drive icepicks into your ears."

Conner drew back in disgust. "What?"

Kirk waved that off. "How long have you been fighting?"

Conner looked at the clock. "Since I got home last night from the hangar. Evidently, she expects a Christmas tree." Conner paced a circle, thinking. "When something special happens, I buy her a charm. So last night, when she sounded testy, and on her last nerve, I told her to close her eyes, and then I held out this month's charm. You would have thought I gave her booger. The damn girl went into this sermon about us going out for a tree. Then I really made a cow pie. I told her Christmas was for kids. I don't remember her talking to me after that. She left. I got the damndest little plant Safeway could pass off as a tree." Conner and Kirk stared at each other a beat. "She cleared this huge space for a tree, and that tiny thing looks mighty lonely."

"Women are tricky, son. This argument is not about a tree. What else happened?"

Conner bit his lower lip. "Well, you know the guy at the jewelers said something to me that I blew off while I was buying the charm. I see him every time I buy one. I walked in yesterday at lunch, and he asked me why I hadn't made an appointment to see their holiday selection of diamonds."

Kirk stood nodding, his lips pursed in a knowing smile. "What did you tell the guy?"

"I told him diamonds were for after you have 'the talk'. He looked at me kind of weird."

Kirk wiped a smile off his face. "Have you had that talk?"

Conner gritted his teeth. "The L talk? Hell, Dad, what is that anyway? She's gotta love me, she puts up with me. She's gotta know I love her. I'm here, aren't I?"

Kirk nodded. "I think I know why you're having trouble keeping the fish in your boat."

"Huh?"

Kirk rubbed his forehead. "Sometimes, I wish you were old enough for a drink. I need a drink." Kirk swallowed a long draw of water. "Son, if you don't tell her you love her, how do you expect her to know that?"

"Don't I treat her right? When something important happens, I make a big deal out of putting a charm on her bracelet."

Kirk rubbed at the back of his neck and drew breath through his teeth. "And in your mind, each charm says I love you. In her mind, that charm is a souvenir. What do you say when you give it to her?"

Conner flinched. "Lemme see your bracelet, I have something for you…"

"Yeah, that's a little foggy on the subject of I love you."

"Yeah, but Dad, in the past, we kind of argued about the Air Force. She let me know clearly she wasn't following me from base to base."

Kirk nodded. "And the two of you went separate ways, and we see how that ended."

Conner shrugged. "I figured when I couldn't get into the military, she'd know I wanted to make a life with her. We came back here and living with her has been heaven every day. I can't even imagine when we're adults with careers."

Kirk threw up his hands. "Conner, you are almost twenty, she is nineteen. You live better than many newlyweds. But you guys are in limbo, and she needs you to step up and stake your claim."

"Isn't that what Hank told you?"

Kirk nodded. "Yeah, don't take eighteen years."

****

Quiet music lilted through the speakers as the sound of servers with trays cut through the warehouse rented for this event. Tall white walls, erected to display art were lit perfectly to flatter each piece.

Why did we argue? Do I really want to leave him, just to see if he'll chase me? I don't play games. I love him. The big question is, does he love me?

Lara Nakamura, a young woman of the uncommon parentage of Norwegian and Japanese, picked up when Rando Kane left for a show in San Francisco. Rando's last conversation assured Sky she would show well beside these other artists. "Confidence, Sky, always remember your singular talent."

Tonight was different from the afternoon when the local news covered her mural's unveiling. That day was casual. Tonight was the biggest night of her artistic career with nerve-wracking details robbing some of her enjoyment. Sky verified her small crossbody bag held her business cards, a pen, and one lipstick. *Check!*

Sky's opening night would be over before she knew it. Kirk and Jordan assured her their fitness center memberships were up since televising the mural unveiling.

Imposter syndrome leaked in with a nagging thought about the ridiculous escapade in Sarasota. She wished she had never left for college in September. *Stop thinking about that!*

Gliding right up to Sky, Lara held out her hands, ready to caress the young artist's face. "You are the sweetest, young thing I have ever promoted." Once she was there, her face in Lara's hands, Sky's lashes lowered, and she smiled.

Lara convinced her to use a rough wood frame on the provocative pastel of Conner, saying she had a specific buyer in mind.

"The patrons, the couple I told you about, they are going to be at the after-show party. I can't wait for you to meet them. The check is as good as written, dear Skyler."

"If they're so eager, why aren't they here?" Sky's brows knitted.

Lara's gaze swept the gallery, and her attention returned to Sky. "He said something about dinner with the Governor."

"Ahh." Sky nodded. *Yes, I will be there for a hot minute.* Then, she'd get home to finish the ongoing argument with Conner. She was still irritated at him.

Wearing a Mona Lisa smile and holding a sparkling cider, she moved through the patrons. Sky wore an island-style dress Aunt Jordan bought her for this occasion. The batik print flattered her tan skin and creamy blonde hair. She was over the fact that Jordan wasn't her mom, their relationship was growing in different ways.

The Rat-Pack era romantic music vibrated negatively within her, reminding her of Page's stalking behavior. First, it was Eric's persistent texts reminding her of assignments or impromptu meetings. It escalated to him waiting for her at the coffee house, standing at a fruit stand in her neighborhood when she walked from her residence hall, and the penultimate fright? The day Eric Page sat at the pharmacy when she picked up her birth control refill. Sky shivered at the thought that the sordidly reworded fairy tale rhymes sent to her phone were his creation. She blinked hard and flushed those thoughts out of her mind.

No squealing friends rounded out her night at the gallery. She was alone living this dream. This was a fantasy to have a five-figure price tag on her life-size canvas, so she behaved the way she thought adults behaved. Shaking hands, making polite small talk, and avoiding any mention of returning to art school in Sarasota.

"Sky!" Lara waved above the thinning crowd as the lights were dimmed twice. The partying hoard dropped empty glasses on small raised tables and left via the front door. Their art purchases were marked 'sold' and waited for packing and delivery. "I can't wait for you to meet your patrons."

"Yeah, I have patrons. The first of many, right?

"They have a limo waiting for you outside."

"Limo? My car is here. I drove."

Lara's arm swept around Sky. "Did you not hear me? Your patrons are expecting you at the party. The limo is outside. They will bring you back to your car with a check after you absorb their praise."

Sky grimaced. "I don't want to rely on a limo to bring me back to my car, Lara. I'll drive myself."

Lara turned and pointed to her assistant. "Let Paki drive your car down to the party, then you can go home from there. When your patrons are the ones sending the limo, it's all about meeting them halfway, Sky." Lara plucked the keys from Sky's fingertips and turned her toward the sidewalk, ushering Sky to the sleek, black limo.

I'm alone. Who arranges a limo for an artist alone? The chauffeur sat silently on the other side of the privacy wall. Faint twinkle lights faded in and out in the ceiling.

Sky watched Paki drive off in her blue hatchback. *Please don't wreck my car.* She looked at her phone, ten-fifty nine. She shivered in the air-conditioning and startled when Lara ripped open the door and bent into the cavernous limo.

"Help yourself. There's water and more of that cider for you. I alerted them you are nineteen."

Perturbed, Sky's lips went straight. "Thanks."

The limo merged into late-night traffic for the thirty-some mile trip to Waikiki. Sky grabbed the only bottle of water and sank back in the plush leather. The catered food was salty. The cider wasn't thirst-quenching. She drained the bottle, and within minutes her phone slipped from her hand.

In the back of the limo, Sky sat on the passenger side, almost asleep and safely belted in the three-point restraint. When the limo slowed at the brightly lit entrance to a dance club, the pulsing music and lights disoriented her.

Chapter Forty-Three

Who is this guy? The fella in the Tom Ford suit, his deep blue shirt open at the neck, leaned into the limo and caught her around the waist. *Do I know you?* Her head swam, and she felt weightless as he propelled her through a shoulder to shoulder crowd. She bounced off people lubricated with liquor, and who knew what else. In a sea of overly made-up women in glittery evening wear, she stood out.

"When I first saw your work, I was blown away, Skyler. You have no idea the impression you made on me." His lips barely cleared her ear. *If whiskey had a voice, it would sound like his.*

The doormen saw them and held open the doors, nodding their welcomes.

"When you see what I have planned for tonight, I think you will be … amazed." His voice carried the promise of forbidden pleasures.

She didn't want that with a stranger. All she wanted him to do was sign a check and buy her art. *Wasn't that what an art patron did?*

Sky shook her head, mentally grasping for reality, it was a silly millimeter away. She could not discern truth from fantasy. But, damn, he was sleek. Freshly shaven at nearly midnight, he wore a savage scent she could not place. As beautiful as he was, there was no question of his masculinity. By the way the throng moved around them, he was the alpha dog. A sheen of sheer perspiration shown on his upper lip, and he smelled of peppercorns and black sandalwood.

His hands were smooth and strong as hell. Sky didn't feel her steps as they wended their way through the throbbing room of sight and sound to a booth raised in the back corner of the main room. Sky squinted into the flashing lights to look for the other artists or Lara. Nobody. She recognized no one.

He led her to the sleek leather booth and pressed her into one side of it. Before he could sit, Sky raised a hand. "You know I don't drink, I don't even know how they let me in."

"You are my guest this evening. I have vouched to keep you from… drinking."

Small plates arrived before them, but the sight of the edamame made her stomach flip. *Is it moving?* A tall frosted glass heavily decorated with fruit arrived at her hand. She blinked at his smoky, hypnotic suggestion, "Go ahead, it's a Virgin Mai Tai, just rum flavoring…" Sky brought the glass closer and sipped. She didn't taste the alcohol. *Could I taste the alcohol in this drink? I'm so thirsty.*

He chatted incessantly to her. Her eyes were dry, and she sat staring at the food, the drinks, and his hand over hers on the white tablecloth. She wanted to recoil. Somehow, she was unable.

"On any other night, I'd want to dance." He gestured with his tall drink to the floor below. "But tonight, it's enough sitting with you, Sky. Is there anything I can get you?"

She shivered as she remembered the opening dance club scene from Blade. She pressed into the plush booth, inadvertently falling into his arm across the back. "Did you ever see that vampire movie with the pulsating throng of people … and the sprinkler system comes on, and they're showered with blood?" She shook her head, disorienting herself. Would that happen tonight? Would she witness that, unable to stop it? Her blood rushed in her ears.

"You have quite an active imagination. That was a hell of a scene." His words were too close to her ear. His lips brushed her earlobe as he smoothed her hair back.

****

"Is that who I think it is?" Dreama tossed her head up toward the couple in the concierge seats above them.

Joy stared long and hard. "Well, she's not with Conner. Wonder how that went south?"

"Aggie, that guy, have you ever seen him at the fitness center?" Joy nudged Agnew on the shoulder to break him from staring into this bourbon.

"He's absolutely not the cowboy., but it's months since I was allowed in."

The girls frowned at his mention of 'the incident' Fog hovered, and confetti fell after the last unrepentantly sybaritic dance partners stopped quivering on the center floor. The throng stumbled to their seats. The D.J. made a detour from the latest self-indulgent Madonna club song to synthesized house music.

Agnew shook a cigarette out of a hardpack and motioned to the door, the unlit cancer stick dangling from one side of his mouth. They waved him off, still staring at Sky and the stranger.

"Whoodda thunk Conner would be with a girl like that?" Joy sneered as she waved the server over for another round. "Maybe that's why he dumped her? That little princess is blitzed."

Dreama shook her head and rolled her shoulders, itching to dance. "He looks… I dunno… skeezy. Keep an eye on him." She ran her finger around the rim of her glass and bit her bottom lip. "Keep your eye on her, too, there are some bad vibes there."

"Wait, wait, look at that." Joy jibed. "She's going face-first into the edamame in a second. Where did Prince Charming go, leaving her like that?"

Dreama snorted. "Well, I'm not going to leave her like that. People can drown in a half-inch of water…" She set off for the concierge level. Joy grudgingly tagged along.

They reached Sky just in time to keep her face out of the food. Dreama slid into the man's seat, and Joy slid beside Sky. Joy dialed the after-hours gym number and requested a call back from Kirk regarding a sick family member.

The two women propped Sky up. Dreama's brows knit in concern. "Sky, what did you have to drink?"

Sky gestured to the virgin Mai Tai and knocked it over. She slurred. "It's fruit juice. I don'… feel good."

Joy sniffed the righted glass. "I don't smell booze."

Dreama's concern deepened. "Yeah, you don't look good. Did you take any drugs tonight?"

Joy's phone rang. "Kirk, I'm at Won Ton Louie's Dance Club. Sky is here, we think she's been drugged. No, we won't leave her."

Sky's head fell back, and her eyes followed the club lights. She garbled fragmented sentences. "I don'… do drugs… I don'… drink."

"Kirk's on his way." Dreama's gaze met Joy's. They jumped as the man returned to the table.

He snapped, "We're leaving." He waved at them dismissively.

Joy looked him up and down. "Sky, who is he?"

Sky's eyelids shuttered, and her head lolled. "Is he real? Do you see him, too?"

Dreama's mind was made up. She looked up at the menacing stranger. "She's not going anywhere with you. Sky's a friend of ours. She's coming home with us."

"Like hell, you don't even belong up here." He turned and snapped his fingers at security. A Samoan man and woman in yellow polos advanced to their table. "These women don't belong here."

Dreama spoke directly to the woman. "Our friend looks like she's been drugged. She doesn't know this man. We're taking her home."

The woman in the yellow shirt nodded and stood guard as Dreama and Joy pulled Sky from the booth. Dreama implored the woman as the man pulled Sky's date to the side. "You do know she's underage, don't you? You need to hold him for the authorities. Don't let him get away."

The security guard nodded discretely and nonverbally got her partner's attention over the stranger's shoulder. The mountain of a male guard hovered over the stranger. "Will you come with me, sir?"

Sky sagged between Dreama and Joy. The female guard stepped in between Joy and Sky and assumed the majority of Sky's weight to walk her toward a more discrete office.

Joy ran ahead and opened the door the guard nodded toward and poured water from a decanter onto a bar cloth. They lowered Sky to a comfortable sofa. Joy sank beside her to wipe her sweaty face.

Sky looked up at her with a crooked smile. "You're so nice, you made him go away."

Within ten minutes, a third security guard knocked on the door. "I've got Kirk Roman asking about Sky?" The door opened, and Conner pushed past everyone to kneel before her.

He took her hands in his. "She's burning up, where's an ambulance?"

****

Kirk pulled Joy and Dreama aside with the security guard. "I can't thank you enough for what you did." His gaze narrowed at the guard. "What's the next step with that predator?"

The woman shrugged. "We've called the police."

Kirk nodded. "Were you able to get a name on this guy?"

The other women retreated to sit in chairs across from the sofa.

The guard pulled a business card from her pocket. "My name is Sefina, Mr. Roman." She extended her hand to shake, and then she consulted a tablet. "He made his reservation with us as Eric Padgett. The credit card he used was Eric Page, they didn't catch the difference."

"Eric Page. He stalked this young woman on the mainland." Dreama and Joy gasped at Kirk's declaration.

Sefina nodded. "That does add another layer to this crime." She turned to the ladies. "The police will want to talk to you."

Kirk ran a frustrated hand through his bedhead. "If it hadn't been for you two, she could dead or worse with this kind of a psychopath."

"Unfortunately, things like this are hard to prove. The officers will speak with everyone involved, and if Ms. Kingston presses charges, he'll be detained."

Conner spoke over his shoulder. "Detained would be the safest thing for him." By now, Conner was seated next to Sky, using the cool rag over her arms and neck. She lay across Conner's lap, now more deeply sedated.

Paramedics, with a stretcher between them, cleared everyone from the small office. Conner turned to his father. "I'll call Jax and Kameo on the way to the hospital." Within minutes Conner climbed into the ambulance with Sky.

****

The interrogation room in the Honolulu Police Department was the same as every other police interview room. Jax stood with his friend, Detective Palakiko, behind the two-way mirror. He nodded toward Page, who sat cuffed to the table while he spouted back at the questioning detective.

"I told you, I'm saying nothing until my attorney arrives."

"You know, Page, you blew in here from the mainland three days ago, and you have an attorney that can show up at a moment's notice? I'd say you came ready to party."

"Don't be ridiculous. I have friends." Page looked down his nose at the detective. "I would like a glass of water, please. That's the last thing I'm saying until my representation is here." He slid into a diffident posture and glared at the two-way glass.

Jax shook his head. "Well, that's it for him until arraignment. Unless you guys learned something when you ran him."

Palakiko raised an amused brow. "You know I can't tell you anything, brah."

Jax shrugged and grinned as he ran his thumb over his bottom lip. "No, you can't. But if you could, what would you say?"

The detective shook his head with jovial exasperation. His index finger brought up a page on the tablet before them. "This guy gets around."

While the detective watched the perp in the room, Jax pulled his phone from his back pocket and snapped a photo.

Chapter Forty-Four

Jax moved out of the police station with urgency, his phone to his ear. "Kami, how is Sky?"

"She's coming around a little better now. They found scopolamine in her blood. They're dumping a liter of normal saline IV right now to help clear her system. We'll take her home after that. She's starting to wake up."

"Why was there a limo? She had her car." Jax enlarged the photo he took of the police file. "I'll see you at home, I need to read this report, and I'm thinking of calling Gideon, my friend on the mainland with the Marshal's office."

Jax drove to his home to meet Jordan, Kirk, and Conner.

****

Jax brewed a large pot of strong coffee and printed out copies of the purloined police file. Kirk read the dryly factual report to put the puzzle together. Conner read it with controlled rage.

"I hope Sky ends up owning that damn school. Did they even do a background check? He has six aliases, and three of them have prior charges. The most art he's done is phony IDs."

While Jax poured coffee, Jordan checked the linens in the guest room and turned down the bed. Jax waited for Jordan before he sat down calmly to discuss the known timeline.

"Jordan, were you able to get the gallery owner on the phone?"

"Rando is in California. I tried to call Lara, that's his assistant who ran the show, but I'm not getting an answer."

"The police report Sky's car was not at the gallery. Do we know anything yet?"

Conner had Sky's iPad. "According to the Find my iPhone app, her phone is sitting in a limo service lot near the airport."

Kirk scratched his head. "That fits, but why was she in a limo?"

Jordan gestured, making a timeline in the air. "The show was up on the North Shore, what is going on? Someone somehow got her in a limo."

Jax pressed a finger on the police report." That 'someone' was Eric Page. But he had help, who helped him?" Jax answered his text alert. He read the text. "The detective says Page's attorney is delayed. Page is a guest of the Honolulu P.D. for the night."

Kirk looked heavenward. "Who travels with an attorney?"

Jax deadpanned. "He said he has friends. Apparently, they're in Maui."

Conner drew in a deep breath. "I want to attend that arraignment."

"If there is an arraignment." Jax shook his head. "Kid, I've got bad news for you. It will be hard to charge him with anything at all. He did not serve her alcohol. He did not molest her. Any drugs were given before he pulled her out of the limo. The surveillance photos showed her impaired when she came in."

Conner's fist slammed the table. "And that's not illegal?"

Jax nodded. "As I said, he had help. It's a matter of identifying the chain of possession on the drugs."

****

Jax stripped to his boxers shorts, and around 4 AM, he slid into bed next to Kameo. With both arms wrapped around her, he spooned and whispered an 'I love you'.

She nuzzled back into his embrace. "I know that, salty. What took you so long to come to bed?"

"Plausible deniability." He whispered his voice heavy with fatigue.

"Plausible deniability?" Kameo flipped on her back and nuzzled into his chest. "You called our favorite white-hat hacker again, didn't you?"

He lifted a finger to his lips. "Shhh."

"You know, I have ways of making you talk." Her hand traveled down his chest.

Jax caught it, kissed her palm, and grinned his trademark crooked grin. "Don't you have a patient down the hall?"

Kameo shook her head. "My capable assistant, Conner, is with her, she's feeling better now. So spill."

In a drowsy drawl, Jax chuckled. "That dirtbag has six known aliases. None of them are going to be able to get on a commercial airline flight for at least a month."

Kameo propped her head on her hand. "Did you have Norah put him on the no-fly list?"

"The no-fly list has a specific purpose."

"Uhuh."

"We just want him on the island until we identify his conspirators." He put a finger to his lips. "Shhh, I've told you too much."

****

The next morning around 8 AM, Detective Palakiko looked at a message from Jax, referring the force to Lara Nakamura through her personal cell number.

After a face to face meeting with the Detective, Lara was more than eager to pick up Eric Page when he was released around 11 AM.

The thirty-something gallery assistant manager reapplied her powder for the second time. "He told me the limo was there because he and his wife were dining with the Governor. The limo was supposed to pick Sky up and get them at the Governor's mansion. I had no idea Mr. Padgett was dangerous."

The Detective shook his head. "Only if you've spurned his romantic advances."

She withered. "I never got that vibe off him. He thought it might be a thrill for Sky to meet the Governor."

"Psychopaths are great liars. He was charming, wasn't he?"

She put her head in her hands. "Who knew? I was late getting to the party, there was an accident I was stuck behind for a good forty-five minutes. When I finally got to the party, no one admitted seeing them. I couldn't find her. I called her phone, and it rang to voicemail. I figured they made it an early night."

Palakiko's gaze hardened. "You didn't call Padgett?" The detective was not sympathetic.

"The same situation. My call went right to voicemail."

"You understand how bad this looks. You put a nineteen-year-old girl alone into a limo to meet a strange couple."

Lara was dumbfounded. "Am I going to be prosecuted over this?"

"Not if you agree to help us." Palakiko rose off the end of the desk he leaned on and waved in the technician at the door. "Our tech will wire you for sound, we'll have a safe word if he makes any threatening moves. When you two are done, I'll come back in."

By 11:15, Lara's cell phone rang. Sheepishly, she answered. "Hello?"

"Ms. Nakamura? This is Eric Padgett. You left me a message to call if I needed a ride this morning?"

She stared at the detectives and drew in a breath. Palikiko made a wind-up gesture with his hand. "Yes, where are you?"

"Kamehameha Highway where it becomes Dillingham. I'll be on the corner."

She bit her bottom lip. "I'm driving a silver Hyundai. I'll be there in about twenty minutes." She ended the call and turned to the detective. "That is a terrible part of town."

"It's the corrections facility neighborhood. Drive by and don't turn off the car."

Chapter Forty-Five

In Jax's guestroom, Conner woke before Sky. He slipped out silently and brought back coffee, juice, and toast. As he returned, she stirred in the king-size bed and looked at his indented pillow. "Where have you been?"

"Kameo suggested I bring you coffee for the caffeine, juice for the sugar, and toast for your tummy. Then I'm supposed to wake you up. But you're already up."

Sky scooted to sit against the pillows and looked at the tee-shirt and sleep shorts she wore. "Where are we?"

"We're at Jax and Kameo's. What do you remember?"

"What day is this?"

"Sunday."

"What happened to the show?"

"You had the showing. I hear you were a huge success." Conner sat on the side of the bed and caught her hand in his.

"I don't understand." Her gaze inspected every foot of the elegant guest room.

"Can you think back and tell me the very last thing you remember?"

"Friday morning, after I cleared a place for the tree… I remember breaking my fingernail getting the pastel into my hatchback. I need to get that fixed…" She pulled her hand out of Conner's and saw the repaired nail. "Oh, when did that happen?"

"Today is Sunday. The gallery show was a huge success. Everyone loved your work. But something happened Saturday night after the show." He got quiet.

She raised the bedcovers and looked at her legs while she wiggled her toes. "Did I have an accident?"

Conner slid into bed and pulled her into his lap. He smoothed her hair and kissed her forehead. "I love you, Sky. I want you to know that."

She stared at him and asked in a hushed voice, "Did I kill somebody?"

"No! I love you, and I realize I could have lost you."

"What happened? You're scaring me."

"Eric Page…"

She groaned and reached for her genitals and peered into the tee-shirt at her bare breasts. "Oh, no. What did he do?"

"He drugged you, he took you to a club, and if two fitness center clients hadn't seen you and realized something was wrong, we don't know where you'd be." She whimpered, and he held her closer. "They told security and called Kirk. Security protected you until the ambulance arrived. Kameo met you at the hospital, and then around 4 AM, we put you to bed here." They sat together in brutal silence. "The reason why you don't remember is the drug he used causes amnesia."

"Is that good or bad?"

He shook his head slowly. "I don't know. The important thing is, he didn't get the chance to do anything to you."

"Where is he now?"

"The last I heard, he was in jail."

"So, what do we do?"

"Kameo says we hang out here for a couple of days. Enjoy the pool. Did you know they have scores of love birds? They've been on the property since it was built."

Sky pursed her lips, and upon not seeing birds outside their balcony, she turned to Conner. "So, how much money did your tooshie make?"

"I dunno. Doesn't the show close on Christmas Eve?"

"Oh, Conner, I want to go home. We need to get the tree, and we need ornaments and stuff. Aren't you going with me tonight to the show?"

✳✳✳✳

Lara fretted to the detective. "I don't know how you expect me to get him talking?"

"This is what you do. Flatter him. Pretend to buy every word he says. Listen to him. When he sounds like he's about to spill, stay quiet."

"Huh?"

"Let his ego take him down."

Lara drove cautiously through the correctional facility neighborhood. 'Spill the beans' was the only thing that ran through her head. The detectives said they needed him admitting every step of the crime without being led.

She turned the corner, and Eric Padgett ripped open the car door and threw himself into the seat. He looked around the car. "You have any snacks?"

"No, let's stop at the Rainbow and eat in the car. Where is Mrs. Padgett?"

Page flipped down the visor, checked his teeth, and smoothed back his hair. What was a runway coiffure last night now looked like the result of electroshock therapy. He straightened his jacket and rested his arm on the window sill. "We had a spat and she decided to fly to Maui yesterday afternoon. How about you get me the hell out of here?"

****

As they ate, Lara was all sympathy. She asked, "Were you able to come to an agreement on the price of the pastel?"

Eric sneered. "No."

"Why ever not?" She picked at her food.

"Two of Sky's friends stuck their noses where they weren't needed."

Lara nodded without seeking his gaze, swallowing hard. "Did you and your wife find the suite to your liking? I do throw a lot of business their way."

Eric gestured with the plastic fork. "We decided on another hotel."

"I'm so sorry your plans for the night caved. The things I did for you, were they okay?" *Why won't he talk?*

"You did your job. You got me the girl." Lara's food caught in her throat. "My limo contact took it from there…"

"Oh?"

Eric preened in the visor mirror again. "Limo drivers will do anything for a c-note."

Lara barked out a laugh. "Well they get paid to drive, what more could you want?"

He snickered at her. "Sometimes, I like to get some strange. Young women are often reluctant, and they need something to help them relax. I knew if I had the time alone with Skyler, she'd come around to my point of view."

Lara winced inside at his cavalier attitude. Swallowing hard, she pandered. "Any girl would be throwing herself in your path…"

He poured hot sauce on the rice and waved a finger. "Some women need to be taught that."

Lara broke the plastic knife with the pressure she felt to get him to talk. He wasn't admitting to being held, he hadn't admitted giving the driver the drug-laced water. *Can I get him to plan it again?* "If at first, you don't succeed, try, try again. The show runs until Christmas Eve."

He chuckled. "So it does. Only this time, I'm not relying on a bunch of lamebrains. I'll dose her myself and drive her directly to the hotel. I don't know what I was doing, putting her on display like that. I thought she'd dig it. You know?"

"Wouldn't she see you coming this time?"

He balled up the empty paper boat and stuffed it in the bag. "What I used last night? She won't remember."

"Oh, I thought amnesia drugs were only in the movies."

"They have better stuff now. I get it in Canada, grind up a few pills. It's tasteless, odorless. If I get caught with it, I tell 'em I get airsick. Bingo! I'm off the hook."

"So, Eric, where am I dropping you?" She cast a slight side-eye at him as she wrapped up half of her food.

"Drop me off at the Mira Del Mar."

Lara could not drive fast enough. When she dropped him off, she didn't even put the car in park. A couple jumped to move out of her way as her car squealed out of the resort. When she was down the road, she spoke. "Did you get all that?" She drove directly to the police station.

Chapter Forty-Six

Sunday night was a family affair. Kirk drove the six of them in his SUV to the North Shore gallery show. Jax silently eyed and acknowledged the serving staff, all volunteers from the police academy.

Music played, art lovers laughed and circulated, as Sky nervously moved from station to station. Although Conner seemed surgically attached to her hip, her head was on a swivel.

They bumped noses, they were so close. "Ohh, let me kiss that so it doesn't bruise."

Their foreheads pressed together as their lips met in a soft kiss. Conner pulled her closer, and when their hips bumped, she let out a little swoon. "You're sure being nice to me tonight."

He caught her face in his hands and inhaled her breath. "I love you, angel. I don't tell you enough."

"Well, I love you too cowboy."

Kameo came around the corner and caught both of them with a hug. "Don't look around. Page has just entered the gallery."

Conner slipped out of the group hug, and he made a face. "Can't I open a Texas-sized can of whoop-ass?"

Sky wagged a finger at him and nodded to Kameo. "Let's make him jealous."

Conner leaned her back over his arm. "Cara mía." He crooned, playing the romantic. He deliberately kissed up her arm to her neck. People around them applauded their ardor. "This is only the beginning." He snapped her upright and kissed her until she blushed bright pink.

A geriatric lady, her program in hand, and her equally aged husband shuffled over near them. The woman held up the page with the image of Conner and adjusted her glasses. After she elbowed her hubby, she wagged a plump finger at Conner. "Walter, that is him." She gestured from Conner to his nearly nude image."

Walter caught his wife and dragged her off. "Well, his gal isn't so bad herself."

"We looked like that once." She turned awkwardly toward Conner and Sky, keeping them in her view.

Walter put an arm around her. "You still look like that to me."

They disappeared into the crowd, and Conner's eyes twinkled at Sky. "I want us to be like that someday."

She cocked her head and viewed him with pursed lips. "What are you saying?"

"You know what I'm saying." He brought her left hand up to his lips and looked at her through those impossibly thick eyelashes. With one sweet kiss, he marked her ring finger.

"Oh, well. Let's talk about that at length, later." She caught him by the waist of his trousers and shook him.

"Okay." He looked around, blushing, and smiling.

Out of nowhere, Eric Page walked up with two flutes of sparkling cider. Gesturing with the bubbly drinks, he sucked up to Sky, working to separate them. "I had to be here for this night. My, aren't you my most successful student?"

Sky's expressive zircon blue eyes flared flame as her lips curled in an odd smile. "Mr. Page, I did not expect to see you here."

He shuffled closer to her, his back to Conner. "I wanted this to be a night you've never forget." He spun on his heel to give a glass to each of them. Conner, without fear, raised the glass to his lips.

"I wouldn't do that if I were you." Detective Palakiko barked from about five feet away. A young cadet dressed in a white shirt and black tie brought a tray for Sky and Conner to surrender their glasses.

Eric Page startled and bolted. He elbowed other servers out of his way and ran for the front door.

Conner looked to heaven and joined his hands in prayer. "Please run, you slimy sonnofabitch. Run."

The murmuring crowd hushed as the sound of a body hitting a concrete slab broke the party atmosphere. Jax nodded to Kameo. "I don't care how much adrenaline is running, that has to hurt."

Eric floundered on his belly as the woman detective read his rights and cuffed him. Once Eric was pulled to his feet, he sneered. His nose was bloody, and his lip cut.

Kameo nodded back to Jax. "And stitches. I'm just sorry I don't get to be the one repairing him."

Jax nodded with a grimace. "No Novocain?"

Kameo leveled a look at him. "I'd stitch him back like Frankenstein's monster."

"There's cold blood in you. You fit right in this family."

****

Monday evening, once the dinner dishes were washed and put away, Conner opened the cumbersome cardboard box with the eight-foot Christmas tree. He sat on the hassock and admired the space Sky had cleared last week. As Sky brought root beer floats to the great room, she sat them down and began attaching hooks to the decorations.

Before Conner pulled out the last piece of the tree, he shook his head and stopped.

"Is something missing?" Sky peered into the almost empty box."

"A confession."

"What? Oh?"

"We've had a completely unconventional relationship from the minute I met you. Even when we didn't see eye to eye about my future, I wanted you in my life."

Sky melted at his words. "Well, that's the way I've felt about you. That's why I got mad about the Air Force."

"I've loved you for so long, I can't remember when it began."

"I can. It began when I said, 'I believe I have the window seat'. And then you dropped the bomb about having a girlfriend. That was a downer."

He pulled her into his lap. "Sorry about that, angel, I just hadn't met you yet." They spent a few minutes chuckling about that, but Conner held up a hand. "Although I knew I loved you, I made the gross error of not telling you because I was scared. I wasn't raised with romance in our family. You and I are so magical, I'm not sure what we are."

Sky wrapped her arms around him and rested her head on his shoulder. "Oh, cowboy, you rode off with my heart."

He pressed a finger to her lips and then found the Christmas tree charm on her bracelet. "The other night, we fought, and I said some hurtful things. The bad part was I didn't realize how our different upbringings would affect us."

Sky's brows knit, and she began a soft pout. "Did I act ugly?" She scrunched her nose and nodded.

Conner winced. "We both were. It wasn't our best night. When Page drugged you, that memory was wiped out. But I can't go on from here without apologizing."

Sky shifted in his lap. "I'll bet, I better apologize, too."

He let her kiss him mercilessly until his jeans became uncomfortable. "Sky, angel…" He slid her off his lap, and he went to the mantel where a gold stocking hung. "Wait right there, don't move."

"Should I close my eyes?"

"Why not?"

He crept silently back to her and knelt before the hassock. He popped open the ring box, and the sound of it made her jump. "Open your eyes."

She blinked. "Is there supposed to be a ring in here?" She caught the box from his hand and dug into the crease with her fingertip.

"Funny thing… it's an imaginary ring. You have to imagine it into existence when I take you to the store tomorrow."

"Uhuh?"

"I could never buy anything and expect you to wear it for the rest of your life. You pick the ring you want as you picked me."

Sky flattened him on the floor. "This is the best Christmas ever."

The tree did not go up that night. Something else did.

Chapter Forty-Seven

Monday morning, Conner and Sky sat under their decorated tree and called Hank.

"Peanut, I was going to call you Christmas Eve."

Conner jested. "This is the big nut, sir."

"Conner, this is unexpected. How's your arm?"

"All healed up, thank you. I'm here with your beautiful daughter, and I confess I'm tardy asking you this. She's already said yes, but I would like your blessing…"

"That can only mean one thing."

"Yes, sir, I asked her to marry me, and the crazy woman said yes."

"Well, before you go shopping, I always promised Sky her mother's engagement ring. Her aunt has it. Have her ship it out to you. Spend that money on a honeymoon, as if you're not living one now."

"Thank you, sir. You know she's my everything. I'll treasure her forever."

Hank's chuckle traveled around the world. "Good to know."

Conner smiled at Sky. "Want to talk to your peanut?" He handed her the phone.

"Daddy, can you believe I've met my one and only?"

Hank's voice carried his smile. "I'm happy for you, peanut. Your mother and I married early. Am I presumptuous about the ring?"

"Oh, no, I love Momma's ring. I'll be proud to wear her diamond."

"Okay, kids, I've got to go review the troops. I'll see you on December 30th, okay?"

****

Conner spent the first two minutes of his Christmas morning studying the play of light in Sky's engagement ring. "It truly is a work of art. What a timeless setting."

Sky giggled and rolled over his chest. "I'm so glad it got here by Christmas."

"We need to create some traditions of our own." He kissed her palm and placed it on his chest.

"What types of traditions?"

His hands caught her hips and pulled her over him. "The first thing I want to do every Christmas morning is get into your stockings. That's my kind of celebration."

Sky sat up and straddled his hips. "The stockings are out there…"

Conner ran his flat palms up and down her thighs. "These stockings…"

Sky threw back her head and giggled. "Oh! Well, you know that will work just fine until little Conner comes along."

He faux frowned. "You never called it little Conner before."

She collapsed laughing on his chest, shaking her head. "When we begin playing Santa Claus for real, we'll have to be careful to schedule Mommy kissing Santa Claus."

The penny dropped, and Conner broke out in a belly laugh. "Yeah, let's hold off on that for about six or seven years."

Sky stuck out her pinky. "Pinky swear." They hooked pinkies and then got on with the traditions of their day. She snagged a red hair ribbon from her bedside table and tied a bow around him at the nest of ebony pubic hair. "Now, I get to unwrap you."

She scooted back and bent toward his morning wood. "I know a way to celebrate."

Conner propped his hands under his head, and his holiday spirit rose to the occasion. "Starting a fire with the yule log?"

Sky shook her head. "If you didn't have such a fantastic body, I'd have to swat you for your bad puns."

"Awe, angel. Don't make me beg."

"But I like you on your knees. You do the most wonderful things to me."

"I promise to return the favor if you let your lips do the walking." He nodded at his bobbling erection.

She grabbed him with a firm hand. "I'll hold you to it…"

Conner stretched out and watched Sky's devilishly sweet assault on him. While her lips danced around his crown, she ran her fingertips along his hips, occasionally marking him with her nails and nibbling with greater intensity.

He watched dawn's warm light overtake their bedroom as she drove him into ecstasy. "I want to love you, Sky…" She mumbled back an answer that sent a shockwave through his flesh. "You're doing that again." She chuckled, and that left him speechless. When she whipped her loose hair back and forth over his belly, the extra tingles of sensation sent him over the edge.

Lying back, Conner stretched luxuriously under the warm and tantalizing strands of Sky's thick hair. Her fingers hit a particularly sensitive spot on his chest, and he wanted to purr like a cat.

"You have magic hands…" He opened his eyes.

Sky smiled down at him with the warmth of the Hawaiian sun.

"Why am I the luckiest cowboy in the world?" He gave her one of her favorite crooked smiles and watched her melt a little.

She gave him a demure smile and lowered her lashes.

"You mind if I sit up while we….?" Conner asked. "I need to stretch out a little."

Sky nodded and rolled away from him, watching with quiet appreciation as he swung his long muscular legs to the bedside and sat up. Conner stretched his arms out behind him on the tumbled bedsheets and looked around. *This is the life! What a fantastic woman. How did I get so lucky?*

He watched Sky's mesmerizing sway as she slid off the bed and sashayed to stand before him. The dawn's light radiated from her like a goddess appearing in his bedroom.

Standing before him, her light hands on his shoulders, she blushed. "It is a beautiful day, isn't it? We're having another first…"

"I agree, just another wonderful first, like the rest of our lives together."

Her fingertips danced over the muscles in his arms, shoulders, and neck. "Everything here is paradise."

Conner's arms wrapped around her slim waist and he wiggled her closer to him. "It sure is," he agreed.

She giggled again and pressed a light fingertip to his lips. "Only very lucky passengers on Hawaiian Air get to meet their soulmate."

He chuckled and couldn't resist touching the softness of the bush at the apex of her thighs. "Let's just say, I paid extra for the soulmate package. It came with the extra five inches of legroom."

She reached out and tugged his reawakening flesh. "You paid for five inches and look what I got." She winked at him.

"Well, what are you going to do with that?"

"It's not what I do with it, it's what you do with it." She nudged into him, dropping her knee onto the bed next to his hip. "Time to start our Christmas party, cowboy." She pushed him playfully, and he fell back, inviting her to straddle him. Once perched over him, her heat just an inch above him, she gave a throaty laugh.

Conner's gaze danced over her. He adored everything about his angel. From her warm, husky voice like silk, dazzling face, and fabulous legs. …

"Hey, penny for your thoughts!" Sky called him back from his reflections. "You could make a girl feel neglected with that far-away look." She pouted prettily as she glanced her sex over his teasingly. "You wouldn't want to neglect me, would you cowboy?" Her lips edged enticingly towards his.

"A cowboy never neglects a lady," he whispered seconds before his lips tasted hers.

She leaned into him, running a graceful slender hand gently from his temple, down the side of his face, along his jaw, and settling at the nape of his neck to encourage him to deepen the kiss.

Conner didn't need much encouragement. His angel was hot as a volcano, and he greedily wanted more. *There was something so enigmatic about her…so sweetly seductive.*

She broke the kiss and stretched, lifting her graceful arms high up. "You know, the family is expecting us there for brunch."

Conner smirked. "Oh, yeah, like Jax and Kameo are going to be there at ten. Hardy, har, har." He stared longingly at Sky's pert breasts tipped with shell-pink nipples. He felt his length grow tall and hard, his erection tapping at her heat above him."

She laughed knowingly. "We have plenty of time." She teased as she lowered herself onto him. "Like the way I ride the range, cowboy?"

Conner licked at lips suddenly gone dry. "Yeah." He caught her hips and rose to meet her.

Her intense azure eyes flamed with passion as she watched his reactions to their quickening rhythm. Conner groaned. *She is perfect. Perfectly proportioned, perfectly soft, perfectly round...perfect for me.*

"I'll bet you never wondered what it's like to be a woman." He shook his head, biting his bottom lip, holding on to reason. She ground deep on to him, and her hands rested on his cheeks. "I am so fortunate that you appreciate a soft, warm, and wet woman."

He bucked up hard, caught her around the waist, and rushed her under him, not missing a stroke. "I sure as hell know what it is to be a man who wants to bury himself in your warmth." He gloried in the feel of her melting around him as his lips claimed ownership of hers. Her mouth opened to welcome him inside.

God only knew what other pleasures she possessed, and Conner would spend his life seeking them. Keeping their dance alive, she looked up into his heavy-lidded eyes with such wanton intensity that he gasped.

Her legs rose around his waist. She held him there, never losing eye contact. Her hands traveled to his back, marking him with her need. "Don't stop..." Her hair crowned her luscious face on the pillow as her eyelids fluttered in reaction to his deep and steady thrusts. She whispered huskily, "Never stop."

Conner's thumb wedged between them, stroking her and bringing her blush to full bloom. "I won't stop until I have you wailing..." He watched fascinated as she writhed beneath him. With a few more strokes, her breath caught, and her moans escalated. "I love it when you come for me, Sky." He claimed her neck with a kiss as he poured into her.

Conner swore softly and rolled her over him. "Damn, woman, I didn't want to come this fast. I wanted hours with you."

"Well, I am thirsty, we can grab a coffee and come back for another hitchin'."

He used both hands to grab her ass and give her a good shake. "Hitchin'. I like the sound of that. Nobody will know what we're talking about. That's a good word."

With all the composure of a heaven-sent angel, she looked down at him and whispered on a breath, their foreheads touching. "Merry Christmas, Conner."

Chapter Forty-Eight

December thirtieth Sky drove out to the airfield to pick up Hank. She bit at her cuticle, thinking of all the things she had to tell him in person. Best to begin with Page.

Hank hugged her fiercely and caught her left hand. "Kirk warned me you'd grow up."

"Oh, Daddy, I'll always be your little girl."

He removed his patrol cap as he sat in her car. "What's for lunch?"

"We can pick up Rainbow and swing over to Kirk and Jordan's they are at their fitness center. You can shower and change. I'll lay out lunch. I want to talk, just you and me."

"What's up now, peanut?"

As Sky maneuvered through traffic, she stayed stoic. "Just want to fill you in on life since I saw you last."

He pushed the seat further back, reclined, and nodded agreement.

✳✳✳✳

As Hank sat at the lanai table in his shorts and Aloha shirt, Sky carried their food and drinks on a tray. Hank raised a beer to the landscape below. "Beautiful view they've got here."

She sat, and they dug into their lunch. "I know there's a condo in this building for sale, you could be neighbors. You should snap it up."

Sky skewered some pork and thought about the wedding. "When do you expect to be out of the Air Force?"

"Four years last June, why?"

"Conner and I want a nice long engagement and graduation under our belt. We're caretakers for Evan Silver's home, so we don't have to worry about housing. I do want you around to plan the wedding."

"Then, I guess I have to buy that condo."

"Yeah, Daddy, that would be very cool."

"Are you ever going to explain to me why you left that crayon college before the semester ended and flew back here? It wasn't about Conner, was it?"

Sky wiped her lips and swallowed hard. She began a narrative of every horrid detail of her time at Central Coast Art Institute. When Sky brought him up to the day they signed the police report on Page, he shook his head.

"I was worried about harassment at the Air Force Academy. I heard of some bad behavior, but the way your college handled Page is appalling. If filing suit didn't bring back every nasty memory, I'd pursue it. Frankly, you sound like you've made good decisions, and you'll save a bundle going locally."

"Oddly, Page has about six aliases, and he's going to jail somewhere in the United States if not here. He won't harass another student ever."

****

On their way to pick up Hank's rental car, he asked. "This engagement... I'm a bit surprised."

"Oh?"

"You were dead set against him as long as he enlisted, that's coming up in a few years, isn't it, peanut?"

Sky winced hard and shook her head. "Conner and I have gone through quite a bit since you left. He was attacked in a self-defense class by a guy whose girlfriend paid a little too much attention to Conner. The guy blew out his shoulder, and Conner had emergency surgery."

Hank shook his head and threw up his hands. "I go away, and I miss all this? I'm not on the moon."

"Yeah, but when it happened, it was hard to discuss. Sometimes the words weren't there. Ultimately, they declared Conner 4F."

"Poor Conner, he has the heart of a fighter pilot. He has to be grieving."

Sky nodded. "Daddy, I believe he has taken the pain and turned it around. He's going to flight school now, we're registered for college in January."

"That's some focus. I'm proud of both of you."

'Yeah, but he's still got some hair-brained ideas about flying."

Hank waved her off. "He's not going to be an airshow pilot, is he?"

"Worse than that." Hank frowned. "Conner wants to fly medivac, and when there's a wildfire, he wants to fly into the damn thing." She pulled into the rental car lot.

Hank patted her arm as she parked. "That's years away, he'll come to his senses."

****

New Year's Eve, Sky stepped out of the dressing area in her flirty golden dress. She wore her hair up with sparkling crystal stars pinned into her curls. Glittering star earrings brushed her bare shoulders when she moved. Conner buttoned his suit jacket and straightened his lapels in the mirror. This was his first Hugo Boss suit, but it wouldn't be his last. *This might be my lucky suit.*

****

"Give me a minute, angel, I've got to get something." Conner darted out the front door toward the main house.

Sky leaned into the dressing room mirror to finish her makeup. "Okey-dokey." She pressed her lips together to set her cherry pink lipstick and then sat in the great room, thinking about leaving the tree up until Epiphany in January.

Conner returned with a bottle of champagne and two crystal flutes. "Since they're coming to pick us up, why don't we have a private toast?"

Sky slinked toward him like liquid gold. "You're so naughty. I like that idea. Where did you get that bottle?"

Conner unpeeled the foil and levered his thumbs under the cork. As the top flew across the great room, he winced. "Evan's wine cellar. I'm letting him know it's our Christmas bonus."

Sky laughed. "Oh, God, it probably costs as much as my car."

Conner poured and raised the glasses. "Then enjoy it wisely."

She accepted her glass, and they walked to the lanai to make their toast in the sunset. The love birds Jax and Kameo gifted them at Christmas had nested nicely in a tree outside their door. The peach-faced birds cooed and loved on each other until they flew away to feed their babies. "Our little family has grown. I saw all three eggs hatched."

"Here's to the first of many New Year's celebrations, my love." He raised his glass and embraced her with one arm.

"When we started counting our blessings, our lives turned around. Here's to ending this year to build a great beginning."

Sky giggled, and Conner mugged it up to keep her laughing. They made a few dance moves until they heard Kirk's SUV arrive out front.

Conner tucked Sky's hand into his elbow. "Come, almost Mrs. Jameson."

****

After lights, cameras, and leis, the seven of the Roman family enjoyed their New Year's dinner. Not much talking, the food was so savory, and the wine was so plentiful.

Hank raised his glass. "Thanks for bringing the Kingstons into the Roman family."

Kirk raised his glass. "Teflon, we've always felt like you were family, and now it's official."

Everyone toasted enthusiastically. The tables were cleared, dinner lights dimmed, and the emcee announced, "Ladies and Gentlemen, prepare yourselves for the revelations of Hawaii's most gifted mentalist, Xavier the Oracle."

The spot hit Des, who was dressed in a sleek black tuxedo. The women in the crowd ooh'd at his blond good looks. He amazed them by guessing birthdates, hometowns, and performing card tricks.

After his warm-up, Des went from table to table, inviting couples to choose one card each from a Tarot deck in the center of their table. From those, he would read their destiny.

"Let's do the lovebirds." Des approached their table. He gestured towards Sky and teased Conner. "How do you keep your hands off her?"

"Dust her for fingerprints, you'll see I can't."

Des swooped up the Tarot deck, fanned the cards in a semicircle on the table, and pointed. "Each of you pick one card."

Sky picked hers, and Conner followed. Des held up the cards. "You have picked the World card, lovely lady, which is stepping out into a new beginning in the world." He held up her left hand. "Do I see a diamond sparkling on that hand?"

Sky blushed. Conner pulled her hand from Des. "I staked my claim already."

"And what card do you have there, sir?" Conner shrugged and handed it over.

"Ah, the Magician. You are adept at manifesting your desires into reality. He spread his arms to include the whole of the table. "These cards speak of a life of adventure."

Everyone applauded as Kirk and Hank whispered humorously between them. Des put a hand to his ear. "What was that?"

Kirk shook his head, "A year ago, you predicted something for me that unbelievably came true. So be kind, I'm an old guy."

Des walked closer to Kirk and rested his hands on his shoulders. He surveilled the table and spoke softly. Des groaned. "What is it about the Roman men? Can't you put the glass slipper on the girl and live happily ever after? Adventures keep finding you."

Kirk and his sons raised their glasses in a toast. "And they always will."

Epilogue

One evening, the following Fall, Sky, and Rando stood with their heads together, deciding on the order of art for her first solo exhibit.

"What if we hang the nature series at the back? They are the largest, we can space them along the wide wall."

Rando nodded. "What a reward for walking all the way through the exhibit. The way you painted them, the animals are life-sized. You show details most people will never see first-hand." He pointed to the layout on the tablet. "If we space out the nudes, people will simply end up in the back."

Sky laughed. "That's mean, feed them a hearty diet of gorgeous semi-nude men and reward them with sea turtles and dolphins…"

The gallery's front door opened and whooshed closed. As Rando turned, he spoke. "I'm sorry, we're closed this evening…"

His voice caught at the sight of the radiant redhead as she lowered an emerald green chiffon scarf. The pooling scarf matched her sparkling eyes. Sky and Rando stood transfixed. From the top of her glossy hair to her black patent leather Louboutins, she personified refinement.

Her heels clicked as her smooth gait glided her closer. The Veronica Beard shorts suit in a celadon shade flattered her porcelain skin. Speaking of skin, the shorts suit revealed lots of leg. She wore an ivory husband shirt with the collar popped. Emerald earrings danced on her earlobes. Once she stood before Sky and Rando, she peeled off ivory kid gloves, revealing impeccably manicured oval nails polished bright coral.

They stared hard. Rando found his tongue. "May I help you, madam?"

Her voice was Midwest cheerful. "Miss Kingston, I'd like to buy your art."

Sky stepped forward with a smile. "Have we met?"

"My husband's business partner is an artist, he doesn't do things like this," She gestured with a flip of her gloves. "But he saw one of your large pieces, it was a mural, last year…and suggested we look you up."

"Is there a particular piece?"

The young woman turned on her heel and strolled down one wall. She returned to them and motioned where the art leaned against the wall, frame to frame waiting to be hung. "Oh, all of it."

Rando stepped forward. "Excuse me?"

"Yes, yes." The redhead nodded decisively. My husband's partner said when we completed our Hawaiian resort, we should look you up."

Sky gestured around her. "But, there are so many different mediums and subjects. Why would a resort want that?" She nodded to an ink drawing of Conner in repose.

"Oh, isn't he a work of art? We have a place for him."

Rando cleared his throat. "You're opening a resort? Where?"

The redhead handed him a business card. "We're currently furnishing The Sand Castle. Have you heard of it?"

Sky and Rando looked at each other and shook their heads. Rando smoothed the perspiration from his top lip. "Where is it?"

The young woman smiled secretively. "We built the entire resort on piers west of the Mermaid Caves. Our clientele arrives by boat or helicopter."

Rando nodded. "Of course." He passed the card to Sky. "It's your art, my dear. But part of having a show is exposure. You've worked hard for this. Kyoto is sending people from their national museum."

The woman extended her hand to Sky. "I'm Anna Hiatt." She paused. "I understand your situation. You deserve your night in the spotlight. Perhaps you'll consider this. We pay your asking price, and your gallery can announce that an anonymous buyer has purchased everything. That is glorious publicity for one so young."

Rando sunk his hands in his trouser pockets. "Why anonymous?" he nodded to Sky. She looked hard at this young woman, barely older than she. "Yeah, it would make the headlines."

Anna smile secretively. "We have a select clientele, we're not open to the general public." Sky played with the engraved business card as Anna continued. "When people express an interest in a piece, you offer a new commission. Mr. Kane, I can arrange a wire for your asking price. Are we doing business?"

Rando cleared his throat. "Thirty-three pieces, at an average of seventy-five hundred each with tax and shipping, two hundred and sixty thousand."

Sky's knees trembled as she bit her bottom lip. Anna leaned toward her. "Is that enough, Miss Kingston? Some of these could engender a bidding war. It might drive up the prices…"

Sky and Rando shared eager expressions. "Mrs. Hiatt, may I have a word with my artist?" Rando nodded toward a table and chairs at the front of the gallery. He caught Sky by the elbow and marched her to his office.

"Sky, this is one of two things. An elaborate con game or the biggest art purchase I've handled for an emerging artist. I wish we could announce the buyer, but her resort could be one of those exclusive playgrounds that cater to uber-rich. It could bring you the wealthiest of clients. This is on you. Either accept her money or let her down gracefully."

"Are you kidding? I'm young, I can paint more. Sell the art."

When Sky and Rando strolled back to Anna, her expression was expectant. She stood and took Sky's hand between hers. "What a wonderful way to begin a friendship. I can't wait to see everything hung."

She turned to Rando. "Two hundred and sixty thousand has been transferred to the wire address on your website." Anna showed her phone to him.

He nodded. "You were pretty confident."

"I had a feeling…" She hitched her glossy leather bag over her shoulder. "Sky, when my friend Cat sees those pieces." She pointed to Conner, "she will lose her mind." Anna made to leave and then spoke over her shoulder. "Keep drawing him."

Sky ran the business card's edge over her palm. "I can't wait to see my art hanging in a resort. I wonder what else Consort Group International does?"

The End

We hope you have enjoyed Conner and Sky's story. We invite you to follow and engage with us on social media.

When you Follow, Like, and Comment, it sends our message farther than we could ever pitch.

We invite you to our website to sign up for our email list. Your bonus for this good deed: you'll be the first to hear about giveaways and new book launches.

We do a blog on GoodReads, but not excessively. Please, follow us there. The more eyes, the better. We love to hear your comments. Please share your favorite books with your friends.

And here are the big ones- When you thoughtfully review our books, it is the highest compliment a reader can give an author.

Please add us to your Goodreads lists. Let your fellow bookworms know Amber Anthony is on your 'to read' or 'currently reading' list.

And if you have gotten this far- Take a selfless selfie. Share a photo of you with the book on social media and tag Amber Anthony. Surprises abound!

-Thank you!

Where to follow Amber Anthony

https://www.bookbub.com/profile/amber-anthony
https://www.facebook.com/WriteAmber/
https://www.goodreads.com/author/show/17062164.Amber_Anthony
https://twitter.com/WriteAmberA

Do you enjoy Tea?

Find our custom blended teas at Adagio Teas
https://www.adagio.com/signature_blend/my_blends.html

Fly Boy
This high-caffeine blend will keep you aloft, just like Conner. Made with Assam Melody, Mambo, Lapsang Souchong Accented With Cocoa Nibs, Chocolate Chips & Cardamom

Sky's Palette
This low-caffeine tea is as peaceful as our artist. Made with White Eternal Spring, White Peony, White Pear teas. Accented With Rose Petals, Freeze Dried Mango & Hibiscus Flower

When you purchase these teas, 5% of the sale will benefit Malama Na Honu. Their mission is to protect Hawaiian sea turtles through education, public awareness, and conservation, all in the Spirit of Aloha. https://malamanahonu.org/

Other Books by Amber Anthony

Paranormal Romance
Appetite for Blood
Blood Rising
Blood Emerald
Blood Dragon
Blood Fugue

Metaphysical Fiction/Romance
Arise, My Darling

Contemporary Romance
Becoming Gabriel

Action/Adventure Romance
Roman's Revenge
Roman's Rules
Roman's Return

Seasoned Romance
Roman's Rules

New Adult
Roman's Return